FIRE ON MONROE BRAVO

The Jack Collier Series

Fred Lockwood

Copyright © Fred Lockwood 2024
This book is sold subject to the condition that it shall not, by way of trade or otherwise, be lent, resold, hired out, or otherwise circulated without the publisher's prior consent in any form of binding or cover other than that in which it is published and without a similar condition including this condition being imposed on the subsequent publisher.
The moral right of Fred Lockwood has been asserted.
ISBN: 9798325324536

This is a work of fiction. Names, characters, businesses, organizations, places, events and incidents either are the product of the author's imagination or are used fictitiously. Any resemblance to actual persons, living or dead, events, or locales is entirely coincidental.

Author's Note

As you start to read this novel, you will immediately notice something is different: the text is 'left-aligned' rather than 'justified'.

The print layout for most novels is justified. This is where the line of text starts precisely at the left-hand margin and ends precisely at the right-hand margin. Justified text stretches and compresses the normal spacing within and between words so they fit on a line of specific length. You will have noticed this when some lines in a novel are severely compressed, and others have words with an odd spacing between them. There are many who believe that justified text looks more professional or neater than left-aligned text. However, research evidence reveals justified text is more difficult to read! This is because as we develop as readers, we recognise and read clusters of letters and shapes of words rather than individual letters and words. In this book, there are more than 85,000 words – that's a lot of reading – and it's all left-aligned.

I do hope you enjoy *Fire on Monroe Bravo,* and that you find it easy to read. A description of other novels in the Jack Collier Series is provided in the final pages of this book.

Dr Fred Lockwood

About the Author

© Turtle & Ray Productions (2022)

Dr Fred Lockwood is Emeritus Professor of Learning and Teaching, Manchester Metropolitan University, UK. He is also a PADI Master Scuba Diver.

His career in higher education has involved consultancies in over one hundred universities in more than thirty countries. Fred has travelled extensively and dived in the waters of Central America and Africa, the Middle East and South-East Asia, Australasia and the Pacific Islands.

Once a keen runner and squash player, he is now an equally keen cyclist, walker, skier and diver. He lives in Northamptonshire with his wife, Beryl.

Acknowledgements

I would like to thank the following:

Muhammad Saleen, photographer, who captured the dramatic picture of the fire on the Abtatun Permanente Oil Platform in the Gulf of Mexico, and which is on the cover of *Fire of Monroe Bravo*. For further examples of his work, see: https://www.pinterest.co.uk/muhammadsaleem99999/

Turtle & Ray Productions (see https://www.turtleandray.com) for permission to use the photograph, taken by Layla Elise Boul Ema, of the author diving off the coast of Curacao in October 2022.

Alamy (see https://www.alamy.com) for permission to use the image of the MV *Athina B* on the cover of my next novel, *One Way Ticket*. The ship ran aground on Brighton Beach, 20th January 1980.

Stephen McGinty (author of *Fire on the Horizon*), and John Konrad and Tom Shroder (authors of *Fire in the Night*) for the inspiration they gave me in their accounts of the *Piper Alpha* and *Deepwater Horizon* disasters.

Andy Hillier, PADI Master Instructor, for his advice on diving with a rebreather, gas mixes and decompression tables, and ensuring the diving sections of *Fire on Monroe Bravo* are plausible (see http://wwwdivenorthampton.com)

Aakanksha Sharma, Barbara Askew, Bob Flanagan, Kevin O' Regan, Janusz Karczewski- Slowikowski and Andy White for reading through the manuscript and offering numerous improvements. Their insights and attention to detail were humbling.

Other books in the Jack Collier Series

Total Loss (2016) Cambridge: Vanguard Press

Overdue (2017) Cambridge: Vanguard Press

Missing Presumed Lost (2018) Cambridge: Vanguard Press

Unlisted Cargo (2019): Kindle Books

Gross Negligence (2020): Kindle Books

Wreck Site (2021): Kindle Books

Non-Hazardous Material (2023): Kindle Books

CONTENTS

Author's Note i
About the Author ii
Acknowledgements iii
Other books in the Jack Collier Series iv
Chapter 1 An expensive and self-indulgent celebration 1
Chapter 2 A blow against the West 6
Chapter 3 Shared on Facebook 11
Chapter 4 Multiple fires 15
Chapter 5 Race to save the Platform 22
Chapter 6 Emergency response 30
Chapter 7 Searing heat 39
Chapter 8 EPLAST 46
Chapter 9 Before the incident 53
Chapter 10 One percent frantic action 60
Chapter 11 Evacuation 66
Chapter 12 Recovery 74
Chapter 13 Desperate journey 78
Chapter 14 Into the void 87
Chapter 15 'We've got a hit.' 95
Chapter 16 Callum Jeffrey 105
Chapter 17 High risk options 112
Chapter 18 Change of Plan 121
Chapter 19 We've got a problem 129
Chapter 20 Plan B 135
Chapter 21 Reluctant hero 145
Chapter 22 Message to Houston 150
Chapter 23 Lucy 'Mad Dog' Rottmuller 156
Chapter 24 Towards a new life 164
Chapter 25 Lost contact 172
Chapter 26 Stavanger … we've got a problem 177
Chapter 27 Breakthrough 183
Chapter 28 Conspiracy to undertake an act of terrorism 191
Chapter 29 Lover, sleeper, or agent? 198
Chapter 30 The analyst 204
Chapter 31 An unusual decision 209
Chapter 32 TV updates 214
Chapter 33 Our man in Tehran 224

Chapter 34 Meeting with Colonel Zand 231
Chapter 35 Knight in shining armour 238
Chapter 36 Praise and promotion 244
Chapter 37 Double agent 253
Chapter 38 Playing the long game 257
Chapter 39 A Good News Day 259
Chapter 40 A few minutes of fame 264
Postscript 270
Future Reading 281

Chapter 1

An expensive and self-indulgent celebration

Tuesday 4th April 2023, 1:00 pm

Jack Collier and Sandro Calovarlo, joint owners of the *Marine Salvage & Investigation Company*, were enjoying a smooth transfer from the MV *Stavanger* to the *Monroe Bravo* Oil & Gas Platform in the North Sea, one hundred and eighty kilometres east of Aberdeen. From the ship, the sea looked calm but once on the water they were aware of a pronounced swell. The helmsman had to limit the speed of the RIB (Rigid Inflatable Boat) to ensure it rolled over the swell rather than butting into the crests and dropping into the troughs. Even so, both Jack and Sandro held on to the safety ropes along the side of the RIB and jammed their boots under the taut webbing that stretched beneath them. They were relaxed, protected by full waterproof gear, and there was no rush. This was all part of an expensive, self-indulgent trip to celebrate securing a contract with TransGlobal Oil for the MV *Stavanger* to function as a support vessel to the *Monroe Bravo* Oil & Gas Platform. The contract guaranteed the survival of their company for an entire year and a little beyond.

From the bridge of the *Stavanger*, the Platform looked big. On the water, and as they got closer, it became massive and towered over them. What's more, as they approached the docking point, they could see the rise and fall in sea level as a swell moved towards and then under the Platform. It was going to be a tricky job coordinating the rise and fall of the RIB as they grabbed safety rails and stepped onto the floating landing stage. Jack was now wondering if they had made the right decision for the helicopter transfer from Aberdeen to land on the *Stavanger* rather than *Monroe Bravo*. However, the thought of landing in their own helicopter, on their own ship, was too much to resist; it was a celebration – and too late now.

Jack's anxiety faded as two crew members from the *Stavanger* nimbly managed lines, fore and aft, to position the RIB. It was just a case of keeping his balance as the RIB and floating stage rose and fell before he stepped off and was grabbed by a member of the smiling welcome party. In their bulky yellow and red waterproofs the two of them, and the two crewmen looked indistinguishable. There was just a narrow slit, enough to see, between the high collar and low hood of their suits. One of the welcoming party led Jack and Sandro up stairwells and along gangways to a small, anonymous building where they peeled off the waterproofs. It was only then that the difference between the two visitors was clear. Whilst they were both about 185 centimetres tall, just over six feet, Sandro stood out. Although about the same height as Jack, he appeared taller and more athletic. His tanned complexion, five o'clock shadow and slightly long, curly black hair confirmed his Mediterranean origin. He could have just stepped off a luxury sail boat or cruiser rather than a RIB in the middle of the North Sea. In contrast, Jack looked stocky rather than athletic, and a couple of kilos heavier than Sandro. He was clean shaven, had short brown hair, and would blend into a crowd rather than stand out. However, when he spoke and acted, he commanded attention.

Jack and Sandro exchanged their waterproofs for orange boiler suits, thick soled boots, heavy protective jackets, helmets, goggles and gloves. After a sobering safety briefing, they were escorted along more walkways and up more stairwells to yet another anonymous building. Inside, it looked like a small lecture theatre with tiered seating, a large screen and adjacent lectern. Jack and Sandro were introduced to their guide.

'Welcome to *Monroe Bravo*. Good to see we've got you properly dressed and briefed. As I'm sure you'll appreciate, safety is paramount onboard the Platform. Whilst I'm delighted that your impressive ship will be on standby for the next year, we try to do all we can to reduce risk.

'I know your time is limited on the Platform. I've been asked to give you an overview of what we do. It's a short presentation prepared for our visitors. We've also arranged a tour of our Command and Control Centre, the Drilling Deck and the Dive Centre. If there is anything else you'd like to see, just ask. About three o' clock you'll meet the Off-Shore Installation Manager, Dr Rick Johnson, in the galley. Rick is the boss on the Platform and will be answering any questions. I'm informed the weather will remain calm and so you should have an easy return to your ship and flight back to Aberdeen.'

The presentation was superficial and predictable. It was more of a public relations exercise than a detailed presentation, with emphasis on TransGlobal's contribution to the UK economy, the health and safety of those working on the Platform, as well as preserving the North Sea environment. The scenic tour of the Platform to Central Command and Control was much more interesting. The sheer scale and intricacy of the Platform, the labyrinth of pipes and ducting, tanks and machinery became clear. This was reinforced when they entered the Central Command and Control building. The contrast between the slate grey buildings, heavy metal grid decks, connecting walkways, stairwells and smell of petroleum was stark. It was like entering a sterilised, hi-tech world. Jack's first reaction was that it was remarkably quiet and clean. Even the orange overalls that the people were wearing looked clean and ironed. About half a dozen were sitting before banks of computers and monitors. Some were typing away whilst others gazed at the screens. There were several large, multicoloured data screens around the walls, showing numbers that were constantly updating. Two men were standing before one of them, deep in conversation. It could have been the control centre for launching a rocket into space.

The tour continued to the Drilling Deck. However, a few minutes watching the men working convinced both Jack and Sandro that it wasn't a job they wanted to do. Working with heavy machinery and powerful subterranean forces while exposed to North Sea weather wasn't attractive – despite the high wages.

Jack and Sandro felt more at home when talking to Konrad, a Dive Supervisor, inside the Dive Centre. The main difference between the *Stavanger* and *Monroe Bravo* operations was that on *Monroe Bravo* it was 24/7, week after week, month after month. It was unrelenting and in one of the most unforgiving environments in the world.

A few minutes before three o' clock, the guide escorted them to the galley to meet Rick Johnson. They'd seen all they wanted to see and meekly followed the convoluted route from the Dive Centre to the galley. It was yet another dramatic change as they entered the galley. The rich smell of food and warmth washed over them as the door was opened. Inside, a dozen or so men and women were sitting at tables – eating and drinking. There were bright curtains against the windows, a shining laminated floor and a long, stainless steel serving counter, tiers of glass shelves and everything you could wish to eat and drink.

Rick Johnson was sitting at a four-person table near a window. He was gazing at a lap top screen and looked deep in thought. Rick looked up as the guide, Jack and Sandro approached. Jack held out his hand.

'Hi, I'm Jack Collier.'

He turned and gestured to Sandro.

'...my business partner and close friend Sandro Calovarlo. Many thanks for the invitation to visit *Monroe Bravo*. It's been a fascinating tour.'

'Glad you enjoyed it. Let's grab something to eat and drink before we chat.'

Rick was making complimentary comments about the MV *Stavanger* as they returned to place their drinks and snacks on the table. As they sat by the table, Jack noticed the open laptop.

'Working on your tea break?'

'Yes and no. I was scanning Platform production levels and everything is looking good. We're maintaining production of both oil and gas levels in a 94% to 97% band. We've maintained it for the last six weeks which is above expectations. There have been no glitches, no problems, simply good weather and high intensity, unrelenting work. Oh, and before you ask, I'm not tempted to open the taps to full and reach the 100% level. I'd rather have a few percentage points of leeway. Maintaining a one hundred percent level of production is a theoretical goal rather than a practical or sustainable one. Supply and maintenance schedules as well as rotation of staff are all under control. It's early April with the worst of the winter storms behind us.'

It was exactly three o'clock when Rick reached for his mug of coffee.

Chapter 2

A blow against the West

Tuesday 4th April 2023, 3:00 pm

The digital timer counted down and triggered the release of the spring-loaded plunger. It smashed the glass phial, the chemicals were combined, and heat was generated from the chemical reaction. As the temperature rocketed, it ignited the complex mixture of metal powder and metal oxides to produce a violent exothermic reaction. In the world of chemical engineering, the well-known thermite process had started. Nothing on earth could stop it now. The positioning and strength of the thermite device had been discussed at length by chemists and metallurgists, structural engineers and demolition experts. Computer simulations had been created to determine the ignition sequence and optimum level of destruction. It was to destroy the Backup Command and Control System of the Western owned gas and oil production platform, and to do so as quietly and efficiently as possible.

As the milli-seconds passed the core of the thermite device got hotter and hotter until it glowed. The surrounding mixture ignited and the temperature continued to soar. In seconds it rose through one hundred degrees centigrade towards two hundred degrees and the plastic sleeves around the wiring and data transmission cables were bubbling and smoking. As the first whiffs of smoke, and rising heat were detected, sensors were triggered and klaxons sounded. They shattered the peace and calm of the galley just as Rick was about to grab his mug of coffee. The tone of the klaxon told Rick there was a fire. Almost immediately a second klaxon, with a different tone, told him toxic gases had been identified. His attention was intensified as he watched tiny concentric rings form on the surface of his coffee, travel across the surface and collapse against the side of the mug. This had to be something major. There had been a collision, an explosion… a jolt somewhere on the Platform that had caused a fire. Perhaps a piece of machinery had overheated and burst into flames, a short circuit in an electrical system had gone off with a bang …something had created those ripples. Something had triggered the alarm and Rick couldn't ignore it.

Ignoring Jack and Sandro, he glanced at his laptop. A red warning light was blinking at the foot of the screen. He didn't need to check what it was; he knew. The warning light was linked to the Backup Command and Control Centre … and there was a fault. Rick moved his finger tip across the touch sensitive pad and clicked on the blinking red light. The pop-up menu merely said "SYSTEM OFF LINE"; this was unusual. People were now streaming out of the galley as Rick turned to both Jack and Sandro.

'The alarms are telling us there is a fire and toxic gases on the Platform. There's also a problem with our Backup Control and Command System. The two may be connected, it may be trivial, but I've got to investigate. You can't stay here … grab your things and come with me.'

Rick slipped on his heavy protective jacket, clipped on his helmet and jammed the laptop into his grab bag. He knew some on the Platform thought he was odd – carrying a grab bag everywhere but it was a long standing habit. It was a small ruck sack that contained everything he needed in an emergency. It contained detailed Platform plans and emergency breathing apparatus, evacuation plans, a satellite phone, first aid kit, torch and a whistle. He even had some high protein snack bars in a side pocket. He slipped it over his shoulders as he ushered Jack and Sandro towards the door. Together, and in silence, they walked quickly toward the Central Command and Control building.

It was a short distance from the galley to Central Command

and Control. A simple right turn out of the galley, right again at the corner of the building, straight ahead for twenty or thirty metres, a left turn and the Command and Control Centre was dead ahead. Although it was mid-afternoon the day was dull with a weak, watery sun still trying to break through. Rick was approaching the left turn when more klaxons sounded; there was another fire and more toxic gases somewhere ahead. He increased his pace and was about to turn the corner when a massive explosion threw him off his feet. He was flung against a safety rail, rebounded off it and crumpled onto the steel mesh walkway. Jack and Sandro were blown off their feet, landed on their backs and slid backwards a metre or so due to the sheer force of the blast.

Two minutes earlier, in the Central Control Room, bright LED lights flashed onto the main display board and a warning screen burst onto the main monitor. The Chief of the Fire Team and the Platform Controller had been alerted at the same time. There was no panic, sensors were triggered all the time, but they had to be checked out. Inside Central Command and Control, the Platform Controller responded automatically. He pressed a button on his control panel and was connected by phone to the Fire Chief.

'Chief, heat and toxic smoke detected inside the Backup Command and Control Centre, Level 3, Grid A6. Repeat, heat and toxic smoke detected Level 3, Grid A6, Backup Command and Control Centre. Investigate immediately.'

At six hundred degrees centigrade the tubular steel canister, clipped across the main wiring harness and fibre optic feed, was glowing red hot. Black pungent smoke was billowing through the cabinet air vents and into the remote backup control room. Toxic smoke and heat sensors had triggered two gut-wrenching "Awooga, Awooga, Awooga" sirens which deafened everyone close by and alerted everyone on the Platform. Vents from tanks of carbon dioxide above the building released a flood of CO_2 through ceiling vents to smother any flames. However, the thermite device would even work under water; it didn't need oxygen to complete its task. It just got hotter and hotter.

The standby Fire Team were already suited up, harnesses and breathing apparatus already in place. As helmets and gloves were pulled on, the Platform Controller, sitting before the main console in the Command and Control Centre, punched the button again to speak to the now scrambling Fire Team chief. Before he could speak to them, the temperature at the centre of the thermite device exceeded two thousand, five hundred degrees centigrade. Metal melted, plastic and fibre optic cables vapourised alongside the crackle of burning. The resultant gases expanded dramatically. The sides of the heavy steel cabinet that had contained the nerve centre of the Backup Command and Control System began to deform under the internal pressure. The cabinet door latch and hinges failed about the same time. The cabinet door blew open and vented a super-heated cloud of gas and pungent smoke into the room.

Those who designed and constructed the thermite device knew that the building housing the backup Command and Control system was designed to withstand violent North Sea weather. The computer simulation they created confirmed the building could absorb the modest blast that would be produced. Two reinforced glass window panes simply popped out of their frames and the single door blew open. Black smoke poured out of the building and was wafted away by the breeze and flood of CO_2. All communication between the Central Command and Control Centre and the Backup Centre was lost.

A second, much more powerful, thermite device and bomb had been placed inside the cabinet that housed the main wiring harnesses and main data transmission and control cables. The cabinet was housed inside a side room within the Command and Control Centre of the whole Platform. It ignited within two minutes of the first detonation with devastating results.

There were eleven people inside the main control room when the thermite device ignited and its temperature soared. Pungent black smoke again billowed from the cabinet as the sound of crackling increased to a crescendo. More sensors were triggered and more klaxons blared; clouds of pressurised CO_2 poured into the control room as the front of the cabinet began to glow red hot. There was panic inside the control room before an explosion and shower of white hot metal and super-heated gases swept all before the expanding blast. It resembled the pyroclastic flow of a volcanic eruption. The walls and roof of the control room, all inside, and the bowser of CO_2 above it were transformed into deadly shrapnel. The blast killed all the afternoon shift, one-third of the senior management team, the team that provided the leadership and managed the *Monroe Bravo* Oil & Gas Production Platform.

The Platform was still working but without any control. The strategically positioned thermite devices and bomb had destroyed both the main and Backup Command and Control Systems but not the basic operation of the Platform. Power to the pumps and lights, compressors and turbines still worked. Automatic safety valves and well shut-down sequences had been circumvented. Thousands of barrels of hot crude oil were still being pumped through a thirty-inch steel pipe from the seabed ninety metres below, into the separation plant and then into the shore-bound pipeline. Liquified natural gas, at 1800 psi, was still being pumped, at over one hundred kilograms per minute, through an eighteen-inch diameter pipe that was one inch thick. The pipeline disappeared over the side of the Platform and through miles of pipework to distribution points on shore … but not for long.

Chapter 3

Shared on Facebook

Tuesday 4th April 2023, 3:02 pm

A non-descript supply boat is moored alongside the MSV *North Guard,* the multi-purpose store, workshop and fire tender. The supply boat resembles a tiny cleaner fish attending to its massive host. A young deckhand, Angus, has positioned a fourth pallet containing stores onto the steel, reinforced loading bed and signalled the load is ready for transfer from the supply boat to *North Guard*. One of the cranes, lining the edge of the huge floating platform, will lift the sling holding four pallets out of the supply boat's hold and onto its deck. There is no rush; up, around, down and wait. A forklift truck is waiting on *North Guard* to move the pallets towards the provisions store. More men will unload the pallets, slide the boxes down a conveyer belt to more men. These men will stack the stores inside the cold store or position it for transfer to *Monroe Bravo.* It will take just a couple of hours to transfer the provisions, another hour or so to transfer dumpsters full of waste and the job will be done.

Angus will be able to have a bite to eat, then get his head down for a few hours, before repeating the process at another rig or platform somewhere else in the North Sea. It's a mind-numbing job but it pays well. It's mid-afternoon but the weather is dull with a watery sun. The lights in the hold are poor and so Angus has switched on the lights on the forklift so he can see better. Suddenly, echoing inside the hold, Angus hears the unmistakable sound of klaxons from the Platform. It has happened before on other rigs and so Angus isn't unduly worried. He's paid to load and unload not to be an emergency responder. He's happy to wait for the next load to be shifted.

As Angus looks up he can see the empty sling hovering above the hold. In an almost bored tone, he uses the walky-talky to direct the crane operator on *North Guard*.

'Lower away ... five ... four ... three ... two ... steady, steady ...'

Before Angus can complete the set up for the next lift there's an explosion that echoes all around him. Klaxons pound out their message as the crane operator shouts into his ear:

'Clear the sling, clear the sling ... have to disengage ... need to recover the sling now ... stand clear ... confirm ...!' was the urgent request.

Angus is shocked. Nothing like this had ever happened before and for a moment he doesn't know what to do, he simply says "clear" and sees the sling disappear. He stands for a moment wondering what to do and then decides to climb out of the hold to see what is happening.

When he saw *Monroe Bravo*, for the first time, he'd been unable to take his eyes off it. The Platform towered above the supply boat and everything around it. At the time it was festooned in lights; an intricate, three dimensional jig-saw of steel pipes and tanks, decks and stairwells, gantries, walkways, girders and cranes. It seemed to hum like some slumbering giant. Now there was a fire in the middle of it. He could see the flames leaping up the Platform. It was as though the sun was setting behind it as black smoke billowed and twisted upwards.

Urgent shouts behind him broke the spell.

'Slip the mooring ... for'ard and aft ... forget the transfer ... we've got to get clear!' was the call from the skipper.

A deckhand ran past him, and shouted:

'*North Guard* 'll be slipping anchors … moving … we've got to get clear.'

Angus moved quickly for'ard, eased the mooring line, waited for the man on *North Guard* to release it so he could pull the line in. Within seconds of the blast, the supply boat was easing away and moving clear. Angus watched the fire as it continued to grow, and ducked as another dull boom sounded across the water. There had been another explosion on the Platform.

'Shit, this is a bloody floating bomb … and it's about to go off!' he said to himself as he stood on the deck, frozen, simply watching the drama unfold.

'Secure the forklift … secure the forklift!' shouted another deckhand as he rushed to pull up the fenders and stow them.

Angus shimmied down the ladder and ignored the violent movement of the boat as he slammed the forklift into the corner of the hold, jumped off and rigged the chains to hold it in place. He was tightening a chain when there was yet another explosion from the Platform. He looked up and could see an orange flickering glow in the sky above. By the time Angus had secured and covered the forklift, the movement of the boat was calmer and it was easy to climb the ladder and make his way aft. As the supply boat veered away into open water, he stood alongside the other deck hands, open-mouthed. A few moments ago, it was just another Tuesday afternoon; now it was an unfolding drama. Angus slipped his mobile phone out of his pocket. A quick click, a few deft strokes and a photo that would charge around the world was sent to his girlfriend and to his list of contacts. His message was simple: 'Fire on *Monroe Bravo*.'

Angus's girlfriend, and many of his online friends, heard the 'ping' and checked their phones. The message and picture were dramatic. More deft strokes and Angus's picture and message began to circulate on Facebook, Instagram and the other social media sites. Within minutes the number of shared photos and messages began to grow exponentially. News of the fire on

Monroe Bravo was spreading around the country …and the world. Just like the thermite device, once it had started no one could stop it. Nobody checked the facts, everybody added a little embellishment to the story.

Chapter 4
Multiple fires

Tuesday 4th April 2023, 3:02 pm

When the Fire Team reached the backup site, they knew what to do; they practised daily. Two men grabbed the hand grips around the nozzle of the adjacent Foam Bowser and ran towards the building; thick black smoke was still billowing out of the windows and door. Energetically, colleagues threw the concertina of hose to one side and hit the lever to emit the foam. A torrent of foam sprang from the nozzle and through the open doorway as the Fire Team began to douse the fire. On the other side of the Platform, more klaxons, a simultaneous flash of light and another explosion added to their confusion. They would soon discover it was the Central Command and Control Centre. Anyone who was on the Platform and who was exposed, felt the pressure wave as it vented its force between the steel grated levels and into the North Sea.

'Jimmy, Bob, Ron … with me!' shouted the Fire Chief as he turned and started to run towards the next fire.

Two minutes after the main control room was neutralised a third thermite device ignited. It was on the other side of the Platform and a level down from Central Command and Control. The device was attached to the high pressure liquified gas pipeline. A pipeline that stretched across the Platform, down to and along the seabed, to the onshore control point one hundred and eighty kilometres away. At first it was like the ignition of an oxy-acetylene blow torch. Witnesses later described a deafening "pop" that could be heard over the sound of the fire above. A small jet of liquified natural gas broke through the ruptured wall of the pipe and immediately burst into flame. It was followed, moments later by a deep rumble that quickly changed to resemble the start of a jet engine. The sound increased in intensity and pitch from a low rumble to a deafening scream. The full jet of intense flame hit the Ground Floor of the four-storey accommodation block with massive force. A whole section of cabins collapsed before they could be melted. Internal walls simply couldn't withstand the onslaught. They were blown away or incinerated as the white-hot flame bored through the building. Even when the flame broke through the devastation continued. Nearby metal support beams began to glow red hot and distort as the weakened structure couldn't support the weight of the storeys above. As the accommodation block sagged more storeys were fed into the resultant inferno. There were twenty-seven people inside the accommodation block when its incineration began.

The jet of intense flame from the ruptured high-pressure gas pipeline not only destroyed everything in its immediate path, but anything close by. The intense heat caused cables and lines, plastic pipes and anything that could burn to smoulder and burst into flame. This included the main umbilical that supplied the Diving Bell with a mixture of oxygen and helium. The surfaces of the rubber hoses were already bubbling in the heat and would burst into flame at any moment. When this happened, pressurised oxygen would feed another fireball. Gas supplies to the divers below would be cut off.

Two minutes after the high pressure liquified gas pipe was severed a fourth thermite device, attached to the main crude oil riser, ignited. The main crude riser was simply a large pipe that brought the oil from below the sea bed to the surface. Once at the surface, it was filtered for debris and the volatile gases drawn off. The oil and gas were further refined before being pumped along lengthy pipes to the shore.

The thermite device had been positioned on a flange, a steel collar, below the elaborate mechanism that allowed heavy drilling mud to be pumped down the drilling shaft. The mud, under huge pressure, would force the crude oil back to below the seabed; it could make the well safe. The housing and valves were made of specialist steel, able to withstand massive internal pressures and high temperature before failing. However, they were never intended to resist a temperature of over two thousand degrees centigrade. As a result, it really didn't matter if the device was above or below the housing. Within seconds, the thermite mixture would soar, melt the steel pipe, anything nearby and ignite the crude oil.

The effect wasn't immediately spectacular. As the thermite device began to melt the steel pipe, crude oil gushed out and was ignited to form a spray of flame. As the seconds passed, and more of the pipe was ruptured, the flame intensified into a solid column of burning oil. Some of it shot through the metal grating of the main drilling floor above, but the majority was deflected onto the deck. Within seconds, it had doused everything within sight with hot crude oil. The volatile gases, which had been trapped inside the oil thousands of feet below the seabed and under immense pressure, were suddenly free. There was a dull boom as these volatile gases ignited and a fire ball shot between the floors of the platform and into the surrounding air. The Fire Chief and his three colleagues were lucky. Had they been on the same level as the fireball they would have been incinerated and blown off the platform and into the cold waters of the North Sea. For an instant the fireball sucked all the oxygen from the air around it, but the heavy metal grid, which created one of the levels of the Platform had shielded them from the worse of the blast and the heat. In the aftermath, blue flames began to flicker around the housing that had supported the main riser. Although the bulk of the crude oil was hot, it was far below the flash point at which it would ignite. The white hot, molten metal would change all that. It boosted the temperature of any oil that was close and set it alight. These flames heated the surrounding oil to flash point. A blue light writhed and flickered over the surface of the oil spewing over and through the steel grating floor, through the floors below and onto the sea. The light around the Platform began to change colour to orange as flames and smoke erupted. The hotter the oil got the more it burned and the thicker the smoke.

The volatile gases inside the pressurised column of crude oil that was now bursting from the ruptured main riser expanded dramatically. They transformed the once solid column of oil into a massive spray which then erupted like a Bonfire Night Roman Candle - but on a massive scale. As heat soared into the afternoon sky, fresh oxygen was drawn into the fire to change the Platform into a funeral pyre. With an almost endless supply of crude oil, it wouldn't take long for the floor grating above the flames to glow red hot, buckle and collapse. Those on or nearby the main riser when it exploded were incinerated or blown from the Platform into the sea. It would be like falling over thirty metres onto burning concrete. The outcome would be inevitable. If, by a miracle, a person survived the fall the cold water would soon kill them.

Captain Erik Sorenson was on the bridge of the MV *Stavanger*, enjoying the quiet time of his watch. There was a dull hum within the ship as the engines and thrusters maintained their standby position. The replacement dive teams would be arriving shortly; an injured diver had been transferred to hospital and would make a full recovery. The ship was on station early and the co-owners would be leaving in a few hours. Life on the *Stavanger* would soon be back to normal.

He didn't hear the first explosion but saw the flashing sensor, relayed from the Platform. He walked across the bridge, unclipped the binoculars from the rack, and was in the process of scanning the area when the second device exploded. This time he heard the dull boom and saw the dramatic effects; he reached to hit the "*All men on deck*" button. There was a problem on *Monroe Bravo*.

Just as men rushed to their station and onto the bridge, the third device severed the high-pressure gas pipeline. Smoke began to rise from the Platform and it began to burn. Captain Sorenson's eyes flicked to the monitor that provided information on the status of *Monroe Bravo*; it was blank.

'*Stavanger* to *Monroe Bravo*, *Stavanger* to *Monroe Bravo*, report on the situation.'

Captain Sorenson demanded; there was no reply.

He repeated the request three times before he spoke to the skipper of the MSV *North Guard*. The *North Guard* was a huge floating platform anchored several hundred metres away from *Monroe Bravo*. In addition to acting as a store, supply ship and maintenance workshop, it was a Fire Killer. There were sixteen water cannons on board the *North Guard* that could send jets of water a hundred metres and pour one hundred and eighty-thousand litres of water per minute onto a fire. The cannons were so powerful they could punch holes through concrete. They could also wash men off the Platform and into the sea below. The problem was that the *North Guard* was slow to manoeuvre. It was designed to support firefighting taking place on the Platform. Whilst it had enormous capability it would take time to get in place. Time was something *Monroe Bravo* did not have.

'*North Guard, North Guard*, this is *Stavanger*, acknowledge,' stated Sorenson.

'*Stavanger*, this is *North Guard*, over,' was the reply.

'*North Guard*, fire on *Monroe Bravo*. No response from Platform Controller. I am launching a RIB and Fast Rescue Craft to search for men in the water and those abandoning the rig. Will restrict search area to South East – down current. Will proceed to East South-East of Platform and deploy water cannons. Will move away at your request. Over.'

'Message received and understood. I am unable to contact *Monroe Bravo*,' was all the captain of the *North Guard* said.

Captain Sorenson turned to his officers and was about to address them when the main crude oil riser was severed. Within seconds, raging fires erupted from the Platform and thick black smoke seemed to consume it.

Two massive fires now raged on the Platform. The crane that supported the Platform Diving Bell began to feel the effect of the oxy-acetylene-like flame; it was later estimated to be close to three-thousand degrees centigrade. The lattice of steel plates, which made up the jib of the crane, began to glow red hot. Steel plates began to buckle as the jib bent under the weight it was holding. Link after link of the chain slowly disappeared into the water below.

Seven divers, *in sat - in saturation,* were inside the Diving Bell when the crane failed. The pressure inside the Bell had been increased until it was the same as the pressure of the surrounding water - ninety metres below the surface. Inside they were breathing a mixture of oxygen and helium, under pressure, and as a result their body tissues were being *saturated* with the gases. They had expected to spend three weeks living inside the Bell, conducting repairs and maintenance on the Platform in eight-hour shifts. Two divers were on the seabed, working, when the crude oil from the main riser burst into flames. They could see the increasing glow in the water above them.

'Danny, Danny … look up! What the fuck's that?' shouted Archie in alarm.

Archie had never seen such a glow before but knew exactly what it was. It certainly wasn't the glow from an arc light or a torch that had fallen over the side. It was also far too big for the flare burning off excess gas. It was a fire, a massive fire on the Platform above. Before Danny could call the dive supervisor, they heard from him.

'Emergency, emergency, emergency … drop everything … return to the Diving Bell immediately! Repeat, we have an emergency. Archie, Danny, return to the Bell immediately. Confirm!'

'On our way!' the divers said as they dropped their tools, grabbed the umbilical, and started to pull themselves back towards the Diving Bell and the *Wet Well*; the water tight compartment between their living accommodation and where they entered and exited the water. They were 'moon walking' on the seabed, hauling on their umbilical, as they hopped and skipped towards the *Wet Well*. Through the dark Danny could see the glow of lights from the Diving Bell. As he got closer, he could see it was swinging on a ninety metre pendulum and was close to the seabed. Only a few metres in front of him the nine tonne Bell began its' final swing. As it scraped and scoured the seabed in front of him the visibility around the Bell was destroyed. The sheer momentum of the Bell had driven a bank of sediment against the entrance. The short steps he was expecting to climb into the *Wet Well* were now buried in sand and mud; so was the entrance. The current slowly cleared the sediment as they bounded closer – but could they get inside?

'We're going to have to dig a hole so we can squeeze inside,' was all Archie said as he fell to his knees and began to scoop away mud and sand with his hands.

Danny glanced upwards at the dull orange light before falling to his knees and digging frantically. Less than five minutes had passed since the first explosion.

Chapter 5

Race to save the Platform

Tuesday 4th April 2023, 3:03 pm

Rick cradled his right side with his left hand as he struggled to catch his breath. The pressure wave from the blast and fall had knocked the air out of him. The blast had also consumed all the oxygen in the immediate area. As he lay, panting for breath, he knew he had broken ribs but also knew he just couldn't lay there. He tried to twist his body and looked behind him to find the visitors. The sharp pain in his chest stopped him. As he searched for a place to put his left hand, to help lever himself to his feet, he realised his vision was blurred. Automatically he swept a hand over his forehead and eyes. His vision cleared but his hand was covered in blood. There was also a roaring sound in his head, his ears were ringing as he pinched his nose and blew to clear them.

Jack scrambled to his knees and looked forward. There was a bright, orange, flickering light illuminating the walkway ahead of him and he moved hesitantly towards it. As he cautiously looked around the corner the drab, utilitarian, Central Command and Control Centre had been replaced by a roaring inferno. For a moment he couldn't remember what the Centre looked like – the walls, position of the door, the windows, the shape of the roof and what was next to it. All he could see was a gaping hole, two steel beams sticking up at odd angles and a roaring fire where the building once stood. The construction materials and everything inside the building had become flying debris. The Centre had been transformed into shrapnel that had damaged parts of the surrounding area. Steam and liquids were spurting from dozens of ruptured pipes. Sparks and smoke were venting from damaged conduit and trunking. There were already small fires burning and twisted metal littered the walkway. Even though it was mid-afternoon flames lit up the Platform area. The acrid smell of burning plastic wafted over him.

As Jack turned away from the inferno Sandro was helping Rick to his feet. Blood was streaming down Rick's face from a deep cut on his forehead. The way he was standing, and holding his side, told Jack that the man was injured, but he was the only person around who could help them. Jack had no choice but to give Rick the shocking news.

'The Central Command and Control Centre has been totally destroyed; there's nothing left … it's ablaze and I doubt anyone could have survived the blast. What do we do?'

Despite his obvious pain and bloody appearance, Rick was back in control.

'We've got to get to the Dive Centre.'

He started to strip the rucksack from his back but stopped and winced in pain. Sandro intervened, undid the straps and eased it off his back as Rick struggled to control his breathing. He wiped his forehead and eyes again with his hand. The blood was still flowing.

'How bad is it?' he asked.

'Looks like a deep cut … about three or four centimetres long. Have you got anything to cover it?'

Rick fumbled in his pocket and brought out a white handkerchief. Sandro quickly folded it into a bandana and wrapped it over the wound; not pretty but it would do the job.

'There's a satellite phone in the pack … switch it on, scroll down to Ridley, the Fire Chief, and press the green button.'

The Chief Fire Officer recognised the caller's name, and answered immediately.

'Ridley here … confident we can get this fire under control … but there's just been another explosion. I'm on my way to it.'

Jack could tell immediately that Chief Ridley was agitated. His voice was almost drowned by the background noise. Jack was also aware of the noise surrounding him and the danger of conveying panic through his tone and language. He knew it was vital that he sounded cool, calm and collected. Desperately controlling his own emotions he spoke slowly and deliberately into the phone.

'Chief, my name is Jack Collier. Sandro Calovarlo and I are visitors on the Platform, and I'm using Rick Johnson's phone. He's been injured in a blast but I think he'll be alright ... Central Command and Control has been destroyed in an explosion. Repeat, Central Command and Control is destroyed, what little is left is ablaze ...'

Rick paused because an explosion off to his left was deafening.

'Nobody inside the Centre could have survived the blast ... assume everyone inside is dead. I'm handing the phone to Dr Johnson now.'

Rick had been listening; he took the phone and suppressed a grimace.

'Chief, we're making our way to the Dive Centre. I'm going to instigate a shutdown of the Platform at the seabed. If I can ...'

Rick paused because of a deafening explosion off to his left.

'If I can shut down, there's a chance we can save the Platform and anyone left on board ... Chief, liaise directly with Yellow and Red Platform Controllers. They'll be assessing the situation and will organise evacuation.'

'Understood ... I've contacted *North Guard* and *Stavanger* for assistance.'

The background noise together with shouts and explosions was so great Rick struggled to hear what Chief Ridley was saying.

'Repeat, please repeat,' Rick shouted into the phone and then regretted it.

Shouting just created stabbing pains in this side.

'I've contacted *North Guard* and *Stavanger* for assistance ... fire at Backup Control and Command under control ... we'll do what we can to contain the other fire sites ...'

'Understood ... I must go,' said Rick as he disconnected one call and started another.

'We've got to get to the Dive Centre ... this way'.

Rick had punched in the speed dial number for Bobby McGregor, the Yellow Platform Controller. Bobby saw the name of the caller on his phone screen.

'McGregor here ... team still arriving at assembly point ... will follow emergency plans ... will assume Backup and Central Command and Control no longer operational ... am unable to shut down the Platform ...'

'Bobby ... Dan O' Neal and all the White Team are dead ... the entire building has gone ... I'm going to try and shut down the Platform at the seabed ... liaise with Chief Ridley and Red Team Controller over fire containment, evacuation and damage assessment ... I'll phone again as soon as I can ...'

Another sound echoed around the Platform. It wasn't the gut-wrenching blast that had destroyed the Command and Control Centre but rather a loud *pop*, that was followed by a dull roar that developed into a high-pitched scream. It must be the site of another fire. Across the Platform the billowing black smoke had changed the afternoon to early evening. The watery sunlight had been replaced by an orange glow that was getting brighter all the time. It was as though the sun was coming up.

'It's the high-pressure gas pipeline,' Rick said out loud. 'If it was one of the gas separation tanks or tanks of liquified natural gas, it would have exploded like a fire bomb, but that may not be far away. There was nothing else in that part of the Platform that would sound like that.'

There was nothing Rick could do about the jet-engine-like scream coming from the gas pipeline. His task now was to get to the Dive Centre as fast as possible and to phone his emergency contact in Aberdeen. The problem was that the Dive Centre was near to the site of the new fire. If it was the gas pipe line, the fire could be a hundred metres or less from the Dive Centre. They'd have to approach it from below.

'Follow me and stay close. We're heading for the ladder that will take us to the deck below,' was all Rick said as he negotiated the maze ahead of him.

Thick, black, toxic smoke was now billowing around the Platform; it was difficult to see and was stinging their eyes. Small fires were burning, streams of steam and fluid were leaking from ruptured pipes. Jack gave Sandro a knowing look – "How is he going to climb down a ladder with busted ribs?" Moments later they reached a latched gate in the safety rail. Rick turned to them. His determination was clear on his face.

'This is what we're going to do: Jack, Sandro, the next deck is twenty metres below this one. I want you to go down the ladder and unlatch the gate, get onto the deck and wait for me. I'm going to climb down slowly … if I slip, I don't want to knock you off the ladder and into the sea. I'll hook one arm around the ladder to brace myself against it. It's just a case of sliding that arm against the rail as I make my way down.'

Jack was about to argue when Rick grabbed him with one hand and brandished the phone in the other.

'We don't have time to argue … every minute counts … I've got to contact Aberdeen … go!'

Jack swung his body off the deck and onto the ladder, began to climb down to the next level and cursed himself for having no form of communication. One of the key pieces of instruction about the visit to the Platform was no mobile phones! The note had explained that the danger of a malfunctioning phone, and a spark, was too great. Rick Johnson must have some special phone. They'd planned to be away from the ship for just over one hour and so it wasn't a problem. However, his girlfriend, Penny, knew he and Sandro would be on *Monroe Bravo* today. In her new job she'd be one of the first to hear about the explosions and fire – and he couldn't contact her. He'd vowed to leave her a message at the first opportunity.

As he reached the lower deck, two Platform workers were tending to an injured colleague. One was wearing a cumbersome survival suit as though he was about to catch the helicopter back to Aberdeen, except Jack knew the helipad was several levels up and on the other side of the Platform. As Rick waited for Jack and Sandro to clear the ladder, and his call to Aberdeen headquarters to be answered, another sound began to build above him. It drowned the background noise and resembled the approach and passing of an express train. Rick knew what it was; he'd heard the sound before. The main crude oil riser was on fire – it was the pipe that brought crude oil from beneath the seabed to the surface for processing.

'TransGlobal Oil Emergency Centre, Aberdeen. How can I help you?'

'My name is Rick Johnson. I'm the OIM on *Monroe Bravo*, Fortes Field, North Sea. We have an emergency on the Platform and I need to speak urgently to Vice President Norton T. Flynn in Aberdeen.'

'Yes, sir ... please give me your twelve digit alphanumeric security code.'

With explosions and raging fires on the Platform, billowing toxic smoke starting to choke him, Rick knew he had to concentrate and recall his personal code. Without the code he knew his call wouldn't be taken seriously. It was a security hurdle he insisted upon to ensure any caller was genuine. He confirmed his personal code.

'I'm connecting you now.'

Rick looked around him while he waited. The whole area was floodlit by flaming torches. Although it was only mid-afternoon, the thick black smoke had blotted out the sun. The sunlight had been replaced with the glow of orange and red flames. As the seconds ticked away, another explosion rocked the Platform. Rick looked up through the lattice of metal beams and girders. At first there was nothing to see ... but then he could feel a rain-like shower of warm crude oil falling on him; furthermore, he could taste it. Eventually, his call was answered.

'Sir, Vice President Norton T. Flynn is not answering his phone; it's switched off. What would you like me to do?'

Rick was stunned. This was highly unusual since he knew the protocol was that all senior TransGlobal executives must be available for immediate contact, 24/7. He stood by the ladder whilst holding the phone to his ear.

'Connect me with the TransGlobal Oil Company Chairman, Walter T. Brachs in Houston, Texas.'

'Connecting you to Walter T. Brachs, TransGlobal Oil Chairman in Houston. Please hold on, Sir.'

Rick tightened his fist into a ball, clenched his teeth and screwed up his eyes as he repeated to himself: 'Come on, come on, come on.'

'Sir, Walter T. Brachs's phone did ring but then clicked into answer mode. What would you like me to do?'

'I need to leave him a message; for both Norton Flynn and Walter Brachs ... just tell me when to start my message.'

'Your message is being recorded now and will be sent immediately to Norton T. Flynn and Walter T. Brachs.'

Rick tried to shield himself from the heat and billowing smoke that was all around him and composed his message.

'This is Rick Johnson, OIM *Monroe Bravo.* At three o' clock this afternoon, 4th April 2023, a series of explosions occurred on the Platform. I believe the first destroyed the Backup Command and Control Centre, the second the Central Command and Control Centre. Two other explosions have, I believe, ruptured the high pressure gas pipeline and the main crude oil riser. The entire Platform is ablaze and out of control. I believe Dan O'Neal and the entire White Team have been killed – there will be many other casualties.'

Rick paused to collect his thoughts. He knew the recording would be played hundreds of times and whatever he said would be dissected over the forthcoming months.

'The Yellow and Red Team Controllers are currently assessing the damage and organising evacuation. I have tried to contact Norton T. Flynn but I'm told his phone is switched off. I have tried to contact Walter T Brachs – but his phone goes to message. I am going to ask divers to shut down the Platform at the seabed using EPLAST …it may be a suicide mission. The time is now 3.08 pm. At the moment I believe this is an act of terrorism. End of message.'

On the Platform, nearby and much further away, others were reacting to the unfolding drama.

Chapter 6
Emergency response

Tuesday 4th April 2023, 9:10 am in Houston, Texas
(3:10 pm on *Monroe Bravo*)

Molly Blackmun is the long time, Personal Assistant to Walter T. Brachs, Chairman & CEO of TransGlobal Oil. She missed breakfast this morning because of her early start; she was in the office before 7.00 am. Walter is holding a 9.00 am meeting of the TransGlobal Oil Executive in the conference room. Molly had prepared and circulated all the papers for the meeting a week ago. She'd constructed the Powerpoint presentation Walter was going to use – but he always liked to recheck the screens, update and add information at the last minute. This was why she was in the office so early. She'd made the changes he wanted, checked the three video links to Senior Vice Presidents currently in Saudi Arabia, Nigeria and Brazil – they were standing by.

About 8.55 am Walter collected his papers, strolled to Molly's desk and, without a word, placed his phone on her desk. Molly knew that Walter didn't like to be disturbed during a meeting of the Executive but his phone must never be switched off – it was company policy. She also knew Executive Meetings were never speedy. He'd be in there for hours. She checked Walter's email, printed out each one and organised them into three piles. The biggest pile were attached to files relating to ongoing issues. The second group merely represented isolated questions or were 'For Information' and the remainder likely to be junk – but Walter wanted to see everything that came to him. It was a never ending process. As Walter left the office to attend his meeting Molly decided to go to the executive dining room for breakfast before starting work on the pile of documents Walter had dropped on her desk.

She strolled by the counters, collected a chocolate croissant, a tub of yogurt, a bowl of fruit and a glass of fruit juice. After selecting an empty table by one of the huge glass windows overlooking the city, she switched on her mobile phone and took a sip of her juice. It would be just a few minutes of indulgence, time to read her emails, check her Facebook page, have breakfast …but there it was. A bold headline that announced: Fire on *Monroe Bravo* with a photograph of the Platform ablaze. Breakfast was forgotten as fingers and thumbs flashed over the mobile phone as Molly checked national news feeds and industry breaking news; there was nothing. It must have been a million to one chance that the friend of a friend …of a friend had forwarded the photo to her. Molly scrolled down the list of speed dial names until she found Norton T. Flynn and punched the button to make the call. She waited, agonisingly, but there was no answer. The phone was switched off. Molly was now alarmed as Norton should always have his phone switched on.

Frantically she scrolled through her contacts for the emergency number for TransGlobal Oil operations based in Aberdeen, Scotland; eventually she found the number and dialled. This time it was seconds before there was a voice.

'TransGlobal Oil Emergency Centre, Aberdeen. How can I help you?'

The flat, dispassionate voice sounded remote and oblivious of the drama that may be unfolding in the North Sea. Molly also knew what was coming. She was going to be asked for the personal security code she had been given a few weeks ago but which she now couldn't remember – and there was no time to find it. Steeling herself, Molly replied:

'My name is Molly Blackmun. I'm Personal Assistant to Walter T. Brachs, Chairman and CEO of TransGlobal Oil, and speaking from my mobile phone at TransGlobal headquarters in Houston.

I've just seen a photo on Facebook of our gas and oil Platform, *Monroe Bravo*, on fire. Can you confirm?'

'Ms Blackmun, before I can release any information, I must verify who you are.'

Molly was surprised at the raw menace in her voice as she replied:

'Young man, listen to me carefully ... Unless you confirm or deny *Monroe Bravo* is on fire in the next five seconds, you're going to be unemployed by the end of the day. Walter Brachs is currently chairing a meeting of the TransGlobal Executive. Tell me what I need to know or I will take this damn phone to Walter and let you ask *him* for the code!'

There were a few seconds pause on the phone line.

'Can you tell me who is OIM on *Monroe Bravo*?'

'It's Rick Johnson; an American.'

'Rick Johnson phoned me a few minutes ago, a verified call, and told me there have been several explosions on *Monroe Bravo*. I tried to phone Norton Flynn, Vice President, Scotland but his phone is switched off. I relayed messages from Rick Johnson to Norton Flynn and Walter Brachs. That's all I can say.'

'Thank you, you did the right thing, gotta go,' said Molly before starting to run back to her office.

Molly hasn't run anywhere in years. She's not built for running or dressed for it, but she's running now. She bustles past clerical and secretarial workers, managers, and visitors with only one goal in mind. She burst into her office and can see the red light on Walter's phone blinking. She snatches it from the desk and starts to run to the Conference Room. Molly doesn't bother to knock and simply pushes open the double doors and strides to the head of the table. She's gasping for breath, trying to regain her composure, and ignoring everyone around her. Walter is unphased and guesses this is serious otherwise Molly would never interrupt an Executive meeting. Between gasps Molly explains:

'You need to see this … it's circulating on Facebook,' says Molly as trembling hands show the photo of *Monroe Bravo* on fire to Walter.

She then gives Walter his phone. He can see the message light flashing.

'I've checked the national news feeds and industry news flashes … no mention of the fire yet, but it's minutes not hours before it makes the news. I've just spoken to the TransGlobal Emergency Centre in Aberdeen. Rick Johnson has reported a series of explosions and fires on *Monroe Bravo*. He tried to phone Norton in Aberdeen, but Norton's phone is switched off. He tried to phone you, but I left your phone on my desk when I went for breakfast. His message is on your phone now.'

There is murmuring around the conference table as people wonder what is happening. In a sharp tone, Walter calls the meeting to order.

'We have a problem on *Monroe Bravo,* off the Scottish coast. I'm suspending the meeting but please do not leave. I need to listen to this message, talk to you individually and decide what needs to be done.'

Walter closes his eyes as he concentrates on the message dictated by Rick Johnson a few minutes ago. He can hear men shouting and a roar, like a jet engine, in the background. He can guess what it is. It took only minutes to listen to Rick's message and only moments to decide what to do. Walter wasn't CEO of one of the biggest companies in the world by accident. He turned to his colleagues around the conference room table.

'I've just had a message from Rick Johnson, OIM on *Monroe Bravo*, our Mega Platform in the British North Sea. He's reported a series of explosions and fires at key points on the Platform and suspects a terrorist act. The Backup and Central Control and

Command Centres have been destroyed by explosions within minutes of each other. The main gas and crude oil pipelines have been ruptured and are ablaze. The Platform is out of control.

Rick believes there will be a large loss of life. This includes Dan O' Neal and his team of Platform controllers that were inside the Central Command and Control room when it exploded. Rick is attempting to initiate EPLAST ... but we have no further information at this time.'

An undercurrent of whispered comments rumbled around the conference room before Walter coughed to gain everyone's attention.

'There is also concern about the whereabouts of Norton Flynn, our VP, in Scotland. Our Emergency Centre in Aberdeen was unable to contact him. We believe his phone is switched off. I'm initiating our Disaster Response Plan, Level Three. You all have a copy and know what to do, but I want a quick word with everyone before you all head off.'

Over the next few minutes, Walter speaks to each member of the Executive to confirm the actions to be taken. The Chief Financial Officer is instructed not to sell stock and to arrange a meeting with the US Treasury as soon as possible. The Communications and Media Advisor is told to draft a reassuring press release. Eventually, there was only one person left in the room: the Head of TransGlobal Security. He was speaking into his mobile phone when Walter approached him.

'Marvin, I've a high regard for Rick Johnson. If he thinks this is terrorist action, I'm prepared to act accordingly. What have you done so far?'

'I've already contacted the US Department of State and arranged a phone call at ten this morning. I may have more information by then but will request the FBI and Homeland Security work with UK security to investigate these explosions. I've asked them to consider it a terrorist act until proven otherwise. I've also spoken to our Head of Security in Aberdeen. He's urgently checking on the whereabout of Flynn before we report him as missing.'

'Good, give me an update in an hour.'

Walter collected his meeting papers and started to walk back to his office. He's so deep in thought he fails to notice Molly walking towards him until she speaks.

'Walter, a message from *North Guard*. It says current observations confirm multiple fires on *Monroe Bravo* … and they are out of control. Many of the injured are receiving treatment on *North Guard* and some are to be flown to hospitals in Aberdeen. They are still trying to account for everyone but fear there will be much loss of life.'

'Let's get back to the office and see what's happening,' said Walter as they made their way back.

Molly switched on the TV and trawled through the news channels. They are confronted with the same photograph of *Monroe Bravo* ablaze on one channel after another. They stumble upon impromptu discussions of the possible death toll, the impact on the environment, on oil prices; it is the major national news headline.

'How did they get the news of the fire so quickly?' asked Walter.

'TV and radio producers probably have their phones set to pick up any breaking news,' Molly replied.

'OK, I've seen enough. Can you switch it off?' asks Walter as he moved to his chair and switched on his computer.

On industry websites there is headline after headline about the potential impact of the disaster. It's only when Walter clicks onto a stock market channel that the financial impact of the fire was confirmed. A graph with the heading of 'TransGlobal Oil share price plummets' filled the screen. It showed TransGlobal Oil share price falling off a cliff. It's not even 10.00 am in Houston but the NYSE and NASDAQ are reacting as though it's a TransGlobal

Fire Sale. Walter is aware that NYSE and NASDAQ account for almost fifty percent of all share trading in the world. When they act the rest of the world tends to follow. Millions of dollars are being wiped off the price of TransGlobal Oil each minute.

Walter switched to the FTSE index in London. London is still trading but the picture is the same. The price of TransGlobal Oil is tumbling. It's the same in Amsterdam and on Euronet, the European Stock Exchange. He's aware that Riyadh is two hours ahead of London, so the Saudi Exchange will have closed for the day. It's little comfort; they will be selling on FOREX. The other big stock exchanges, in Shanghai, Tokyo, Singapore and Hong Kong will open in ten hours. By then the market will be in a frenzy and the selloff is likely to continue.

The phone rings on Walter's desk; it is Molly.

'Harvey Blickstein is on the line.'

'Thanks, Molly, put him through.'

Harvey Blickstein is the United States Deputy Secretary of the Treasury. He's not exactly a friend but he is someone Walter can talk to, share high level and confidential information, and from whom he can seek advice.

'Walter, just seen the news about *Monroe Bravo*. What can you tell me?'

'Harvey, we have direct reports from Dr Rick Johnson, our Off-Shore Installation Manager on *Monroe Bravo*. He believes terrorist action caused the explosions and fires on the Platform. Let me explain. He confirms that sensors detected smoke and heat in the Backup Command and Control Centre before it was destroyed. Seconds later, other sensors detected heat and smoke in Central Command and Control before it exploded. According to Rick, it was a massive explosion and killed everyone inside ... but there was nothing in the Centre or close by that could explode and create that amount of devastation; it has to be a bomb. The effect of these two explosions was to destroy all command and control

… and this is the critical point … allow the gas and crude oil to continue pumping. Two more explosions, in rapid succession, ruptured the high pressure gas pipeline and main crude oil riser. We have a Mega Platform, with no control, pumping burning gas and crude oil into the North Sea. We also have a large number of casualties.'

'Any more bad news?'

'Afraid so. Firstly, the death toll is probably at least a dozen and likely to increase. It's going to take time to account for everyone and for injuries to be assessed. Next, the price of TransGlobal Oil stock is in freefall. A few minutes ago, TransGlobal had lost almost ten billion dollars … and the stock is still falling. So, with the scale of these losses, we will have no choice but to offset our losses against our tax liability. We won't be paying billions of dollars in tax to the US government. Another point is this – if the explosions and fires on *Monroe Bravo* are a result of terrorist action, who benefits? So far, no group has admitted responsibility. We may find evidence of explosive devices but the chance of linking these to a terrorist group or even a country is unknown. So, who benefits? Certainly not the US or UK governments. Loss of revenue, reaction against oil pollution in UK waters and so on. As the price of TransGlobal Oil shares falls, those of other oil producing companies has gone up, and so has the price of their oil and gas. I've got some of our analysts working on patterns of share sales, but nothing has emerged yet.'

'Any good news?'

'Well, a glimmer, Rick Johnson is trying to initiate a Platform shutdown …but we don't know if it's been successful. Eye witness report massive fires close to the Dive Centre. The tanks supplying breathing gases to the Bell and divers are at risk. If Rick Johnson has managed to send divers to shut the Platform down they may not have enough gases to breath to survive. It may be impossible to shut the Platform down.'

'If this unwelcome news continues, the price of TransGlobal is going to continue dropping like a stone. You need time ... some breathing space. I'll authorize a blackout of news about the status of *Monroe Bravo* for forty-eight hours.'

'Harvey, that's not enough time. We need more time.'

'Seventy-two hours ... and that's stretching it. There's no way we can keep a lid on this for any longer. Let's talk again soon ... we'll agree the timing and nature of any announcement,' was all Harvey said before he rang off.

Chapter 7

Searing heat

Tuesday 4th April 2023, 3:10 pm

Rick looked down at his feet and could see the splatter of oil as globs of it hit the deck and surfaces around him. The unreal, flickering orange light was being reflected off the sheen of crude oil that was covering everything. Crude oil was dripping off the handrail, running down trunking and pipework, creeping along the edges of the metal grid deck and dropping through to the deck below. His head ached, his chest ached and an icy cold wave of fear washed over him as he acknowledged what was about to happen. At the moment the space around him was well below the flash point of crude oil; but it will warm. The heat from the fires above will warm the oil to its' flash point and it will ignite. The fire will slowly, but inextricably, work its way along every surface of the installation until the whole Platform is ablaze. Fed by an infinite amount of crude oil the Platform will be destroyed. Within hours all that will be left will be a massive pool of burning oil on the surface of the North Sea. A pool that could burn for months. The human, ecological and financial impact would be staggering.

    Gingerly Rick held the rail of the ladder in one hand and pulled himself against it. He winced at the pain in his chest but placed his weight on a rung. "So far so good", he told himself. Swinging his body onto the ladder and placing his other foot sent another sharp pain through his chest, but he knew there was no alternative. Three short breaths and Rick slowly bent his right arm around the ladder and agonisingly pulled himself against it. Step by step, grimace by grimace, Rick climbed down the ladder. He had closed his watering eyes and merely concentrated on one rung at a time; slide his arm down and stop, one foot down to a rung, second foot down to a rung, free hand one rung lower ...repeat. He wasn't sure how far down he had managed to climb until he heard a voice. It was Jack Collier.

'Just hold on. Sandro is going to climb onto the ladder next to you and we'll both help you off.'

It was awkward and painful but Rick managed to get off the ladder and onto the deck.

'We're not far from the Dive Centre; it's this way,' he said.

Rick knew where he was and began to lead the way to the Dive Centre, but in the last few minutes the fires had got worse. A wave of heat and pungent, choking smoke suddenly washed over him. He could hear explosions all around and feel the pressure waves from them. Suddenly everything was in darkness and the effect was disorientating. "Which way is forward?" Rick asked himself. In the cloud of choking smoke he wondered if it was time to use the emergency breathing apparatus, but discounted the idea. It was only an emergency supply, good for ten minutes, he may need to stay around for more than that. The smoke didn't clear and fear suddenly started as a tingle in his groin. "Are we on the correct deck?" "Have I taken a wrong turn and missed the Dive Centre?" The smoke suddenly cleared to reveal a wall of fire on the deck above. Off to his left, lit by a fire, were the helium and oxygen tanks that supplied the main umbilical to the Diving Bell. He could see the plastic coated umbilicals on fire. He lost sight of them as smoke enveloped the area and billowed towards him.

Rick stumbled into the Dive Centre Control Room. Jack and Sandro followed before they slammed the door behind them to keep out the smoke. Rick bowed his head and held up his hand in a gesture of "give me a minute" as he tried to relax and ease the debilitating pain in his side. It took a few moments to regain his composure. When he looked up he was surprised to see Konrad, the Dive Supervisor, alone and simply gazing out of the window; Rick followed his gaze. The crane holding the Diving Bell was shrouded in smoke and flame. The lattice of metal plates making up the jib were burning and it was distorted. He could no longer see the storage tanks nor the umbilicals delivering breathing gases and hot water to the Diving Bell below.

'What's happening here and below?' Rick demanded.

Konrad shook his head in disbelief as he turned his gaze from the scene before him to a cardboard tray of coffees and tea on the table next to him.

'They've all gone … They're all dead.'

Only minutes before Eddie, one of the crane operators, had called into the Dive Centre with an offer to get tea and coffee; all three of them had placed an order. He'd collected it from the galley and was walking back to the Dive Centre. The cardboard tray of three white coffees, no sugar, one sugar and two sugars, one black coffee, no sugar, for himself was balanced on one hand. Considering the Platform worked 24/7 it was a quiet afternoon, a bit gloomy, but dry with a gentle breeze. He was surrounded by reassuring noises from turbines and pumps, shouts and clatter. He'd decided to have a break now because he'd soon be busy transferring supplies from one of the support boats to the on board store. He'd checked at the Dive Centre in case there was any work for him now or after he'd transferred the stores.

The sound of klaxons jolted him out of his daydreaming. He'd worked on rigs and support barges for years and heard dozens of klaxons but never on *Monroe Bravo*. Although his leisurely pace had been disrupted he was confident that the Controller would be onto it, a false alarm. He was at the door of the Dive Centre when more klaxons and the ear splitting sound of an explosion, had him ducking and grabbing a hand rail. Even from the walkway he could see the flames and smoke; it was at the heart of *Monroe Bravo*.

Eddie threw open the door as Konrad, one of The Dive

Supervisors, was bent over the desk and almost shouting into the microphone.

'Emergency, emergency, emergency! Drop everything! Return to the Wet Well immediately. Repeat, we have an emergency. Archie, Danny, return to the Wet Well immediately! Confirm.'

The urgency in his voice sent a cold shiver down Eddie's back. This was no false alarm. He heard the cartoon-like voice of one of the divers confirm they were on their way back to the Bell. Konrad then desperately tried to contact Central Command and Control but there was no response. As Konrad turned to the others in the Dive Centre, he noticed Eddie.

'Eddie, we need to bring the Bell to the surface. We've two divers making their way back to it. Once they're inside, and the Bell is secured, I'll give you the command to bring it to the surface and drop it into the cradle. Once we know what the problem is, we may decide to start decompression … or return the Bell to the seabed.'

'On my way,' was all Eddie said as he suddenly remembered the carton of drinks in his hand. He quickly put them on the table and almost ran to the door.

Eddie scurried along the short walkway away from the Dive Centre, turned left towards the crane, and then up a couple of steel ladders to the crane and his cab. He'd made the same trip hundreds of times and could have done it blindfolded. As he grabbed the door handle to his cab, he heard the start of a dull roar.

Eddie was a petrol head. On his last leave, he and two mates had gone to the drag racing meet in Newcastle. It was a regular event during the season and when he was on-shore. He loved the noise of the high-powered engines, the smell of the exotic exhaust fumes and the chance to rub shoulders with the racers; it was intoxicating. He could hear a similar noise now. It was a deep, throaty bellow that epitomised power. But as he listened, it changed to a whine and began to increase in pitch and volume. It was coming from the other side of the accommodation block.

Eddie had hesitated for only a moment. He climbed into the cab, hit the start button and tried to relax as the crane hummed into life. He switched on the radio, checked in with Konrad, and gave the dials and warning lights a quick glance. The position of the needles on the dials and green lights told him everything was OK; he was ready as soon as he got the word; it never came.

In the first few seconds of his wait for instructions the whine he could hear increased to a piecing scream. Somewhere in the cab he had ear protectors and started to look around for them. A movement somewhere off to his left caught his attention. Three windows from Ground Floor cabins had blown out and were being followed by smoke and flame. As he watched, the Ground Floor outside wall began to change shape and colour before it disintegrated and a jet of flame began to emerge from the accommodation block. Eddie watched in fascination as the flame got longer and bigger. Thick black smoke was now pouring out of the accommodation block as fibre board and plastic, carpets and cabin furniture were vapourised or burnt to ashes in seconds. The sheer power of the flame was drawing air towards it, oxygen feeding the flame to higher and higher temperatures. It was dragging smoke from the building, but the smoke couldn't keep pace. It fell away from the flame and billowed. Thick, black toxic smoke threatened to shroud the area.

It was an automatic reaction. There was no considering of options, no weighing up of the implications, Eddie simply flung open the cab door and reached for the ladder; he wasn't going to hang around. "The whole bloody Platform's on fire" he said to himself. No sooner had Eddie grabbed the rungs of the ladder he felt a searing pain at the back of his neck. He froze for a moment and could smell burning. The hair on the back of his head and neck were on fire. No time for careful climbing down ladders. Eddie pressed his hands and feet against the outside of the ladder and slid down it to the base of the crane. The pain from the back of his head and neck were so intense they threatened to overwhelm him. As he dropped to the deck he noticed there was smoke coming from the arm of his jacket. He was being burnt alive. Eddie's hands were drawn to his head and neck …to provide comfort, relief or protection no one will ever know. His fingers caught the brim of his safety helmet; it felt odd, it felt different. His helmet was melting onto his head and the molten plastic was sticking to his fingers. He gazed, uncomprehendingly, at the back of his hands and fingers. The back of his hands looked like bubble wrap and there were grape-like blisters on the back of his fingers. Eddie ran.

Two of the Dive Team stood alongside Konrad as they watched the unfolding scene in horror. As they waited for a senior diver, the Bellman, to confirm that Danny and Archie were inside the Bell and all was secure they had watched Eddie make his way to the crane. Two other Dive Centre technicians were on a gantry below the crane. They were completing routine checks of gas pressures and flow rates, water pressures and temperatures. Even inside the Dive Centre they could hear the same dull roar and initial whine.

'What the hell is that?' asked Konrad as they searched for the source of the noise.

A technician moved to the door and opened it to check on the noise. The sound had changed from a high pitched whistle to a full blown scream. In the afternoon gloom they could see smoke rising from beyond the accommodation block. There was a change in the light; there was another fire on *Monroe Bravo*. The technician looked expectantly at Konrad, only to be greeted by the shaking head. There was still no response from the Acting Platform Controller. Before they could speak a movement before them caught their attention. Windows had blown out of the accommodation block. One was spinning like a huge playing card as it swooped towards the sea. Smoke and flames were now roaring out of the Ground Floor cabins and a jet of flame was blasting its way through the cabins towards the crane.

'It must be the gas pipeline. There's nothing else on the Platform that would burn like that.'

Konrad looked in disbelief at the growing inferno that had been his cabin. He knew exactly where his cabin was located. Now it had disappeared. If he'd been asleep, he'd be dead. He threw the switch to talk to Eddie but it was too late. They could see him swing out of the cab, shimmy down the ladder and then pause.

'He's on fire,' was all Konrad said.

It was all over in seconds. One moment Eddie was standing at the foot of the crane. The next he was running along the deck and jumped off. His arms cartwheeled and his leg kicked as he dropped towards the sea and disappeared from view. A faint trace of smoke was following him before the whole scene erupted in flame. The gas tanks below the crane had exploded in a ball of flame. It took only moments for the oxygen in the tanks to be consumed and the heat to drive the smoke upwards. Konrad searched for the technicians who had been working just beneath the crane moments earlier. They were nowhere to be seen. He didn't know if Eddie would survive the jump but had to give him a chance. He turned to the two centre staff still standing next to him.

'He's in the water! Go throw him a line!'

The two Dive Centre staff didn't hesitate. They strode to the door and were gone. The Dive Centre building had shielded them from the heat – but they hadn't taken their heavy industrial jackets. It was a mistake. Outside, it was like walking towards a furnace. Every step they took closer to the crane, the hotter they got. Very quickly, their cautious walk slowed to a halt. They didn't get to within thirty metres; the heat stopped them in their tracks. More explosions and the black smoke obliterated them from view. When it cleared, they were nowhere to be seen. They didn't return to the centre but would join Eddie on a list of *missing, presumed lost*. In just over ten minutes, the Platform had been transformed into an inferno. It had been just over ten minutes since an explosion had destroyed the Central Command and Control Centre.

Chapter 8

EPLAST

Tuesday 4th April 2023, 3:12 pm

'Who's gone? Who's dead?' Rick demanded.

'Eddie, the crane driver … he jumped off the Platform … he was on fire … an explosion … four of our men just disappeared.'

The vacant gaze on Konrad's face suddenly disappeared as he returned to the present.

'I've got nine divers, *in sat*, trapped on the sea bed … the jib on the crane has failed … it's dropped the Diving Bell onto the seabed. I've got to get them out!' he shouted above the screaming noise of the ruptured gas pipeline less than a hundred metres away.

Rick awkwardly, yet gently, held him by both his arms and led him to a chair at the centre of the control desk. The U-shaped desk stretched around three sides of the room, in front of the windows. Mounted above the work surface were multiple video monitors and row after row of dials, gauges and switches. It represented the status of the life support system inside the Diving Bell ninety metres beneath the sea. Rick leaned forwards to make sure the microphone linked to the Diving Bell was off before turning back to Konrad. He was about to speak when Konrad blurted out:

'I've got to get them safe,' and started to rise from the chair.

It was then that he noticed the blood smeared around Rick Johnson's face, the bloody bandana across his forehead, the blood and oil on his gloves. Rick gently but firmly stopped him getting up. The effort caused him to wince in pain.

'Konrad, there's nowhere that's safe for them – look.'

Sweeping his arm across the fiery scene before them, Rick continued.

'The ruptured gas pipeline has punched an eight, maybe ten, metre hole straight through the accommodation module. There will be dozens of people dead. The heat from the jet of flame must be two to three thousand degrees centigrade. Even if you could get to the crane, it would be no use. With the jib bent, you'd never be able to lift the Bell onto its cradle. Any minute now other tanks will explode and feed the fire.'

Rick tightened his grip on Konrad's arm to emphasise his point. As they watched, they could see the jib of the crane sagging even more as smoke and flames erupted from the crane drivers cabin. Rick looked into Konrad's face and, over the noise, shouted:

'The divers are as good as dead! We can't save them ... but they can save the rest of us ... and the Platform.'

Rick pointed to the jet of burning gas.

'That's a ruptured gas pipeline ... 1800 psi ... it's now a massive cutting torch. In a few minutes the heat will destroy the pressurised oxygen and helium feeds to the main umbilical – if it hasn't done so already. The gases to the Bell will be cut off and they'll be on the reserve on-board tanks. There will be a massive explosion that could take us and the Dive Centre out. The reserve oxygen and helium storage tanks will be next. It will be a fireball that will contribute to the destruction of the Platform. The crane and that part of the Platform will soon fall into the sea. You know what's directly below. Konrad, the divers are as good as dead and we can't help them. I'm afraid we've got to accept it.'

There was still a look of defiance on Konrad's face as he refused to accept the inevitable but Rick continued.

'They can't swim to the surface, they're too deep … If they start for the surface, the effects of decompression will kill them. There's no way we can get pressurised oxygen and helium to them in the time available. That's assuming debris doesn't fall onto the Bell and entomb them. We've no Command and Control … we can't stop the flow of oil and gas from the Platform, but we can stop it from the seabed … your divers can do it.'

As Rick switched the microphone on and linked it to the divers below, another explosion rocked the Platform. Rick and Konrad were knocked off balance. The effect of the blast threw clipboards and filing trays, coffee mugs and equipment onto the deck.

At that moment, the radio burst into life; it was the Senior Bellman in the Diving Bell below.

'Konrad, we're in trouble … stuff's been falling on the Bell … we've all heard it, and we've got big problems. Danny and Archie have lost all pressure on their breathing gases … they're still trying to dig through debris to get inside the Bell … we're digging from our side. They've had to switch to pony cylinders ... they've got less than five minutes before they run out of gas. We've also lost all pressure on the breathing gas feeds. The gauge for the reserve oxygen supply is registering zero. We've got just the gas inside – nothing else. Difficult to say how long we've got – but not long.'

Rick leaned across the desk, picked up the microphone and answered.

'It's Rick Johnson here. We're working on it. I'll get back to you as soon as possible … hang in there.'

Rick switched off the microphone and turned to Konrad.

'The first priority must be to shut down the oil and gas pipelines at the seabed.

We've got "An action of last resort"; it's an installation called EPLAST, Emergency PLAtform ShuTdown.'

'I've never heard of it.'

A swirl of black smoke engulfed the Dive Centre and for a moment the vivid orange glow was muted. In that moment, Rick was aware that whilst time was of the essence, it was vital that he secured the help and cooperation of Konrad. He also knew the time available to the divers below was limited.

'It's a last resort feature I insisted upon when *Monroe Bravo* was being designed. It's based on lessons learned from the *Piper Alpha* and *Deepwater Horizon* disasters: uncontrollable fires that eventually destroyed those two Platforms. If all our shut-down options fail, then EPLAST is the last resort; it's a series of physical valves that can be turned off. It's a highly sophisticated design but basically like a massive water tap. There are no electronics, no hydraulics, simply basic mechanical engineering.'

'But where is it? Is it on *North Guard*? How does it work?'

'Two devices are on the seabed beneath us. One unit is between Platform legs 5 and 9, the other between legs 12 and 16.'

'They're the Winnebagoes that we were told not to go near or touch.'

Rick smiled at the description of the EPLAST installations. They did look like huge, sleek motorhomes, sides extended – albeit without wheels. Konrad continued.

'They're next to the crude oil riser and the gas pipeline ... some sort of seismometer ... research stuff ... checking on earthquakes or collapsing oil reservoirs below the seabed. You sent priority messages about them – instructions that none of the divers get close to them, but a few months ago a team came to check them out.'

'It was a special dive team from Houston.'

'I can tell you, our guys didn't get on with them – arrogant bunch.'

Rick could feel the seconds and minutes drifting away as the Platform burnt. He cut the conversation short and simply stated.

'You have two divers suited up and ready to work. They can

shut the Platform down.'

Konrad gazed at one of the monitors in front of him before he replied.

'No, they can't. They're still trying to clear a path to the entrance. They'll be gobbling up gas and they only have a minute or so left before they begin to suffocate.'

The monitor showed the two divers frantically digging, almost lost in a cloud of sediment. Mustering all his stature, Rick spoke to Konrad.

'Konrad, we've got to get two divers to shut down the Platform. Is there any way they can do it?'

Konrad paused for a moment, scanned the monitors in front of him and then looked at the fiery scene before him. In a resigned tone, he replied:

'I don't think there is. It looks like the main umbilicals to the Bell have been destroyed. There's no pressurized oxygen or helium getting to it, no pressurized gases to support a diver. An emergency pony cylinder gives you about five minutes – just enough to get back to the Bell. It's not enough to get you to a Winnebago and back to the Bell.'

Konrad flicked his head to look at one of the other monitors.

'There are two massive reserve tanks of oxygen and helium on the Bell – enough for days. The gauge on the oxygen tank is registering zero; it's either been punctured or damaged. Either way the only gases the guys have to breathe is what is already inside the Bell. It's going to last a couple of hours … max.'

Jack had been standing back, listening to the conversation. He was watching the deteriorating scene outside when he interrupted.

'Are there any other divers who could do the job … any nearby?'

'There are divers around but none nearby. The nearest support vessel with divers is hours away. Our guys would have suffocated by the time they arrive.'

'Could a scuba diver shut down the Platform?'

It was Rick who answered.

'Yes, I guess so. It's a simple task to physically shut the values, but they are at ninety metres, in cold water and in the dark.'

Turning to Konrad, Jack asked:

'Do you have any scuba diving kit on the Platform?'

'Yes, there are half a dozen sets of *Poseidon* Mk VI rebreathers, dry suits, fins – everything a scuba diver needs – in the dive store on the deck below. The rebreathers are all set up and ready to go but we don't use them very often.'

'Do they have comms? Can a diver talk to you here?'

'Yes, the set-up is the same as the full commercial suit. Two-way between divers and control, but it'll only work as long as this radio is operational.'

Jack turned to Sandro.

'What do you think?'

'The *Poseidon* Mk VI is a sound piece of kit. I've seen them but never used one. By the time we are in the water, our Diving Bell could be dropped to ninety metres. We could drop down to the seabed, shut the valves and fin to our Bell. Whilst we are doing that, you can think of ways to get breathing gases to the divers below or to get them out.'

Jack turned to Rick.

'What do you want us to do?'

Rick knew this could be the last throw of the dice. If he got this wrong there could be two more bodies to recover from *Monroe Bravo*. Rick also knew they couldn't stay inside the Dive Centre much longer. The smoke inside was getting thicker. He could see the fires spreading and feel the temperature rising. He grabbed a pen from the desk and a scrap of paper and drew sixteen small circles in a four by four square pattern.

'The Platform is supported by sixteen legs, thirty five metres apart, in a four-by-four layout. It's aligned north to south.'

Rick drew an arrow with the single letter 'N' denoting due north.

'The legs are numbered 1 to 16.'

Rick started at the left-hand bottom corner of the square and labelled the legs 1, 2, 3 and 4. Above these, he wrote 5 to 8, 9 to 12 and 13 to 16. Pen in hand, he pointed to a spot just below the number 2. He started to explain the route to the two EPLAST installations.

He had been concentrating so hard on the instructions to Jack and to Sandro that he had been oblivious to the rapidly deteriorating conditions inside the Dive Centre. Konrad gave Rick's arm a nudge, twirled his finger whilst pointing it upwards at the ceiling. He also gave him a tea towel soaked in water. He then gave similar wet towels to Jack and Sandro.

The smoke was now much thicker than before. Rick could see it trickling through a vent near the floor. His face was glowing from the heat, sweat and crude oil had combined into droplets that were running down his bloody forehead and into his eyes. He blinked to clear them but the sting remained. He could feel the sweat running down his chest and back, and into his waist band. The panels that made up the ceiling were starting to distort and bubble. It was just a matter of moments before melting plastic started to drip on them or the whole ceiling collapsed. He then noticed that the double glazed plastic windows were starting to melt. Bubbles were starting to form on the outside surface and discolour.

'Can we carry the comms equipment with us?'

'No ... but we've got a mobile handset. It'll work as long as the comms system works ... but we can't stay.'

Drips of molten, discoloured plastic started to fall from the ceiling, across the carpet and onto the desk. Twenty-six minutes had passed since the first thermite devise had ignited. The time was now 3:26 pm.

Chapter 9
Before the incident

Tuesday 4th April 2023, 11:30 am

Penny Pendleton Price is a Deputy Director within UK Border Force and a *high flyer*. She is part of a small group of Officers on the Express Route to senior management positions and is enjoying rapid promotion. During her short career she has worked in several different branches of UK Border Force. It's an overview of the Service that will be required if she does achieve her expected potential. However, it's clear that many on the Express Route have failed to progress. Some have decided the nature of the work is not for them, others simply couldn't cope with the demands. Periodic transfer to new branches was too disruptive for some, whilst others made poor operational decisions and did not want to live with the consequences. Her intake has been reduced to two Officers.

Whilst Penny was expecting a transfer within UK Border Force the secondment to the Office for Security and Counter Terrorism (OSCT) within the Home Office, and based within the Metropolitan Police Headquarters in London, New Scotland Yard is a surprise. If she's honest, it's also a bit of a disappointment. She wonders if this is like moving a sick patient in hospital closer to the exit. Her colleagues tell her OSCT is a desk job – or rather a 'sat on your arse' job. She will be the Liaison Officer between UK Border Force, the Metropolitan Police and the Spooks – UK external Security Services or MI6. If there's a terrorist incident, she will be part of a coordinating trio for three arms of government. However, most of the time she will be coordinating massive amounts of incoming data. Page after page of reports as the status of 'persons of interest' are monitored. It was described as ninety-nine percent boredom and one-percent frantic action.

It's her second day at OSCT. On her first day Penny spent about ten seconds in her new office. The rest of the day was spent running the gauntlet of ID checks and verification, photos and finger prints, DNA swabs and issue of passes. Lanyards with a variety of plastic key cards gave her access to virtually every part of New Scotland Yard – and the stationary cupboard. Her UK Border Force phone was taken away and replaced by a secure, OSCT encrypted phone. She was also given a single sheet of A4 paper with a photograph, contact details and brief resume of the Police Officer she will be working with; it's Chief Superintendent Steel. There wasn't a sheet introducing her Security Service counterpart; she was told cryptically "position to be confirmed".

The resume for CS Steel made impressive reading. In just over twenty years he'd risen from a Police Constable, on the beat, to Chief Superintendent and been awarded three commendations for bravery. It also looked as though he'd moved around within the 'Met', the Metropolitan Police. He had worked in armed robbery and fraud, vice and diplomatic protection as well as leading murder enquiries. Penny also noted that there was nothing about interests outside the police, nothing about a family.

So far, day two was an anti-climax. After all the hustle and bustle of day one, she'd been left alone in her office. She had spent a couple of hours reading through a thick file that provided information on everything, from the names and contact details of everyone in OSCT, to evacuation routes, from mission statements to operational protocols. She took an hour off and took a walk around the maze of floors and corridors that constituted New Scotland Yard. She'd found the canteen, armed response unit, forensics and, seemingly, dozens of other units. However, she wasn't entirely sure she would be able to find them again in a hurry!

She had rearranged the furniture in the office, decided to replace the drab picture on the wall with something brighter, and raided the stationery cupboard. Penny had just finished arranging writing pads and pens, staplers and scissors, paperclips and highlighters in and around her desk, when the phone rang. It was her first call, and it was from CS Steel; he was on his way to see her. Two minutes later, there was a knock on her door and it opened.

Penny recognised the smiling face from his photo. He bounced into her office, grabbed her hand firmly in both of his, shook it vigorously, and seemed genuinely pleased to see her. The few people Penny had met so far seemed very formal – courteous, polite, but guarded. Steel was the opposite. He was warm, open, and affable, with a strong London accent. In fact, he sounded more like an East End barrow boy than a senior police officer. Penny could see straight away how this police officer would endear himself to both colleagues and villains alike.

Penny was relieved. She'd heard all sorts of stories about sexism in the Met, the aloofness of senior officers, and 'outsiders' being kept at a distance. She just hoped that the security officer was like CS Steel. After the initial welcome, Penny took a moment to refine her first impression. She knew Steel was in his mid-forties but he looked younger. He was tall, slightly overweight but it was disguised by a well-cut suit. Clean-shaven, healthy looking skin, bright, expectant eyes and a cropped salt and pepper haircut gave the impression of a former athlete. It was his movement that reinforced the impression.

Penny wasn't the only one making an initial assessment of a team member. CS Steel had not only read through Penny's resumé but phoned an old friend at UK Border Force. He'd been given the inside information on Penny and wasn't disappointed. The resumé described an economics graduate on the fast track route to a senior post in UK Border Force. A string of attachments to different branches, several notable successes, and interests outside work. It was when he read that Penny Pendleton Price was a keen horse rider, skier and scuba diver that he felt envy for a person who had a life outside the job. His job had been all-consuming and had cost him his marriage, and alienated a son and a daughter. He also wondered how long this blonde, pretty, slim young woman would retain her youthful glow, faced with the grim realities of human nature. On reflection, he thought it wouldn't be long. Despite the youthful and attractive appearance, Ms Pendleton Price didn't look strong. She barely reached his shoulder, was probably a dress size 10 and well under sixty kilos in weight. Her face had a pale, porcelain white quality that made her appear delicate. He wondered how she would cope with a cat fight on a Saturday night in the clubbing district.

'I'm so pleased to meet you, Chief Superintendent. I'm really looking forward to working with you.'

'Call me Tommy,' said Steel; he could see the puzzled expression on Penny's face.

The puzzlement was nothing to do with his name but the informality. Inside UK Border Force, colleagues were typically addressed by rank and surname. She was expecting to call him Chief Superintendent or Sir. Steel interpreted the look of puzzlement differently.

'My mother loved Rock and Roll and the stars of the 1960s – Adam Faith, Marty Wilde and …Tommy Steel. And so when I was born, my mum called me Tommy – Tommy Steel.'

Penny realised she had vaguely heard of Tommy Steel but not the others.

'Do you fancy going to the canteen for a cup of tea and a chat? I'm sure you've got a hundred questions to ask and I need something to eat,' he smiled.

Tommy led the way. As they passed various offices and departments, he gave her a summary of the key people, who they were, what they did and how well they did it. Tommy knew everyone. When they eventually walked into the canteen, it was clear that all the servers knew Tommy. There was a relaxed, informal banter between them. He asked about husbands, sisters and kids as he introduced Penny. He didn't have to say what he wanted; they knew. A giant mug of tea, a BLT and slice of apple pie.

Tommy had just taken a huge bite out of his BLT when Penny asked him about the other member of the team and the comment 'position to be confirmed'. Tommy pointed to his bulging cheeks, munched away, and washed the food down with a gulp of tea.

'We'll be working with Harry Preece but apparently he's been 'unavoidably detained'. It could be true or he could be sleeping it off. The MI6 guys love the cloak and dagger stuff, and so does Harry. He acts as though he is Harry Palmer ... not Harry Preece.'

There was another confused look on Penny's face and she asked, '*Who?*'

'Harry Palmer ...*Ipcress File* ...Michael Caine ... the 1960's film,' explained Tommy, but the confused look on Penny's face made it clear she doesn't know what he's talking about.

'It's a classic spy film starring Michael Caine. He plays a character called Harry Palmer and our Harry Preece not only looks like him but acts like him – even down to the heavy black framed glasses. He'll probably be in this afternoon.'

Another bite of the sandwich, another gulp of tea, and an endorsement.

'Harry's good ... worked with him lots of times, never a problem ... always delivers and often surprisingly so, but plays up the MI6 bit.'

Tommy went on to explain that day by day they will be reviewing surveillance and cyber intelligence from GCHQ and monitoring *persons of interest*.

'The job is all about trying to foil attacks rather than respond to them. It will be nine to five work. However, if and when there is a suspected attack, it will be full on 24/7, often eating and sleeping in the office.'

Tommy paused and looked across the table at Penny. There was something about her that reminded him of his daughter. He felt protective.

'Penny, I'm old enough to be your dad, so a bit of advice … be careful around Harry. He's a charmer … and will have your knickers off in no time.'

Penny laughed; it was an honest, joyful laugh and she was not at all embarrassed.

'Thanks for the advice … I'll try to keep 'em on! What about Commander Short?'

Commander Alice Short led the Office for Security and Counter-Terrorism.

'She's good, methodical … to the point of being fastidious. She's fair, has no favourites … but all by the book. She doesn't tolerate 'cowboys' or 'Lone Rangers', which is why there's always a bit of tension between her and Harry. Harry cuts corners and uses … shall we say "unorthodox" methods of enquiry. With Alice, it's all a team effort or nothing.'

Penny sipped her tea whilst Tommy demolished the rest of the sandwich, the pie and drained his mug. Over the next forty-five minutes, he gave her an overview of the OSCT and the cases he was currently working on. As the lunch time crowd disappeared, and the canteen became quiet, Tommy made a suggestion.

'I was thinking … why work in separate offices? The Coordination Room is big, plenty of room for the three of us. Why don't we all work together, in the same room? We can try it for a couple of days and see how we get on. I can talk you through what I'm doing, answer any questions you've got and generally get you up to speed.'

It was a generous offer. The active cases that Tommy and Harry were working on required little or no input from UK Border

Force. Penny assumed this was why she'd not been thrown into a frenzy. It was merely a case of keeping UK Border Force informed. With no cases of her own, she followed Tommy from the canteen to the Coordination Office and spent the next couple of hours shadowing his work.

It was mid-afternoon. Penny was trawling through a report and *intel* on a suspicious person. She was watching video footage of a young man standing on a street corner in Fulham. *Is he there to meet someone? Will anything be exchanged? What will be said?* A string of CCTV cameras had tracked him from the Tube station to the street corner. The facial recognition software had confirmed his identity and summarised what was known about him. Another monitor displayed photographs of known associates and *intel* on them.

As she watched the video, a young man in a hoody approached her 'person of interest'. From the descriptions of known associates, officers had narrowed it down to three people. There was a short conversion and a small package was exchanged. Immediately the two men turned and walked away from each other. Penny began to read the report summary and recommended action when Tommy's phone rang. She ignored the distraction and concentrated on reading the recommendations and actions.

'Drop what you're doing ... we've got a meeting with Commander Short in ten minutes ... her office. There's been a suspected terrorist incident on the *Monroe Bravo* oil rig in the North Sea and it's going to be *go, go, go* from now on. We've got five minutes to scan feeds from GCHQ, social media and news outlets. I'll check GCHQ and the news outlets. Can you check social media sites? We need to know as much about the incident as Alice Short before we see her.'

For a split second Penny froze. Jack and Sandro could be on *Monroe Bravo*.

Chapter 10

One percent frantic action

Tuesday 4th April 2023, 3:11 pm

This was the 'one percent frantic action' Penny's colleagues in UK Border Force had mentioned. She only had accounts on Facebook and Instagram, but knew there were dozens more social media sites that had billions of followers. As she opened Facebook on her phone, she was greeted by the dramatic photograph Angus had taken a few minutes ago. She felt physically sick and all her energy seemed to drain out of her.

Jack had told her that he and Sandro were flying from Aberdeen, in the company helicopter, to the *Stavanger* for a visit to *Monroe Bravo.* It was to celebrate their standby contract with TransGlobal Oil. As she scrolled down, the screen captions said the Platform was pumping millions of gallons of crude oil into the North Sea. Banner headlines were saying it was a human and ecological disaster with dozens of casualties. Penny didn't hesitate. She sent a text: "ARE YOU SAFE?" to Jack and Sandro before flicking through linked screens for more information; it was all speculation. She switched to Instagram and was greeted by the same photo as before, but different headlines. Penny suddenly realised how unprepared she was to search for information. In desperation, she typed "*Monroe Bravo* Oil Rig" into her search engine and started to summarise what she could. With the clock ticking, and not knowing where else to look, she went to the Financial Times Stock Exchange (FTSE) web site. News of the fire was plastered all over the home screen and showed the share prices of TransGlobal Oil in free fall.

'What have yer got?' asked Tommy.

Penny read from her notes.

'*Monroe Bravo* is a massive oil rig, sorry oil Platform, in the North Sea with a workforce of about 160 men and women. It's 180 kilometres east of Aberdeen in the Fortes field. It cost close to a billion US dollars to build and pumps crude oil and liquified natural gas to on-shore installations. It's owned by TransGlobal Oil and produces just under fifteen percent of UK crude oil production and almost twenty percent of natural gas. If production is halted, it will have a devasting impact on the oil company and energy supply. The FTSE is showing the price of TransGlobal Oil shares in free fall.'

Tommy was surprised and impressed. He hadn't intended to put Penny on the spot; he didn't want to embarrass her, or make her feel inadequate, he just needed the information asap. What she had produced, in minutes, and under stress, was impressive. It was more detailed and more comprehensive than he had assembled in the same time.

'I've discovered similar info, but less than you … well done. Let's go. Alice doesn't like people being late.'

Commander Alice Short had spent years working within the Met – long days, weeks, months and years of hard graft, gaining experience, building a reputation and gaining promotion. She's worked with some outstanding officers and others who were promoted to levels of incompetence. She's worked with the mercurial and the plodders, seen the guilty go free because of unauthorised procedures or sloppy policing. She's also aware that a single minded terrorist can cause untold damage in a UK city. Her job was to stop them before they could act. In doing so Commander Short had assembled a hand-picked team that she's proud of. They're dedicated professionals who are insightful but also check out the trivia. They followed the leads and do not ignore anything.

As such, Alice was wary of the UK Border Force replacement at Deputy Director rank. Whilst she strongly believed women should be given every chance, she also wanted the best people in post. Before she accepted Deputy Director Pendleton Price, she'd made exhaustive enquires about her; not all the information was from UK Border Force. As a result, she was going to give this officer every opportunity to demonstrate her ability ... or incompetence. It was coming sooner than expected.

Tommy and Penny arrived at Commander Short's outer office a couple of minutes before the meeting was due to start.

'Commander Short is on the phone with a minister. She knows you're here and I'm sure she will be free shortly,' the PA announced.

Both Tommy and Penny simply sank into the large leather sofa. Tommy closed his eyes and thought about the forthcoming investigation. Penny was studying the screen on her phone as she searched the internet for information on *Monroe Bravo* and other Oil Rig disasters. There was no reply from Jack or Sandro.

Tommy stirred as Commander Short opened her door, smiled and invited them in. As she did so, she checked her watch.

'Isn't Harry Preece with you?' she asked.

At that moment, Harry strolled into the outer office. He noticed Alice looking at her watch, pulled up his sleeve, and announced:

'The message said your office, 3:30 pm; it's 3:30 pm,' he said with a smile.

Alice ushered the three of them into her office and sat at one of the chairs around a large circular table. She had a plain folder with a large label reading '*Monroe Bravo*'.

'We have a terrorist incident. About 3:00 pm this afternoon there were four explosions on the North Sea Oil Rig *Monroe Bravo*. The Off-Shore Installation Manager, Dr Rick Johnson, believes the explosions are terrorist related. Two explosions knocked out the Backup and Main Command and Control Centres. The other two ruptured the gas and oil pipelines. We have photographs of the whole rig on fire. There has already been a large loss of life ... which is likely to increase. Actions are underway to control the fires and shut down the rig – but this may be impossible. We may be facing a disaster like *Piper Alpha*. The Police Commissioner, the Director General of UK Border Force and the Head of MI6 have been alerted. Your teams are currently being activated and will be following the off-shore TIP ...'

Commander Short glanced at Penny and clarified.

'Off-Shore TIP ... it's the Terrorist Incident Plan. We have pre-prepared plans for a range of incidents. Your team will be following it now. In this folder there's a copy of the documents sent to your teams – a plan of the oil rig, name of captains of supply and support vessels, names and responsibilities of all personnel who have been on the rig over the last month. There's a separate list of those who left the rig in the last 72 hours. Also included is a biography of Rick Johnson – the person who believes it's a terrorist attack.

'TransGlobal Oil as well as US Homeland Security and MI6 are assuming the explosions and fire are a terrorist incident – if it's an accident, it will become clear. A team from US Homeland Security, and a truck load of equipment, are being assembled. In a few hours it will be somewhere over the Atlantic Ocean. They are due to arrive sometime after midnight and will set up in Room B137 – adjacent to your office. I'm told they will be fully operational by noon tomorrow.

'Speed is of the essence. You are to use our executive authority. If anyone does not actively aid the investigation, let me know. I want an update, in person, here in five hours. Is that understood?' demanded Commander Short. 'I'll be briefing the minister and attending a COBRA meeting with the Prime Minister later today. A spokesperson will be making a statement on the evening news. So, any questions ... any comments?'

'Commander, do you have any more information on the US Homeland Security Team?' asked CS Steel.

'No, only that it will be a team of five. An anti-terrorism Special Agent will be in overall charge. There will be a Border Protection Officer, a Cyber Security Specialist and two support staff. All the information I have is in the file. Anything else?'

'Yes, perhaps I could ask Penny to summarise what she's found out in the last few minutes, since your phone call?'

The tone and intonation of Tommy's suggestion wasn't lost on Alice; she'd known him too long. He gave credit where credit was due … and any blame where it was deserved. The next few minutes would tell her a lot about Officer Pendleton Price and Tommy's opinion of her.

It did, as Penny succinctly repeated her summary. Tommy noticed the faint change in Alice's expression as she listened. He could tell she was pleasantly surprised and impressed. Penny had just finished her summary when she hesitated, but then continued.

'Oh, just a small point … in terms of accuracy, *Monroe Bravo* is officially known as a Platform not an oil rig. Oil rigs are used to drill for oil whilst Platforms process and transfer the products to tankers or to shore. However, *Monroe Bravo* is an exception. In addition to drilling into one of the largest known oil deposits in the North Sea, it is also being fed oil and gas from dozens of other wells for processing. I understand the oil rigs can cut off the flow of gas and oil to *Monroe Bravo* but without Command and Control, *Monroe Bravo* cannot shut down; it could burn for months, if not years. The effect on TransGlobal Oil, as well as the US and UK economies, could be significant.'

It was sobering information. Commander Short turned to Harry.

'No group has admitted responsibility,' he said, 'but if what Penny says is true, they'll soon be queuing up. We're checking with GCHQ for *intel* on any cyber traffic and starting to rattle a few doors …'

'OK, report back here in five hours.'

As Harry, Tommy and Penny walked back to the Coordination Office, Tommy turned to Penny.

'We've got ten to fifteen minutes before all hell breaks loose. Ten to fifteen minutes to get up to speed before questions and reports, emails and phone calls start flooding in. It's going to be manic for days. Don't worry about what Harry and I are doing. Start on the file and ask for regular updates from your team; tea and cake at five o' clock,' Tommy concluded with a reassuring smile.

Chapter 11

Evacuation

Tuesday 4th April 2023, 3:26 pm

'Konrad, what's the safest way from here to the deck below – avoiding the worst of the fires?' asked Rick.

'The south-east ladder … about forty metres along the walkway, due east. Next to the rail is a gate … you can get on a vertical ladder … it'll will take us down to Deck 3 … but we'll be walking towards the drilling platform and the main crude oil riser. We'll be a deck below but it's going to be incredibility hot … probably burning oil dropping onto us. Once we get to the ladder, we'll be sheltered from the worst of the heat but burning oil will be pouring over us. It's going to be tricky climbing down the ladder, but it's our best option. The dive store is just a short walk from the ladder.'

'We need to go,' said Jack as he pointed to a bubble that had burst on the window; a hole had appeared and a flood of smoke was pouring in. The whole window was starting to melt.

Sandro turned to Konrad.

'Do you have any breathing apparatus in here? Have you got any for Jack and me? If so, we need it now.'

Konrad dashed across the room to a metal cupboard, grabbed three sets of apparatus and handed a set each to Jack and Sandro. Each set consisted of a simple face mask linked to a pony cylinder; half a litre of compressed air, good for ten minutes at most.

Sandro helped Rick fit the face mask snugly over his face. He opened the tap, strapped the cylinder into a side pocket of Rick's rucksack and draped it over his head and shoulder. The helmet, gloves and wet tea towel around his chin gave him all the protection he could muster; he was ready to go. A quick glance and Sandro could see Konrad was ready and making his way to the door. As he reached for the door handle, Sandro shouted – but too late. Konrad reacted as though he'd been shot. He spun away from the door and hugged his hand to his chest. The door handle may not have been red hot – but hot enough to instantly blister his palm and strip the skin away.

More panels were starting to droop and fall from the ceiling as flames emerged to writhe above them. Konrad opened the door with his elbow, the volume of noise trebling as he bent into a wall of heat. It was like opening a furnace door but he walked doggedly into it and along the walkway; Rick, Jack and Sandro followed. They were committed; there was no turning back, no alternative route. One moment the walkway was illuminated in the deadly orange light, the next, swirling black smoke obliterated everything. It was only by brushing against the rail of the walkway that they could gauge their position. Konrad was counting his paces and hoping he'd have a clear view of the gate when he got close. However, he was also trying to shield himself from the heat; he could feel the temperature rising on his left side. He was also praying that the closer they got to the gate, the more they would be shielded. Until then, it would get hotter and hotter. They were being cooked alive.

Rick was also counting steps and stole a glance forward when smoke momentarily cleared. At first, he wasn't sure what it was, but the smoke was swirling around Konrad's legs. The soles of his boots were melting on the hot metal deck; his footprints were smoking and would burst into flame at any moment. His clothes were also smouldering. Rick glanced at his own boots and saw smoking footprints. His boots were melting and the sleeve of his jacket was smouldering. They had to get away from the heat.

'Here,' shouted Konrad, as he stood by a gate in the walkway rail.

Get going, we'll follow you.'

Jack unlatched the gate and didn't hesitate. He grabbed a rung in one gloved hand, placed a foot on another and started downwards. Sandro followed almost immediately. Konrad hesitated by the gate.

'We've got to go … we can't stay here!' shouted Rick over the roaring fire above.

'I've no gloves … I'll have to use the end of my sleeves …' Konrad said as he tried to shuffle the sleeves of his jacket down so he could use the ends as protective pads. 'You go first; if I slip, I don't want to knock anyone off. I'll give you a count of one hundred before I start down. You'll be clear by then.'

There was no time to argue. The construction just above them was providing a shield but it was still incredibly hot. Between the continuous spray of hot crude oil, falling like heavy rain, large globs of oil were splattering everything around them. Some were alight, trailing flames and smoke as they fell.

Rick steeled himself for what he knew was about to come. He grabbed a rung and put a foot on another as he looked down. He couldn't see anything because of the smoke but could feel the sharp pain in his chest. He couldn't feel any heat through his heavy leather gloves but could already see oil smeared over them. As he started downwards, Rick closed his eyes and started the count. Step by step, sliding one arm down the side of the ladder and holding on with the other hand, he descended. He was concentrating on the rhythm and his counting when a shout from Jack broke the spell; he'd made Deck 3 and, awkwardly, stepped off the ladder and hugged Jack. Much later, Rick wouldn't be able to explain why he'd embraced him; it just seemed the natural thing to do.

It was still hot, but slightly cooler on Deck 3 than Deck 4. There was also less smoke but every surface was dripping with crude oil. They all knew that it was just a matter of time before the heat and flames above drove the temperature of the oil to flash point and the whole Platform would be engulfed in flame.

'Where's Konrad?' asked Jack.

'He's coming ... didn't have any gloves ... he's using the cuffs of his jacket as pads to protect his hands.'

No sooner had Rick explained when anxiety washed over him – had Konrad decided not to follow? Was the pain in his hand too much? Could he grip the rungs? No sooner had the thoughts arrived, than Konrad appeared – slowly and purposefully. Jack and Sandro grabbed his jacket and helped him onto the safety of Deck 3. Rick suddenly remembered the first aid kit.

Konrad, I've got a first aid kit ... we can bandage your hands.'

Without another word, Sandro slipped the rucksack off Rick's shoulder and rummaged inside until he found the kit. He grabbed two crepe bandages and a tube of antiseptic gel. He ripped the plastic covering off the bandages with his teeth whilst Jack unscrewed the top off the tube of gel. Konrad offered his hand: it looked as though the whole of his right palm was raw and watery.

'This is going to hurt ... but we've no choice.'

Jack squirted most of the tube of gel onto Konrad's palm. Sandro wrapped the crepe bandage around his palm, fingers and wrist until it came to an end. It wasn't pretty but it would give some protection. He did the same for the other hand. More burning oil was dropping onto and around them.

'It's this way,' shouted Konrad as he led the way to the dive store.

He released the heavy, key-coded lock, ushered them inside, flicked on the lights and slammed the door closed. Apart from wisps of smoke, it all looked tranquil and well organised. Half a dozen Poseidon Mark IV rebreathers were hanging on the left-hand wall. Beneath, on a shelf, were spare CO_2 scrubber cartridges and packets of soda lime granules that absorbed the CO_2 from any breathing cycle. It was a key component of the rebreather system. Konrad had said the rebreathers were set up and ready to go. However, he decided to replace the soda lime granules with fresh ones before the dive. On an adjacent wall were dry suits and fleecy all-in-one outfits to keep a diver warm at ninety metres. There were racks of full face masks, fins and boots as well as several rows of weights and a string of weight belts. It was like an Aladdin's cave containing top of the range diving gear but they had no time to marvel. It was Konrad's domain and he took charge.

'I'll set up two rebreathers whilst you decide which dry suits, masks and fins you want.'

Konrad glanced at his watch.

'It's just past 3:30 pm. The current will be from the south-west but lessening all the time. Slack tide in about two hours.'

Jack and Sandro threw off the protective clothing they had been given and pulled on a set of fleecy underwear and a dry suit. It took moments to slip weights into a weight belt and a few more to find a face mask that would fit, some fins, and to confirm the comms were working. Fins and faced mask were strapped to the rebreather and they were ready to go.

'Jack, Sandro, forget the comms … they are never going to last … it's vital you know what to do without me guiding you. I've drawn diagrams and notes on these two slates … I'll go through them.'

Rick held up one of the white plastic slates on which he had drawn identical diagrams and notes. He showed the slates to Jack and Sandro and explained:

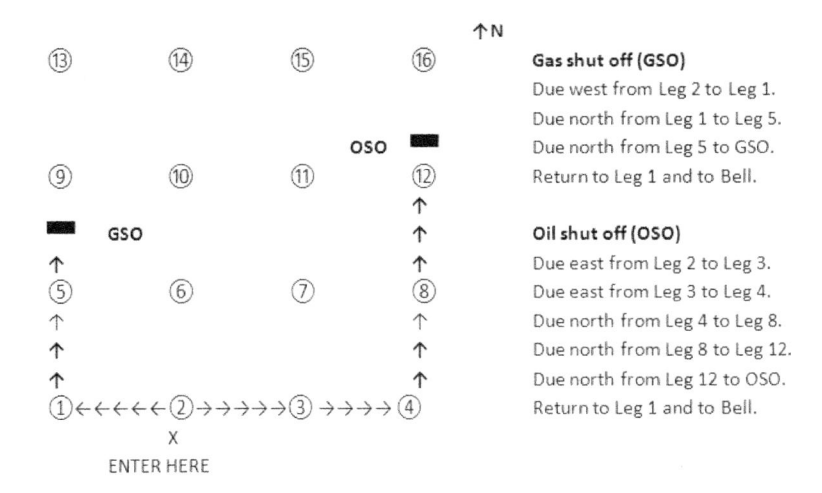

```
                                    ↑N
   ⑬         ⑭         ⑮         ⑯      Gas shut off (GSO)
                                          Due west from Leg 2 to Leg 1.
                                          Due north from Leg 1 to Leg 5.
                              OSO ▬       Due north from Leg 5 to GSO.
   ⑨         ⑩         ⑪         ⑫       Return to Leg 1 and to Bell.
                                    ↑
   ▬  GSO                            ↑   Oil shut off (OSO)
   ↑                                 ↑    Due east from Leg 2 to Leg 3.
   ⑤         ⑥         ⑦         ⑧       Due east from Leg 3 to Leg 4.
   ↑                                 ↑    Due north from Leg 4 to Leg 8.
   ↑                                 ↑    Due north from Leg 8 to Leg 12.
   ↑                                 ↑    Due north from Leg 12 to OSO.
   ①←←←←②→→→→→③→→→→④                    Return to Leg 1 and to Bell.
             X
         ENTER HERE
```

REMEMBER: Open red taps (acw), release 8 clips, break seal & remove cover. Turn wheel 80 turns (cw). Bell on bearing 225° from Leg 1.

'This may not be the quickest route to the shut-off valves but it's probably the safest. There'll be debris falling off the Platform and you don't want to be under it. The shut-down procedure is the same for both installations.'

Jack and Sandro were listening intently.

'You'll be entering the water here, next to Leg 2. One of you has to swim due west for thirty-five metres to reach Leg 1. At Leg 1, swim due north to Leg 5; it's another thirty-five metres. EPLAST is between Legs 5 and 9, another fifteen – you can't miss it. It's the size of a forty-foot shipping container, a big Winnebago with bulging sides. You need to be on the inside end of the installation, the end pointing towards the middle of the Platform.

'You're looking for a dome-shaped cover, about one metre by one metre. It'll be about chest height and will have the word EPLAST painted on it. The edges are marked in a band of yellow and black painted bands.'

Rick was struggling to remain calm. The smoke was starting to find its way inside the dive store but he had to be clear and precise in his instructions. His head throbbed and his side ached but he had to concentrate.

'There are two standard taps, both painted red, one just above and one just below the cover. Open both anticlockwise to release the air inside the cover and to flood the space inside.

'There are eight clips holding the cover in place. They're simple lever clips and you should have no problem releasing them ... there's now nothing holding the cover in place except the seal between the edge of the cover and a rubber insert. Use your dive knife to break the seal and release the cover – just let it fall.

'There will be a large, four-spoke cast-iron wheel, size of a car steering wheel, in front of you. Start to turn it clockwise. It's going to be hard to start but once you get it turning it will get easier. You'll be turning a series of gears and fly wheels. It's basically a simple screw mechanism. Turning the wheel will drive precision-ground steel plates through equally precision-ground steel housings to progressively cut off the flow of gas. You're going to have to turn it about eighty times, that's *eight zero* times.

'Once it's starts to turn, don't stop ... you've got to keep it turning; every turn and it will get easier ... just keep it spinning until it comes to a sudden stop. Once it stops turning you return to Leg 1 and then swim on a bearing of 225 degrees to your Diving Bell. I'll contact your ship and make sure the Bell is waiting for you. It will be as close to Leg 1 as your ship can get.'

Rick was concentrating so hard on giving the instructions to Jack and Sandro that he had been oblivious to the rapidly deteriorating conditions inside the dive store. Konrad gave Rick's arm a nudge and pointed to a rack of equipment on the far wall. It was starting to smoulder from the heat outside.

The smoke inside was also getting thicker. Rick could see it pouring through a vent near the floor. Sweat and crude oil were still running down his bloody forehead and into his eyes. He blinked to clear them but the sting remained. The panels that made up the ceiling were starting to distort and bubble. It was just a matter of minutes before melting plastic started to drip on them or the whole ceiling collapsed. Jack and Sandro were getting hotter and hotter in their dry suits. This was not the way to start a dangerous dive.

'We've got to go!'

Chapter 12

Recovery

Tuesday 4th April 2023, 9:35 am (Houston, Texas)
(3:35 pm on *Monroe Bravo*)

It was as good as he could have hoped. Brachs had seventy-two hours to discover as much as he could and to put plans in place to save TransGlobal Oil. He'd no sooner put the phone down when Molly walked into his office with a slip of paper.

'Just had a phone call from a Mr Baxter, Head of Security at our Aberdeen headquarters. He wants to provide you with an update and believes he's found Norton Flynn. He says it's "delicate". Do you want me to get him for you?'

Moments later the phone on Walter's desk rang and he answered it abruptly.

'Brachs!'

'Sir, it's Baxter, Head of Security, Aberdeen Headquarters. I believe I've found Vice President Flynn … but it's awkward.'

'What do you mean, *awkward*?' demanded Walter.

'Norton Flynn left his office at 1:35 pm this afternoon, UK time, for a 2:00 pm meeting with a company called Kirkpatrick & Barnes in central Aberdeen. However, when we checked with their office, they had no record of such a meeting. His car has a tracker installed and we tracked it to the … er, Best Western Airport Hotel, north-west of the city. His car is in the car park and he's registered as Mr and Mrs Hoffman, in room 227 … checked in at 2:10 pm.'

'Are you sure it's Norton in the hotel room?'

'Yes, sir. I had to lean on the hotel manager but the receptionist confirmed it was Norton and a young woman. They have stayed in the hotel before … er, several times.'

Walter struggled with the strong Scottish accent and for an instant he was confused by the phrase "lean on" but guessed this was a Scottish phrase for coerce or intimidate.

'Could Norton be held in the room … under duress?'

'I doubt it, sir. The receptionist said they have had very few guests so far today. Check-in is normally 4:00 pm. They allowed Mr and Mrs Hoffman to register because they are regulars. People typically arrive late afternoon and early evening. What do you want me to do?'

'I want you to bang on the door and tell Flynn to phone me – now! You got that?'

'Yes sir.'

'Thank you for being so efficient and … er, discrete.'

Minutes later, Molly transferred a phone call from Norton T. Flynn to Walter's desk phone.

'Norton Flynn here, sir. How can I help you?'

'Norton, there have been multiple explosions on *Monroe Bravo*; it's ablaze and the fire is out of control.'

Walter could hear Norton's intake of breath. It was a golden rule that senior executives never switched off their phones. He wasn't particularly bothered about the extra-marital sex – except it was on company time. It was because he was so angry that he decided to give Norton a tough time; to set an example for others.

'People have been losing their lives trying to save the Platform whilst you've been shagging some broad on company time. Well, I'm guessing she's not your wife. Get your arse back to the office and do what we pay you to do. When this emergency is over, we'll talk again.'

Walter slammed the phone into its cradle and turned to other pressing matters.

It was a frantic time at TransGlobal Oil Headquarters, with a steady stream of reports coming in by phone or in person. However, Walter had experienced similar dramas before and knew they were marathons rather than sprints. He'd arranged for a change of clothes and toiletries to be delivered to his office that evening, along with a meal. He would be at his desk, and sleeping on the couch, until the situation stabilised. The next drama would take place when the Shanghai Stock Exchange opened for business. He'd spoken with Harvey Blickstein, the United States Deputy Secretary of the Treasury, earlier in the day. Between them, and a dozen lawyers, analysts and strategists, they had agreed a plan. The question was, would it work?

Within minutes of the Shanghai Stock Market opening, the selling frenzy reached new heights. All the prepared and carefully orchestrated calming messages from TransGlobal Oil were ignored. It seemed that every minute that passed another percentage point was wiped off the price of TransGlobal Oil stock. It continued to be in free fall. As the hours passed, and as stock was liquidated, there was less to sell, and the frenzy seemed to ease. By the time the NYSE and NASDAQ Exchanges opened on a new day, the dramatic fall had slowed as analysts began to recognise the market had over-reacted. With the share price of TransGlobal Oil at less than 50% of their pre-fall level, it looked as though the worse may be over; there was a chance the price of stock had stabilised and may even recover, especially if there was good news from the North Sea. However, the decision to impose a blackout on any news about *Monroe Bravo* did not constitute good news.

Walter slept for a few hours on the couch in his office as he waited for the London Stock Exchange to open. As soon as it did, the selling of TransGlobal Oil stock resumed. The bold speculators were not convinced the price had stabilised and it would be driven lower; it was worth waiting longer before buying TransGlobal Oil even at these rock bottom prices. The mood was reinforced a few hours later in Riyadh. When the Saudi Exchange opened, several brokers began liquidating their holdings, which prompted further selling of TransGlobal Oil shares.

Chapter 13

Desperate journey

Tuesday 4th April 2023, 3:40 pm

'There's a dedicated stairwell from behind the store to a floating stage next to Leg 2. We'll be sheltered from the heat as we leave but exposed at the top of the stairwell. Once we start downwards, we'll be sheltered.

Konrad led the way. Smoke and heat swirled around them as they skirted the dive store. It was no more than five metres to the top of the stairwell but Jack could feel the heat as he padded along the metal deck and hurried down the metal stairs. Konrad had been right. They were exposed to the full blast of heat for only a few seconds before they dropped below Deck 3. It had been hot and uncomfortable in their heavy protective jackets. In a dry suit, with a rebreather on their backs, weights around their waist, it was a trial. Divers tend not to walk far when in full kit: maybe a few metres before they step into the water. By the time Jack and Sandro had clambered down to sea level and the floating platform, they were both breathing hard and sweating heavily. This was not the ideal start to a deep and taxing dive.

Both Jack and Sandro were desperately trying to control their breathing as they completed buddy checks on their equipment.

'Gas or oil shut down valve … between Legs 5 and 9 or 12 and 16?' asked Jack.

'You're the stronger swimmer – why don't you take the oil valve … between 12 and 16?'

Jack leaned against an upright as he slipped his feet into his fins and tightened the straps.

'Don't forget the sequence; open the taps, remove the clips and cover, turn the wheel clockwise – 80 turns. We're all depending on you,' said Rick.

Jack and Sandro took Giant Strides from the Platform, bobbed to the surface and both signalled AOK before starting their descent. In moments they were lost from view. Rick scrolled down the list of pre-set numbers on his phone until he found the new standby ship, the *Stavanger*. The roar of the flames and explosions were now muted but Rick pressed the phone to his ear as the radio operator took his call.

'MV *Stavanger,* my name is Rick Johnson and I am the Off-Shore Installation Manager on *Monroe Bravo*. I need to speak to the captain immediately, and I mean *immediately*. Do you understand?'

The radio operator was fielding radio traffic in the immediate area but recognised the name of the OIM.

'Yes, sir, I am transferring this call to the bridge immediately.'

There was the briefest of pauses before Captain Sorenson answered.

'Captain Sorenson here ... how can I help you?'

'Your two owners, Jack Collier and Sandro Calvolaro, are currently diving to the seabed to shut down the Platform. If they are successful, they will be returning to the base of Leg 1 on the Platform – that's the south-west corner. They will then swim on a bearing of 225 degrees to intercept your Diving Bell.

'We have no communication with the divers. They are using rebreathers with enough gases to complete the shut-down and return to your Bell. You must drop your Diving Bell to ninety metres and as close to the Platform as possible. It must be on a bearing of 225 degrees from the corner of the platform. Do you understand?'

'Message received and understood. I am ordering the Diving Bell to be in place as instructed. Where are you?'

'I'm at the base of Leg 2 … no immediate danger but make sure the Bell is in place.'

'I'm directing a FRC to pick you up. Out.'

Rick's mind was racing. "What else should I be doing?" he said to himself as warm water fell like rain alongside the oil now that less of the oil was burning. He slowly dropped to his knees, braced himself with one arm and rolled onto his backside. With a grunt, he rolled onto his side and then his back. The pain had returned, he was struggling to breathe but felt better lying on his back. He'd done all he could and needed to rest for a few minutes. He needed to compose himself for what was to come. Rick wasn't sure if he fell asleep or just dozed for a few moments before a deluge of water fell on his face and roused him. Through the premature evening, he could see a ship blasting water at the burning Platform above him. He realised it was the *Stavanger*. Despite the noise and drama, Rick tried to relax to ease the pain. When he looked up, he could see that the whole Platform was ablaze. He couldn't see the drilling floor but could visualise where the main riser would be. A black skeleton of the Platform was back-lit by the raging fires. If Jack and Sandro were unable to shut off the oil and gas pipelines, it was just a matter of time before the whole platform collapsed and millions of barrels of oil gushed into the North Sea – where it would remain a hazard for months!

Konrad had been busy scanning the immediate area for rescue boats and hadn't noticed Rick drop to his knees and then roll onto his back. He noticed him now but couldn't really help him if he was seriously injured. He slipped Rick's rucksack off his own back and retrieved the torch before creating a makeshift pillow for Rick. He then began to wave the torch to attract attention. A few moments to relax and compose himself was all that Rick needed.

Rick knew he couldn't wallow in self-pity or self-recrimination, there was still work to do. He asked Konrad for his phone and called Fire Chief Ridley. It was good news. The Fire Chief confirmed the gas pipeline had been shut down. He also confirmed that all but one of the fire sources were under control; the main crude oil riser was still ablaze even though *North Guard* was pouring thousands of litres of water onto it. *North Guard* was also cooling the oxygen and helium tanks, gas separation and holding tanks of liquified natural gas; but it may be a rear-guard action.

Rick then phoned the Yellow and Red Platform Controllers, but only Bobby McGregor, the Yellow Team Controller, replied. He confirmed that his team had tried their best to conduct a systematic check of accommodation, recreation and catering areas. These places were no longer ablaze but shrouded in smoke. All who could be evacuated were being evacuated. He also confirmed that the Red Team Controller had been killed by a blast.

Konrad was still waving a torch when a FRC (Fast Rescue Craft) from the *Stavanger* emerged out of the gloom. There was a man on the bow holding a line and several men from the Platform on board. The men recognised Rick Johnson; two of them jumped off the rescue craft and onto the floating stage. As gently as they could, they helped Rick from the stage and into the boat. It didn't matter that he had done all he could to shut down the Platform and to save the men on it: he felt impotent as he slumped against the side of the boat.

As they eased away from *Monroe Bravo* Rick realises this could be a replay of the *Deepwater Horizon* disaster in 2010. A massive explosion on the rig had been followed by an uncontrollable fire. The multi-million dollar rig was destroyed in hours. It was later estimated that at its peak 800,000 gallons of crude oil per day gushed into the Gulf of Mexico. In the 84 days it took to stem the rupture it was further estimated over 200 million gallons of oil were released – and most of it was still there. Rick recalled reports of a twenty-mile oil slick - not on the surface but hanging at 3,500 feet below the surface. There were also reports of oil particles on the sea bed. In some areas it had created an obscene blanket five centimetres thick and covered tens of square kilometres. It had been an ecological disaster with two million gallons of dispersant used; dispersant that was more toxic than the oil it was dispersing.

It had also been a financial disaster. The shares of the two main companies involved, BP and Transocean, dropped immediately. Months later they were worth fifty percent of their pre-incident value. The disaster wiped US$23 billion off company stock. Those who had designed and operated the rig were vilified in the media and in the courts. Much of the criticism was deflected onto the designers of the rig and its operation. Rick had been part of the design team on *Monroe Bravo* and was also the OIM, the Offshore Installation Manager. It may not sound impressive – but if *Monroe Bravo* was a ship, Rick would be the captain; he was the boss. He had one chance to prevent a disaster and it was now down to Jack and Sandro.

Rick was jolted from his musing when a blanket of heat flooded over him. At sea level, and at the foot of the Platform, they were sheltered from the searing heat. However, as the FRC moved away and back to the support ship, heat began to scorch them. It was a race between being cooked alive and sheltering behind a ship. Men simply cowered in the boat and tried to shield themselves as it roared away. Moments later it swept around the bow of the *Stavanger* and into the shelter of its starboard side. Fenders from the FRC pressed against the sides of a shallow steel tray used to collect transfer stores and to bring divers from the water. The survivors didn't need any encouragement. Awkwardly they transferred Rick into the basket before it was winched up. Willing hands helped the survivors from the tray and onto the deck. They could see the pain in Rick's bloody, blackened face. They could also see determination etched across it. With no pleasantries or thank you he grabbed hold of the first crew member he could see.

'Which way to the bridge?'

'That way,' the crew member replied, pointing.

'Let's go,' said Rick to Konrad as he clutched his side and they made their way towards the command tower and the bridge.

The deck of the *Stavanger* was being swept by torrential rain. *Where's it coming from?* Rick wondered before realising the ship was being doused by an onboard sprinkler system. Dripping in water, he looked back at *Monroe Bravo*; the scene was as he had feared: a black cloud of smoke rose from the centre of the Platform and flames still roared from the crude oil riser. *North Guard* was pouring tens of thousands of litres of water onto it but it was having no effect. What it *was* doing was creating dozens of waterfalls, quenching the smaller fires and washing burning oil off the Drilling Deck onto the decks below and falling like a fiery waterfall into the sea. It didn't look as though Jack had managed to shut down the crude oil riser.

The moments it took for Rick to get to the bridge gave him time to think through what he needed to do next. Chief Ridley would be coordinating the firefighting. If Jack did manage to shut down the crude oil main riser, the fire fighters would be able to gain control. Bobby McGregor was good and would organise water borne and helicopter evacuations of those seriously injured. Neither Ridley nor McGregor needed him pestering them. Rick needed to speak to the captain of the *Guard North* about cooling the Platform and spraying oil dispersant – but he knew they would be doing that anyway. He had to speak to Norton Flynn in Aberdeen; he'd left messages for both Flynn and Walter Brachs. They should have the messages by now and would be acting on them. Mentally, he'd justified focusing on the rescue of the divers below.

Captain Sorenson still had the radio microphone pressed to his cheek when two dishevelled men burst onto the bridge. It wasn't their unexpected and breathless entry onto the bridge that he later remembered. It wasn't the sight of heavily soiled and oil covered high viz jackets, nor oil and soot streaked safety helmets. It wasn't even the pungent smell of burnt oil that flooded the bridge. It was the desperate, wide eyed expression on their faces. He couldn't help but focus on their eyes; they seemed so white against their oily, smoke blackened faces. White lines, creases around their eyes and mouth, seemed to give the eyes even more prominence.

He turned towards them in surprise as one of the men raised both hands in a gesture of apology.

'I'm sorry … I'm sorry to barge in … I'm Rick Johnson … I phoned you a short time ago about Jack Collier and Sandro Calovarlo attempting to shut down the Platform on the seabed. Have you heard from them? Have they managed to get back to the Diving Bell? Are they safe?'

The grim expression on Captain Sorenson's face didn't change but he glanced at his wrist watch.

'We'd anticipated the need to evacuate the divers. It's been *blown down*; the pressure inside the Bell is equivalent to a depth of eighty- five metres. It's deployed and on a bearing of 225 degrees from the Leg 1… the South West corner of the Platform.'

Captain Sorenson paused for a moment before he continued.

'I was speaking to our crew member in the Bell when you arrived. The men have not return to the Bell. We are assuming they are still trying to shut down the Platform.'

Rick turned to Konrad.

'How long would it take to drop from the surface to the seabed, swim, say one hundred and fifty metres, to EPLAST then another one hundred and fifty metres back to the Bell?'

'They probably wouldn't drop straight down … they'd fin along a bearing, from Leg to Leg, before they arrived at the seabed.'

Konrad did some quick metal arithmetic.

'A few minutes to release the cover … I'd say twenty to twenty-five minutes.'

It had been almost thirty minutes since Jack and Sandro dropped below the surface of the North Sea. Rick glanced towards *Monroe Bravo* and his shoulders slumped. The scene looked little different to the one moments before. The whole Platform was swathed in black smoke and there were fierce flames rising from its centre. Jack hadn't managed to shut down the crude oil riser. As the seconds ticked by, and as *North Guard* continued to pour tens of thousands of litres of water onto the Platform, Rick knew he couldn't save it. He couldn't help Jack and Sandro either but he could try to save the nine divers trapped on the seabed. After a deep sigh Rick announced:

'It looks like Sandro Calovarlo has shut down the gas pipeline … but the crude oil riser is still ablaze. If Jack can't shut it down soon, we've lost the Platform – but we have nine divers to save.

'The support crane has been damaged, the jib has collapsed and cannot retrieve the Bell. We're pretty sure the main umbilical, supplying life supporting helium and oxygen gases, has been destroyed. The only gases they have to breathe are those inside the Bell.'

Rick turned to Konrad and asked.

'Konrad, are there any other gas supplies in and around the Bell? How much time do they have left … before they suffocate?'

'They've got a dozen or so pony cylinders … that'll give them ten to fifteen minutes, but that's all. The emergency batteries will give them light but aren't enough to heat the Bell … they're going to get cold soon … very cold … but it's not the cold that will kill them.'

Captain Sorenson had been listening patiently. He turned to his First Officer and asked.

'Could you ask Lukas to join us in the briefing room as soon as possible? Tell him it's urgent. Could you also ask the cook to provide drinks and snacks for our friends? Thank you.'

Alternating his glance between Rick and Konrad, Captain Sorenson continued.

'Lukas is our Dive Supervisor. Let's go to the briefing room and we can decide what to do.'

Chapter 14

Into the void

Tuesday 4th April 2023, 3:50 pm

As Jack dropped below the surface it was suddenly quiet. The visibility was surprisingly good for mid-afternoon in the North Sea. The light from the fires above resembled afternoon sunshine. He started to speak but immediately realised the communications link, the comms, between himself, Sandro and Konrad was down. That alone was unsettling and Jack suddenly felt vulnerable. It wasn't the dive to ninety metres nor shutting down the Platform … it was what he had to do next. He had started the dive with no confirmation that the *Stavanger* had lowered the Bell, that it was pressurised to ninety metres and he could get inside. If the Bell wasn't waiting for him he would have to work his way to the surface, through a decompression sequence, and hope the Platform didn't disintegrate around him. He tried to dismiss the fears from his mind and concentrate on the task in hand.

He guessed the dive store was now ablaze. A few minutes ago, he'd been choking on smoke and trying to shield himself from the heat. Now the glow from the fires above seemed unreal. He'd already decided to fin steadily towards Legs 3 and 4 whilst still fairly shallow. He knew that as he descended, it would get darker and colder, and in the dark, grey void it would be disorientating. Leg 3 came into view quicker than he expected. He was eager to make progress but this job required stamina not speed; he tried to slow down. As he finned past the Leg, he noticed it was encrusted with barnacles and weed. Jack could see the delicate ends of the weed gently swaying in the current. It told him he was swimming across the current. It also made him wonder if the installation would be encrusted with shell fish and weed. Would it be difficult to gain access? At leg 4 he checked his compass, changed direction, switched on his torch and finned due north towards Leg 8 and then Leg 12.

Sandro was just passing Leg 5. He could see the grey seabed two or three metres below him as he finned strongly across the current. It looked remarkably smooth. As he flicked his torch over the surface, a brightly coloured, yellow anemone came into view; it looked abandoned, forlorn. Flicking the torch beam forwards, he could see the container-sized installation ahead. At some time, the word EPLAST had been painted in big, bold letters on the side but most of it was now obliterated by algae and other marine growth. He finned to the inside end of the Winnebago and was relieved to see the maintenance team had cleaned up the area around the cover. He released some gas from his dry suit, settled with his fins on the seabed, and holding one of the red taps, steadied himself in position.

Sandro looked up and thought he could see a dull glow near the surface but wasn't sure. The fires must still be raging. He could remember the sequence but checked the slate attached to his harness. *Open the taps, anticlockwise to release air from the cover.* A stream of bubbles tumbled towards the surface. Sandro knew that the bubbles may be small now but they would expand rapidly as they raced upwards. The surface would appear to boil when the gas eventually broke through.

He released the eight clips and used his knife to break the seal between the metal cover and the rubber insert. He caught it before it fell and he gently pulled it to one side. The metal wheel in front of him, and the surrounding bulkhead, looked brand new. It had obviously been protected by the cover and trapped air but it looked scrupulously clean. Sandro wasted no time in grabbing the wheel in both hands, bracing himself on the seabed, and turning the wheel. It was stiff but he could sense it was moving so, so, slowly. He could imagine flywheels turning, gears moving and metal plates sliding. Sandro maintained the pressure and was now sure the wheel was turning. Encouraged by the tiny movement he applied more pressure and could feel the wheel turning. Imperceptibly slow at first but getting quicker with each passing second. Indeed, within half a minute the wheel was turning so fast he couldn't hold onto it and merely let it spin in his hands. "Eighty turns!" Sandro had forgotten to count and it was difficult to count now. He just let it run until it came to an abrupt halt. It had been easy. The task now was to retrace his path, reunite with Jack and find the *Stavanger* Diving Bell.

Jack's dive computer told him he'd only been in the water seven minutes, was descending at a safe rate, and was close to Leg 12. A few more metres and he would be at the installation. He turned his head and looked up towards the surface. The orange glow was still there but muted. He knew the Platform was pumping thousands of barrels of oil through the main crude oil riser, feeding the flames, and it wouldn't stop. He didn't want to dwell on the scene ninety metres above; he had to concentrate on the job in front of him.

Just a dozen or so kicks and he was past Leg 12 and in the torch light he could see the installation, the Winnebago looming ahead of him. His heart sank as, in the torch light, he could see weed and marine growth festooned over the top and side of the installation. However, as he finned to the end towards the inside end of the installation he could see that someone had scrapped away the growth around the dome shaped cover. It must have been the maintenance team from Houston. "Release the two red taps" Jack said to himself and in the torch light could see a stream of bubbles starting to make their way to the surface. It took only a few seconds to vent the cover. Whilst he was waiting he found the first clips holding the cover in place; they released easily. He guessed he was destroying the rubber seal with his dive knife, but it was expendable. He eased the cover free and let it drop to the seabed. "Just 80 turns on the wheel and I'm done," Jack said to himself. He spoke too soon. As he braced himself against the wheel, took a deep breath and strained …"shit, it's stiff, ugh …won't move." Jack moved so that the valve wheel was side on to him. He reached up and grabbed one of the spokes of the wheel in one hand and the rim in the other. He bent his arms, took his weight off his fins and in a single, arm pumping jolt tried to free the mechanism. It didn't move. In a combination of fear and frustration he bounced up and down, like a keep-fit fanatic at the local gym. The wheel remained rock solid. "A lever …I've got to find a lever …something to give me more leverage." Jack thought back to the route he'd just taken. Had he seen any pipes, any metal, anything on the seabed he could use as a lever? He guessed that in the past there'd be scaffolding poles, conduit and pipework that had been dropped or thrown over the side. That was years ago. Today, if something fell over the side it had to be retrieved.

Jack knew there were tools and metal pipes inside the *Stavanger* Bell, but it would take time to get there, find what he needed and get back. He tried again to release the wheel but realised he must not over exert himself at ninety metres – it could be fatal. It looked as though he had no choice. He'd have to retrace his route and then fin to the Bell.

Sandro shone the torch onto his dive computer. The display told him he was at a depth of eighty-nine metres and had been in the water for fourteen minutes. He also checked his gas supply; he had plenty. The adrenaline he'd generated on the descent, and when shutting off the valve, was gone and he now felt alone and cold. Another check on the dive computer, gas supply and compass, and he was ready for the short trip to Leg 1 and then the comfort of the Bell. He released some gas into his dry suit – just enough to make him neutrally buoyant. It was then that he noticed the small particles of sediment flowing past him. Konrad had said the current was mild and decreasing. It didn't seem that mild as he finned across it to Leg 1.

When he arrived at Leg 1, he shone the torch around it until he found one of the metal loops used by the repair and maintenance crew to tether themselves to the Leg. He clicked on, relaxed, and let the current float him a metre or so from the Leg. He just had to wait for Jack. Time passed slowly as Sandro began to notice the cold more. He scolded himself for taking off the orange boiler suit he'd been given when he arrived. It would have been another layer, another layer to trap heat. However, he also realised the sweat he'd generated before the dive was now cooling his body.

He glanced again at his dive computer. He'd been waiting over ten minutes. "How long will it take for Jack to get to the other installation, close it down and get here?" On the back of the slate, he started his calculations. A descent rate of, say, twelve metres per minute for ninety metres would be about seven minutes. He'd have to fin from Leg 2 to Leg 4, and then to beyond Leg 12 – say a hundred and fifty metres. About ten minutes. Two minutes to get to the valve and close it and then another hundred and fifty metres back to Leg 2: another ten minutes.

Sandro completed the calculation. "Thirty minutes;" he then checked his dive computer. "He'll be here in two or three minutes;" he wasn't.

Jack was about to start finning back to the Dive Bell to collect the longest spanner or metal pipe he could find, when he paused. "If I was a diver working on this equipment ... and knew it was the 'option of last resort' ... wouldn't I leave a few tools next to it? If the valves were stiff when the guys from Houston did the maintenance, what would they do? They wouldn't want to waste time and energy walking backwards and forwards for a length of pipe ... they'd leave some kit here."

Jack fell to his knees in slow motion and started to rake his gloved hands through the silt. The viz was immediately destroyed but it didn't matter. What only mattered was finding any tools that had been left behind. No sooner had he started when he stopped. "Think!" he scolded himself. "Be systematic!" Jack crept forwards and started to run his fingers through the silt that was at the foot of the installation. It was the second sweep when his fingers hit something solid – a bar of metal. Jack couldn't see anything through the swirling silt, zero viz, but he could feel. It was a heavy steel bar, about 20mm diameter and about a metre long. On one end someone had welded a U shaped piece of steel – it felt like a blunt prong. About twenty to thirty centimetres from the prong was a curved spigot sticking out at ninety degrees and maybe ten centimetres long. It had been welded onto the steel shaft. Jack smiled in satisfaction, he knew precisely what this was, a lever that would hook onto the valve wheel and give him enough leverage to close the valve.

Jack could have done it with his eyes closed; just as well 'cos he couldn't see anything. He wedged the prong onto the rim of the valve wheel and made sure it was hard up against one of the spokes. With his left hand he held the bar in place whilst he hooked the curved spike over the opposite spoke. He simply reached up to grab the end of the bar and pulled it down; it was almost effortless. A tiny spring was triggered and he started to turn an equally small fly wheel. The mechanism started to turn a series of gears and the valve mechanism started to close. More fly wheels started to spin and precision machined steel started to slide inside equally precision machined housings. Jack struggled to control the long bar as its speed increased; he tugged it free and let it fall. He could then just stand in front of the wheel and maintain the spin. He was shutting down the main oil riser and saving the Platform. What he had to do next was think about saving himself.

It was taking a long time for the valve to shut. It was impossible to count the number of rotations; he couldn't even see the wheel, only feel it turning. "Have I broken the mechanism? Is it spinning free but not closing the valve? Have I forgotten any of the instructions?" Just as panic started to rise, the wheel stopped turning abruptly. Jack wondered if he should fit the metal bar and make sure it was shut; but decided it must be shut.

The elation of shutting off the flow of oil was short lived and was replaced by a feeling of amazing calm and well-being. Even the prospect of finning over 200 metres to find the *Stavanger* Bell seemed enjoyable. He kicked gently with a fin, turned in the water and started his return. "Sandro will have shut down the gas pipeline ... I wonder what he's doing on the ship ..." Jack asked himself. "Is Penny on board the *Stavanger*?" For a moment, Jack couldn't remember. "The holiday in Grenada was fantastic ... and Penny's a confident diver."

Jack collided with Leg 8. Only his pride was hurt, none of his equipment was damaged, but it broke the spell. He hadn't seen the Leg, he hadn't even been looking for it. Perhaps it was a combination of the stress associated with the task, tiredness due to his exertions, or disorientation in the grey void. Whatever the combination of reasons, he'd been finning aimlessly, but luckily on the correct bearing. He was jolted back to the present. He realised he'd lost concentration, and was both cold and tired. If he hadn't bumped into the Leg, he could have continued finning, into the void, with no idea where he was. He would have got colder and colder, becoming increasingly tired, until he gave up and died. The thought made him physically shiver. "Concentrate!" he said to himself as he checked his compass to confirm the direction of his return route to Leg 1 and on to the Diving Bell.

It was a tense return to Leg 2, and a relief when Jack could see the dull torchlight ahead. Sandro was waiting for him, grinning through his face mask and giving him the AOK hand signal. Together they checked the amount of breathing gases available, set off into the grey void on a bearing of 225 degrees, hoping the Diving Bell was waiting for them.

Both Sandro and Jack were counting their fin kicks and trying to estimate how far they had travelled. They knew the heat from the fires was intense and even with the onboard sprinkler systems working at the maximum, the *Stavanger* would not be able to get within fifty metres. Sandro had just estimated they had travelled about fifty metres when he saw the glow of the *Stavanger* Bell just off to his left. He knew the ship would have been stationary and on the correct bearing – it was they who had drifted offline. Another ten or fifteen metres and Jack was waving at Gunnar at the base of the ladder. Jack grabbed the rungs of the ladder, climbed into the Wet Well, pleased that the dive was over.

Gunnar was helping Sandro get the rebreather off his back.

'Did you manage to shut the Platform down … the gas and the oil?' he asked.

'It was surprisingly easy … it was the viz and the cold that made it difficult,' said Sandro.

In the confines of the *Wet Well* it was difficult for three people to move around, take off kit, wash and store it. Gunnar helped Jack remove the rebreather and stowed it. As he returned he noticed Jack had slipped the face mask from his face. With his elbows on his knees, and head bowed, Jack was merely sitting, eyes closed, and breathing deeply; he looked exhausted.

'Guess you got the short straw,' was all Gunnar said.

Jack smiled and handed his fins to Gunnar.

'Luck of the draw. Getting to the installation was no problem … but turning the valve was a pig … I was about to give up when I found a tool, a lever, somebody had made … once I got the lever in place, it was easy … just took a lot out of me.'

'Let's get all this kit stowed, have a hot drink … 'cos I've got some news for you.'

The time was 4:25 pm, and Jack had not yet left a message for Penny.

Chapter 15

'We've got a hit.'

Tuesday 4th April 2023, 4:25 pm

Penny had contacted the head of her team, worked through the file that Commander Short had given her, and read through the dozen or so pages about Dr Rick Johnson. As the minutes passed, reports from ferry ports and marinas, private airstrips and airports began to flood in. None reported any worker on *Monroe Bravo* leaving the country. She was still waiting for information from the port of Dover, and some of the smaller regional airports, when Tommy announced tea time. Penny hadn't noticed him leave or return with a cardboard tray of coffees and a bag of cakes. As they grouped around his desk, he turned to Penny.

'What do we know about the main man on *Monroe Bravo*?'

'I've read through his full TransGlobal biography; it's long but interesting. It's a collation of contributions from a variety of people … makes him sound exceptional and a committed company man. Let me read you my summary.'

Penny quickly returned to where she had been working, picked up her notes, and started reading.

'Apparently, Rick Johnson is not your caricature of a Texas Oilman. He doesn't wear jeans, check shirts or cowboy boots. He isn't even a Texan – he's from Utah. He is cultured and knowledgeable, as much at home in boardrooms, theatres and academic gatherings as he is running a mega oil platform or working on the drilling floor with machinery. In terms of working in the oil business, he's done it all, and commands the respect of those around him.

'According to the biography, Rick grew up in the small town of Silver Springs, Utah. A boom town in the 1860s when silver was discovered. It survived when the deposits were exhausted; it's now a quiet, unassuming town.

'He's an only child. His mother taught English and Literature at the local high school. His father taught geography at the local community college. It was his mother's love of language and his father's passion for geology that shaped his early life. Although sporting and amiable, it seems Rick preferred regular weekend camping trips with his parents, exploring the amazing geology of Utah.

'As he grew up, his childhood dreams of finding silver or gold were replaced by a fascination for geology. According to his teachers, he also realised early on that reading gave him the key to knowledge, and language the means to express it.

'He won a state scholarship to the University of Utah to study geology. One of his lecturers noted that his prior knowledge of geology, particularly that of Utah and Colorado, matched that of his tutors. He excelled in his courses, and at graduation was awarded the accolade of 'Top Student of the Year'' and 'Most Likely to Succeed'.

'He was head hunted by TransGlobal Oil and offered a scholarship to study Petroleum Engineering at the University of Texas in Austin. It's at this point that Rick became a 'company man'. TransGlobal Oil funded him, part time, to continue his studies and he obtained his PhD.'

Penny, flicked over the page and studied her notes before continuing.

'Johnson progressed through a carefully choreographed route to become a TransGlobal Oil executive. He's moved from isolated drilling rigs in the wilderness of Texas to high pressure operations in the Gulf of Mexico; from politically sensitive roles off the coast of Nigeria to the challenging conditions of the Persian Gulf; from a geologist advising on prospective drilling sites to working on the drilling floors of oil rigs; from part of the platform design team to Chief Engineer and oil platform supremo. He's at the peak of his 'hands on' career.

'According to the final paragraph, he will join the TransGlobal Oil Board in Texas later this year as Vice President, Worldwide Production. He certainly doesn't sound like a disgruntled employee who wants to blow up the Platform.'

Neither Tommy nor Harry said anything, they merely nodded. Penny was about to add more comments when her phone rang; it was a Senior Officer within UK Border Force.

'Pendleton Price,' Penny said.

'Officer Parker, Aberdeen Regional Airport here. We've got a hit on your *Monroe Bravo* list,' he said excitedly. 'I can confirm that Callum Jeffery, a senior health and safety technician on the *Monroe Bravo* Oil Platform, boarded a flight from Aberdeen regional for Amsterdam this morning. We are checking him out and working with our Dutch colleagues to trace his ongoing movements.'

*

Callum Jeffrey did indeed board a flight to Amsterdam.

It had been stressed to him that he must behave entirely normally; he shouldn't draw attention to himself. He'd fitted the last of the thermite devices on Monday and had been convinced that members of the crew were taking it in turns to look at him. He knew that all the forged paperwork was in order, staff had been notified he was 'fitting the sensors', and it would not affect production – he wouldn't get in the way. He'd done similar things a hundred times and so no one should suspect him.

He didn't sleep very well on Monday night and knew he had an early transfer, the next day, from the Platform to the helicopter base on the mainland. It was the worst part of the entire *hitch* – his entire time on the Platform. He knew the survival suits were for his own safety and that if the helicopter had to ditch in the North Sea, the suit would keep him alive for days. Without it, his survival would be counted in minutes in the frigid seawater. However, the suit was hot and cumbersome. He usually delayed clambering into it as long as possible, and joined the disembarkation queue at the last possible minute. This morning he was in the middle of the group and waited close to the exit route to the helicopter. He couldn't afford to be bumped off the flight to make space for someone who was ill, a departing visitor or some piece of equipment. Cal had a timetable to follow and it didn't include missing this transfer.

There was the usual banter in the crowded muster station as the departing crew waited for the call to board. It would stop as soon as they got on board, and would start again when they got off. As the call was made, and crew lined up to sign off the Platform, Cal checked his watch. He was less bothered about the schedule than checking how long he'd have to endure the noise and vibration inside the helicopter. Despite the ear protectors, he always had a dull headache and felt slightly nauseous by the time they landed. By checking the time, he could gauge how much longer he'd have to endure before he could get off.

Once off the helicopter he tried to behave normally. He chipped into the banter and smiled at the odd joke as he hung up the survival suit and made his way to the waiting bus. He was going to the bus station and took his usual seat near the back. He recognised all of the men and knew Arthur and Roco would be heading for the airport. Arthur had a girlfriend in the Philippines. He was catching a flight from Aberdeen to Helsinki and on to Cebu. It was then a ferry to some remote island and holiday resort. Tomorrow he'd be on some tropical beach and soaking up the sun. Roco would be flying to his home on the Costa del Sol and spending the next three weeks with his wife and family. He'd told Cal that he would be spending all the time working on the extension to their home.

Cal sat back as the shuttle bus made the short journey to the long-term car park, the airport, and eventually to the bus station. He joined the last passengers to get off, shouted good bye, and headed for the bus station café; it was all part of his routine. He had been told to keep to his normal routine. He always missed breakfast before the transfer. He'd never been sick on the flight, but made sure he avoided it. Eggs on toast, a mug of tea and a quick read of a newspaper would kill the time before his bus was due to arrive. However, today it wasn't the one to take him home; he was off to the airport. He'd been told that his e-ticket and boarding pass would be waiting for him at the airline information desk. He only had a carry-on back-pack, a short wait for the flight and less than a two hour flight time to Schiphol.

*

Penny was scribbling notes from the brief conversation with Officer Parker, and was about to brief Harry and Tommy when the phone rang.

'It's Officer Parker again. Callum Jeffrey did not exit the airport. He was in transit and boarded the 11:25 am flight to Tehran on an Iranian passport. He'd tried to change his appearance … different clothes, hair style, shaved off his beard, but Dutch facial recognition identified him. It's a seven hour flight and due to land at 21:00 pm local time. He lands in ninety minutes.'

'Thanks, Officer Parker … can you send me confirmation of all this by email asap? Keep looking for any others … and thanks again.'

*

With only a back-pack, and no luggage to collect, Cal made his way through the transit area and towards the transfer desk in Schiphol airport. Near to the desk, there were rows of seats – and his contact. As Cal approached him, he surreptitiously signalled everything was OK. He removed his baseball cap and glasses, put them inside a duty free plastic bag and placed it on the floor next to him. The simple switch had been explained and Cal knew what to do. He sat next to his contact, put his back-pack on the floor, stretched out and counted slowly to one hundred. A couple of minutes would be enough for other passengers to walk past and those around him to lose interest in him. He stretched again, picked up the duty free carrier bag and made his way to the gents' toilet. He'd been told there was a baby changing booth inside the toilet, just what he wanted.

Cal emptied the carrier bag. He put the new baseball cap and plain lens glasses on top of the Heart of Midlothian Football Club supporter's jacket. The rich maroon colour matched the baseball cap. He took the battery powered clippers out of the box and reduced his beard to designer stubble. A brush down, quick tidy up and Cal was ready to leave. He put his own blue fleece jacket inside the duty free carrier bag, slipped on the Hearts jacket, baseball cap and glasses. Cal felt inside the jacket pocket and took out a plastic room key – the size of a credit card. On one side was written the number twenty-four. He glanced in the mirror and decided that even his wife would struggle to recognise him. Another quick check and he walked back to the row of seats and his contact. Cal placed the plastic bag on the seat next to his contact, grabbed this back-pack and made his way to room 24 in the Airport Hotel.

There were guests at reception but Cal already had a room. He smiled and waved the room key in the direction of the receptionist as he made his way to room 24 where another contact was waiting for him. Cal knocked on the door and then used the key to open it. His next contact was sitting in an easy chair facing the door.

'I need to go to the toilet,' said Cal as he dropped the back-pack and opened the door to the toilet.

He'd been told that he would be changing clothes here; removing anything that could identify him. This included the back-pack, his watch, phone and jewellery. Cal didn't want to give up his Omega Seamaster Chronograph. Years ago, he'd agonised over buying it, knowing it was an expensive indulgence. He needed a watch, but not one costing almost US$8000 and that would still work at 300 metres below the sea. The heavy stainless steel body and bracelet, ceramic blue bezel and multi-function watch had seduced him. He'd bought a copy in Aberdeen market, under the counter, for £30, and had it on his wrist now. The real Omega was in his pocket.

Once inside the bathroom, Cal carefully removed the top of the water cistern and dropped the real omega into the water. He waited a moment, flushed the toilet, and joined his contact. The man was standing on the other side of the bed, and looked serious.

'I need your UK passport, phone, wallet … watch, jewellery … keys.'

Cal slipped the fake omega off his wrist and dropped it onto the bed. He'd already taken the SIM card and battery out of his phone and dropped the pieces next to the watch. His wallet, house keys and passport followed. Self-consciously he stripped off and threw his clothes onto the growing pile on the bed. He put on the clothes he had dropped off at the mosque a month ago: shoes and suit, shirt and tie.

'Here's your Iranian passport with all the necessary stamps, e-ticket and boarding pass, new wallet, cards and money. It's all in your real name. There are more clothes and presents in the pull along. Boarding for the flight to Tehran is in about 30 minutes, gate 35. I will tidy up before I leave.'

Cal walked towards the door and was about to leave when he remembered the watch.

'Oh, must be nerves. I need to go to the toilet again before I leave.'

Callum carefully lifted the ceramic top off the water cistern, retrieved his watch, and put the top back carefully. A quick dry with a towel and he put the watch in his pocket with a smile. At least he was retaining some of his old life.

Penny walked briskly to where Tommy and Harry were sitting and relayed the information about Callum Jeffrey's flights. There was a flurry of activity as they blasted off instructions to their teams. Thirty minutes later, a phone call to CS Steel had him scribbling away at a note pad and calling to Penny and Harry.

'According to neighbours, Callum Jeffery's wife and daughter left this morning, on holiday, in a taxi. It wasn't unusual after her husband's three weeks stint on the Platform; they'd go away for a week or so. The house is being searched – we'll know soon if they find anything that contributes to the investigation. We're checking taxi companies.'

'I'll check what we have on Mrs Jeffrey,' said Penny as she returned to her desk.

A few minutes later, she announced:

'Jeffrey's wife and child caught a morning flight to Amsterdam; they had two large suitcases and paid for excess luggage. Dutch immigration confirms Mrs Jeffrey and her daughter are on the same flight as her husband. They're all travelling on valid Iranian passports; they have dual nationality.

'We've checked their travel record. Callum Jeffrey, his wife and child make short, annual visits to Iran to see family.'

'It doesn't mean he's the sole person of interest,' DS Steel reminded them. 'They could be entirely innocent or they could have accomplices traveling in opposite directions.'

Penny stood up and walked around the office to where Tommy and Harry were sitting.

'This is too easy and just enough to be suspicious,' she said. 'If Callum Jeffrey is our bomber, he and his accomplices have been planning this for months, if not years. They'd know that we would be checking ferry ports and airports, and CCTV and immigration checks would be able to track them. Yet apart from a few cosmetic changes for Callum Jeffrey, they get taxis and onto flights to Iran.'

'Could be a decoy,' suggested DS Steel. 'If he has family in Tehran, it explains why he's a regular visitor. On his off-shore salary, he can afford it. There may be a plausible reason why he changed his appearance, why his wife is dragging two full suitcases. Could be presents for the family.'

'I'm getting more detailed background checks on Jeffrey and his family; I've already told my team to continue searching for any other workers who have left the country,' said Penny. 'Oh, by the way, we've identified two more workers from the Platform who have left the country; one to the Philippines and another to Spain. At the moment, they all look like regular trips … neither of them have access to the places where we think the bombs went off.'

'If Jeffrey is our bomber, we've got just over one hour to do something about it. No point asking the Iranian authorities to detain him. They'd acknowledge the request then drag their feet until Jeffrey left the airport. It'd also alert the Iranians and Jeffrey to our suspicions,' Harry argued.

'So, what do you suggest?' asked Penny in obvious frustration.

'We track him,' said Harry as though it was the obvious thing to do. 'We've got people in Tehran and I've already got one mobilised. I'd suggest we target Nazarene, his wife. If Jeffrey is the bomber, he'll be on full alert, but she'll be distracted by her daughter and all the activity around her. We stick a tracker on her suitcase and see where it leads.'

'If Callum Jeffrey is going to be on 'full alert', isn't he going to spot a lump of plastic stuck to a suitcase?' asked Penny sarcastically.

Harry smiled, slid his hand inside his jacket and took out his wallet. Very deliberately he thumbed through the contents until he found what he was looking for: a small, thin, rectangular strip of plastic. It was multicoloured, had a bar code on it and writing so small one would struggle to read it. He offered it to Penny.

'What do you think it is?'

'Looks like a baggage security sticker, the type they stick on suitcases.'

'Very good. It does look like a baggage check label, doesn't it? What if I told you this is the latest generation of tracker? Wafer-thin semi-conductors, electronics and solar battery. Good for a three-kilometre radius, five-day battery. If the label is exposed to daylight, the built-in solar cells will charge it.

'Our people stick this on Mrs Jeffrey's suitcase as they help her get it off the baggage carrousel. As long as we are within three kilometres, we know where she and hubby are going and staying. We identify his contacts and those who interact with him. It'll take time but we ID the network. When we're ready, we can lift him, squeeze him until pips pop out and then dump him somewhere. We don't have to depose of him, his friends will do that for us once they learn he's talked.'

Penny was shocked by the casual way in which Harry described an abduction, interrogation, and murder of a suspect. She then thought about the dozens of people who may have been already killed on *Monroe Bravo*. She was also aware she had no news from Jack or Sandro.

'What are the risks of anyone finding the tracker?' asked Penny.

'Remote ... it's basically graphene, plastic, and undetectable with their generation of scanning equipment. Our current generation of scanners can't even detect it.'

It was CS Steel who took the lead.

'I suggest we ask Harry to confirm use of the tracker. We also need to find out more about Callum Jeffrey. Penny, can you get your colleagues to check his movements in and out of the country? I'll organise a detailed background check on him and his wife. Harry, can you check if your guys have found any links to national or international groups?'

Chapter 16

Callum Jeffrey

Tuesday 4th April 2023, 4:30 pm

Chief Superintendent Steel had been right; all hell had broken loose. Penny was fielding email after email, report after report, and each time trying to fit the information into a timeline. She was also answering one phone call after another, adding this information to her growing narrative, requesting clarification or further enquiries on the main person of interest: Callum Jeffrey. The phone had just stopped ringing when Chief Superintendent Steel called them together for an update.

'Just heard who will make up the American team. Special Agent Gene Dilks, Anti-Terrorism, will be in overall charge. There will be a US Border protection officer called Pamela Edwards, a Cyber Security Specialist called Dave Perry, and two support staff. Penny, what have you got on Jeffrey's movements?'

'Callum Jeffrey, aka Khalid Jaffra, came to the UK for the first time in September 1988 when he was eight years old; he's now forty-three. As a child, Khalid made annual return visits to Iran during school holidays for the next ten years. He was eighteen when he changed his name to Callum Jeffrey and continued his visits to Iran for the next three years.

We've no record of his movements until almost two years ago when he arrived from the USA with a wife, Nazarene, and a young daughter. He and his family have resumed their annual visits to Tehran. The current trip could be just another visit like the earlier ones.'

Steel picked up the account.

'Dilks and Co. are going to love this; just listen. Khalid's parents, two brothers and a sister were killed when Iran Air Flight 655 was shot down by the US guided missile cruiser USS *Vincennes* on 3rd July 1988. All of the 290 passengers were killed. For his father it was going to be a business trip to Dubai … to be combined with a family holiday. Young Khalid should have been on the flight but days before the trip, he broke his leg and couldn't travel.'

CS Steel looked up from his notes and explained.

'Iranian culture dictates that Khalid should have been taken into his uncle's family but they didn't like each other. The solution was simple. As guardian, Khalid's uncle controlled his nephew's inheritance and used it to send him to a prestigious private school in England, the King George V near London. It's over 4000 kilometres away, and his inheritance was more than sufficient to pay the fees and allow him to return to Tehran each year for a few weeks. This satisfied social expectations, and he eventually became a UK resident.

'King George V school has a good record of university entrances. Khalid was bright, and after his school exams, he went to Loughborough University where he studied electrical and electronic engineering. It was no hardship because on his eighteenth birthday he received US$900,000 in compensation from the Americans for the death of his family. It was US$300,000 for his father and US$150,000 each for his mother, two brothers and sister. Straight away he donated half of this to the mosque his father use to attend. He didn't do anything else extravagant; he doesn't have expensive tastes and lives a very modest lifestyle.

'On graduation he went to the USA, to the University of Texas in Austin, to study for a master's degree in the monitoring and control of petroleum and gas production systems.

'It's a bit of a coincidence that both Rick Johnson and Jeffrey went to the University of Texas. It may be just coincidence. It's likely the place specialises in courses linked to the petroleum industry. From what we have been able to establish, Jeffery is a well-regarded, Senior Health & Safety Technician on the Platform. He was recruited from within TransGlobal Oil and was part of the original crew, joining *Monroe Bravo* at the time it was commissioned and before it became operational. From all accounts, he's not demonstrative but strives to ensure all Health & Safety regulations are observed. Occasionally these impact on local, unofficial practices on the Platform, require more form filling, and affect production. Although this irritates some of the workers, it's generally recognised that he's doing a good job. He's got sound academic qualifications, considerable international experience, and an unblemished off-shore record. Harry, what have you got?'

'We monitor anyone who comes to the UK who may have reason to harbour resentment. An orphan, whose parents, brothers and sisters are killed when their plane is shot down by a western power, is high on the list. He's comes from a religious background and is a practising Shi'a Muslim. The school he attended made special arrangements for him to attend the mosque every Friday. When he moved to Loughborough, he continued his attendance. There's no evidence the Iman, or groups within the mosque, were radical. There's a prayer room on the Platform but we don't know if he used it or not.'

Harry eased back in his chair as though he had finished his contribution but then continued.

'If Cal Jeffrey, aka Khalid Jaffra, is an Iranian *sleeper,* he's been well prepared for his current role as a key figure on the largest, most expensive, and most productive oil and gas platform in the world.'

*

What the intelligence didn't capture, couldn't capture, was the smouldering resentment that Callum had carried, and hidden, for the last thirty-five years.

Callum could now only vaguely remember being told the Americans had murdered his family. At the time, he was stunned and the following days and weeks were a blur; they were unreal. The condolences from neighbours and friends didn't console him. Indeed, the loss was so great he felt guilty for not being killed. He should have been on that plane with them, not in a hospital bed; he felt abandoned. All he had heard from relatives was a call for vengeance, but he felt powerless to act.

His broken leg healed slowly and poorly. On the day he left the hospital to live with his uncle's family, a sympathetic doctor had tried to explain the problem. All he could remember was that he wouldn't have full function of the leg and should avoid playing football and other sports. If he was honest, it was a convenient excuse not to mix with other children; he felt apart from his friends. In the months following the death of his parents, life followed a new routine; it revolved around school and the mosque. At this time, he sensed a coolness, even resentment, in his uncle, and began to avoid him and his family whenever possible. When it was suggested he attend school in England and live there, he was happy to go. It wasn't going to England that was the attraction – it was leaving his relatives behind.

Academically, Khalid did well at the British school; in maths and science subjects, exceptionally well. He was bright, worked hard and passed exams. However, he didn't mix with the other children. His broken leg reduced his physical activity and he didn't like sports. School staff tried to encourage him to take part in the numerous clubs and societies, but he wasn't interested. He wasn't bullied, staff ensured that, he was simply ignored by the other children. His only extra-curricular activity, if you could call it that, was Islam. He was the only practising Muslim in the school and it set him apart. The school timetable was altered so that he could attend Friday prayers and receive instruction from the local Iman. As Khalid got older, he was drawn more towards Islam and was influenced by growing radicalism both within Islam and via the local Iman. He began to resent the western culture into which he had been forced to live, a culture that he believed denigrated Islam. He was ripe for radicalisation.

It was after his school exams in England when a careers guidance lesson gave his life a new direction. All those leaving had to give a brief talk about how a book, a film, a play or an incident had influenced their career choice. One of his class mates was to join the British Army as a junior officer. He described how the ancient book, *The Art of War* by the Chinese War Lord Sun Tzu, and his mantra of "know your enemy", had spurred him to apply. Khalid wasn't really interested in military tactics but the phrase "know your enemy" changed his life. He realised that the only way he could avenge his family was to strike at the Americans. The only way he could know his enemy was to study, live and work in America. Only then could he learn its strengths and exploit its weaknesses.

The award of compensation from the Americans merely strengthened his desire for vengeance, but he was still unsure how he could achieve it. His own future was still pending when he returned to Tehran in the long school summer holiday. His uncle had reluctantly acknowledged his nephew's academic success and noted the school's prediction that he would obtain excellent examination results and be a strong candidate to go to university. He took more notice of the letter from the Iman of the mosque his nephew attended. His nephew was not only a devout and committed Muslim, but keen to promote Islam – even aggressively. Even so, the uncle didn't want Khalid to return to his home and needed a plan that would keep him away.

The solution was fortuitous. His brother-in-law was an officer within the Islam Revolutionary Guard Corps, the IRGC, and had heard that the Quds Force was looking for recruits. Khalid's uncle had heard stories about the Quds Force – allegedly a group engaged in unconventional warfare and military operations. He assumed this was a myth, a legend, but it wasn't. School reports and the Iman's letter were shared with his brother-in-law and, miraculously, progressed through the Byzantine system that characterised the IRGC, a system that was complicated, convoluted and secretive. More by luck than good management, Khalid came to the attention of an officer within the Quds Force. Under the guise of continuing his religious education, Khalid was interviewed by an Iman linked to the Quds Force and then by a series of military officers and government officials.

He was willingly recruited as an overseas asset – to be developed and refined into a strategic weapon against the West. Khalid was an enthusiastic recruit but initially struggled with the idea that it may take years before he could demonstrate his commitment to the cause. He was to develop skills and knowledge in the West that he could eventually deploy against the West. He was instructed to change his name to Callum Jeffrey and was helped to do so.

Once back in the UK, Callum was instructed to apply to Loughborough University to study electrical and electronic engineering, and attend the local mosque. Three years later he graduated towards the top of his class and continued to confirm his commitment to Islam. It was his Iman who passed on documents directing him to a master's degree course at the University of Texas at Austin, USA. The IRGC made sure his application and references would be successful. He was to specialise in the monitoring and control of petroleum and gas production systems. He was assembling an impressive Curriculum Vitae.

Over the next fourteen years, he had a succession of jobs with American oil and gas companies in Texas, northern Canada and Mexico; the Al Sawadi oil platforms in the Red Sea and an installation in Kuwait; Platforms off the coast of Venezuela; and Norwegian oil rigs in the North Sea. They were all designed to create the perfect candidate for a special job.

On an annual visit to Iran to see his relatives, Callum met his Iman contact. He was informed that his destiny was close and he must prepare for the next three years. . He was instructed to marry and become a family man; his ultimate job would require a family man. A future application would be for a position on the new *Monroe Bravo* Platform, currently under construction. It would begin operations in the Fortes sector of the North Sea. He was to be part of an inaugural crew to be formed – he must be part of it. His marriage was rapidly arranged and completed in Tehran. Callum married Nazarene, a woman from a well-connected family, a graduate, attractive, and a devout Muslim. She was unaware of Callum's role of *sleeper*. Their daughter was born within the first year of their marriage.

On merit, but with some background help from influential people, Callum was appointed to *Monroe Bravo,* and joined the work-up team on the Platform. He was on board when it was towed to its position in the North Sea and connected to the underwater structure. His job was to monitor and report on safety procedures associated with oil and gas production.

Chapter 17

High risk options

Tuesday 4th April 2023, 4:30 pm

Lukas, the Diving Supervisor, joined Captain Sorenson and two oil and soot smeared visitors in the briefing room. Sorenson quickly summarised the challenge and then turned to Konrad.

'What can you tell us about the *Monroe Bravo* Diving Bell and the divers?'

'If you've got a laptop, I can show you.'

A laptop was housed in a small lectern. Whatever was on the screen could be viewed on a large, wall-mounted monitor. Konrad typed in a series of search commands and an image of a Diving Bell appeared on the screen; it looked ugly and nothing like the sleek, streamlined Bell on the *Stavanger*. It looked like a collection of half a dozen or more shipping containers and huge gas tanks, in steel frames, bolted together.

'This is a Neptune SDS Mark IV. It's a twelve-man, state of the art, saturation diving system. There are twelve … er, do you have pointer?'

Sorenson gave him a laser pointer.

'There are twelve modules on two levels. On the upper level are the Dive Control Room, Saturation Control Room, Bell Machinery, winch, batteries and the gas reclamation unit. On the lower level, there are three living chambers, showers and toilets, equipment store, transfer chamber and emergency gas tanks. The emergency gas tanks are good for eighty-four hours. Each unit is protected by a steel frame; it's all attached to a ridged sled.'

'What about the divers?' asked Lukas.

'Only nine divers on this hitch, er, this working session on the Platform; it's called a *hitch*. I can get their names and details, but they're all experienced and good.'

'Any injuries?' Lukas asked.

'Don't know ... the guys in the Bell should be safe ... unless it's been damaged by anything falling off the Platform. Danny and Archie were working under the Platform. They both had emergency pony cylinders – enough gas to get them back to the Bell ... but we lost communication with them when we had to evacuate the Dive Centre.'

Quickly looking at Lukas and Konrad in turn, Sorenson asked:

'What are our options?'

Before they could answer a crewman interrupted.

'Sorry to interrupt, sir, but a submersible marker buoy and a slate have been recovered close to the Platform. It's a message from the Diving Bell.'

Konrad grabbed the now deflated marker buoy and focused on the attached slate.

'They've lost all gas pressure from the Platform. They've tried to switch to the emergency supply – but the oxygen is registering zero. The only gases they have to breathe are what's already inside the Bell. They've got a couple of hours before they suffocate.'

The announcement stunned the group. It was Lukas who answered first.

'We could try and connect our reserve umbilical, the back-up to the *Stavanger* Dive Bell, to your Bell. I've never done it under water and I just don't know if getting sea water into the system would have major consequences. It's less of a problem with the oxygen and helium lines, and gas recovery lines, but a problem with the comms, power and data transmission lines. If we get seawater in the gas hoses, they've got bleed valves in the Bell and back on the ship. It would take time to bleed the system ... depends how much water gets in. The comms, power and data lines are sealed units. If water gets into the electronics, it'll blow them. We'd have to ask the company that make the umbilical and its link to the Bell. It's a possibility we can explore alongside others. The bad news is that we have limited time to find out.

'However, this option has other problems. Who connects the umbilical? It can't be those inside the Bell. The onboard system controls the flow of gases into the Bell, but there's not enough pressure to supply gases to their umbilical. It would have to be a diver, or divers, from our Bell and we've only got one. That's Gunnar, and at the moment he's inside our Bell! The chopper that brought Collier and Calovarlo to the ship took our divers and other dive supervisors back to Aberdeen. Gunnar was due to fly back tomorrow, after our relief divers, supervisors, and technicians arrive ... but that's been postponed. Again, it would take time to get divers and back up staff here and *blown down* – pressurised to ninety metres. Time we don't have.'

'Do they have divers on *Guard North*?' asked Rick.

'Not *in sat*, not divers use to working at depth in commercial dive suits,' replied Konrad. 'I know they've got a couple of scuba divers ... but just for routine monitoring and maintenance of *North Guard*.'

'If the *Stavanger* remained close to the Platform, and if we could transfer umbilicals from our Bell to the one on the *Monroe Bravo*, could the divers walk from one Bell to the other?' asked Rick.

'We'd have the same problem as with the main umbilical ... the connection between the umbilical and dive helmet would be exposed to seawater. The Kirby Morgan helmets have non-returnable valves so the gas lines wouldn't be flooded with seawater but somebody would have to drag two or three some distance from one Bell to the other one and then walk back.

Hauling one can be challenging work, hauling three would be exhausting … but it's possible,' replied Lucas.'

'Can we get the Bell off the sea bed and on-board?' asked Rick. 'Would it be possible to disconnect or cut through the shackles connecting the Bell to a lifting chain? If we could connect our Bell to your crane, we could bring it to the surface. Once on the surface, supplying gases, power and comms should be easy … and the crew would have a much better chance of survival.'

'The *Monroe Bravo* Bell is on a reinforced sled. Dragging it a short distance over the seabed and then hauling on board the *Stavanger* would be straight forward,' Konrad replied.

'There's always the chance of fouling,' commented Captain Sorenson.

'We'd need to check any debris in the vicinity, winch the existing chain clear, be aware of the current before anything was attempted,' offered Lukas.

'Could the divers walk between the two Bells using their pony cylinders?' asked Rick.

'Big, big risk,' replied Konrad. 'The cylinders they have are good for about five minutes – enough to drop what they're doing and get back to the Wet Well. If they try to transfer from one Bell to the other, they have to get into their dive suits. They'd have to flood the suit with gas – that's a lot of litres. They've then got to get out of the Bell and walk – on a bearing and in the dark – dozens of metres to safety. Problem is the divers seldom venture away from the Platform; we're not sure what's on the bottom twenty, thirty metres or more from the base. If there's debris, they have to walk round it. There may be soft sediment, forcing them to wade through it knee-deep. Once they find your Bell, they've got to get inside and get the helmet off. Five minutes is tight. They'd also be anxious, maybe breathing heavier than normal … gobbling up the gas. I reckon that's the last option.'

There was a pause as those in the Briefing Room thought

about solutions to the problem.

'We're forgetting the obvious,' said Lucas. 'What about three scuba divers, on rebreathers and *buddy breathing*, ferrying three divers at a time between the *Monroe Bravo* Bell and ours?'

'Gunnar always takes his scuba diving kit onboard the Bell. Jack and Sandro are fully equipped and are saturated at 90 metres. There's the three divers we need.'

There was silence inside the briefing room. Those present knew Jack and Sandro were overdue. If they returned to the Bell, they could replenish the gases in their rebreathers, but they'd be exhausted after shutting down the Platform. It was Lucas who broke the silence.

'Of course, there's also the risk of Cold Water Shock, hyperventilation and hypothermia with the divers inside the Bell being exposed to cold water ... it's probably four degrees centigrade at ninety metres.'

'They'd get cold, very cold, but they wouldn't be in the water long enough to suffer hypothermia,' Konrad replied. 'How long would it take you to haul a diver a hundred meters?'

'It'd depend on the current. With no current, a compliant diver, steady but not frantic finning, I'd say over one kilometre per hour. A hundred metres in four to five minutes max.'

'There are sets of stubby fins and a few masks in the Bell ... but that's about all. We're geared up for deep commercial diving, not recreational stuff.'

'Captain, how close could you get to *Monroe Bravo* if the fires are under control?' asked Rick.

'There are strict regulations about how close any ship can get to the Platform. In the current, life-threatening circumstances, it depends on how close you wish me to get. We also have the Bell deployed. We have to be careful manoeuvring with it below us.'

'Could you get within fifty metres?'

'Yes, but the risk wouldn't be to the ship or the Platform, but to anyone in the water. I'd have to use our dynamic position to maintain our position. That means our propellers and thrusters would be working all the time. We'd also risk being fouled by floating debris or injuring anyone in the water. The closer we get to the Platform, the higher the risk.'

'Are there any underwater scooters on the Platform or on *North Guard*?' asked Lukas.

'Not on the Platform and none on the *North Guard* that I'm aware of,' replied Konrad, 'but we can ask.'

'What about your Diving Bell?' asked Rick.

'In position, fully operational, fully stocked, with the key people onboard. But remember, it's *blown down,* and operating at ninety metres. Everyone inside is tied to the Bell and that includes Jack and Sandro. Everyone will have to decompress together for days. We can bring the Bell to the surface in minutes but it will not be operational for days. The *Stavanger* will have limited functionality at this time,' Lukas added.

'Looks like we have a couple of viable options. Raise the Bell onto the *Stavanger* or ferry divers from one Bell to another. Which would be the safest and quickest?' asked Captain Sorenson.

'Bringing the Bell to the surface is the safest and quickest … but we need a plan A and a plan B,' offered Lucas. 'The Bell is directly below the crane and I've seen debris falling into the water in that area. If the emergency oxygen tank is damaged, there may be other damage. The Bell may be flooded, and then it's recovery rather than rescue. My suggestion is to check the status of the Bell and that they're all alive. There are no comms, so it'll be a case of manually checking the integrity of the Bell. If they're all dead, we leave the job to a recovery team. If they're alive, I'd say haul the Bell to the surface so we can work on it.'

Lucas scanned the faces of those round the table; they accepted the reality.

'OK, looks like we have a plan A and a plan B. Plan A involves disconnecting their main umbilical, lifting chain and hauling the Bell to the surface. I'm sure we can re-attach a shackle and new chain or cable to the Bell and cut the existing chain free in minutes. I know we've got all the kit we need on board. Gunnar can ratchet our lifting cable into position and help Jack ... if he's available to attach it. Sandro, er ... likewise, could disconnect their umbilical and ratchet the existing Bell chain clear. They can do a quick survey of the seabed, check for obstructions or entanglements, and check the Bell. I reckon they can do all that in less than 45 minutes. They'd be back in our Bell in less than one hour and their decompression time would be in hours not days. By the time they're out of our Bell, the *Monroe Bravo* Bell will be on deck and decompressing.'

'What's plan B?' asked Captain Sorenson.

'Towing divers, with no dry suit, fifty metres or more – much more dangerous.'

Lucas and Konrad both nodded their heads in agreement. Captain Sorensen confirmed, that with Rick Johnson's agreement, they would position within 50 metres of the Platform and attempt to lift the stranded Bell to the surface. He then added:

'OK, we have a plan A and a plan B ... assuming Jack Collier and Sandro Calovarlo return to the Bell and are prepared to attempt plan A.'

Captain Sorenson and the group were suddenly interrupted by one of the officers on the bridge.

'Sir, I'm sorry to interrupt but we have an urgent message for Dr Rick Johnson. The caller is President and CEO of TransGlobal Oil, the company that own *Monroe Bravo*. He insists that Dr Johnson take the call immediately.'

The officer escorted Rick away from the group and to a nearby telephone. As Rick grabbed the phone, he noticed his hands were blackened and smeared in oil.

'Rick Johnson here.'

'Rick, good to hear from you ... are you safe?'

'Yes, sir, I'm safe but I'm expecting a high death toll ... afraid we will not know the numbers for several more hours ... some of the explosions have been so violent, and fires so fierce that some of the crew will never be found ... they'll remain missing. Bruce, Bruce Gilling, the Yellow Team Controller, has been killed by a blast. The Red Platform Controller is coordinating the evacuation of injured men and women.'

Rick paused for a moment as he reflected on the death toll but realised he couldn't mourn for them now; that would come later.

'The two owners of the MV *Stavanger*, Jack Collier and Sandro Calovarlo, have dived to the seabed and are trying to shut down the Platform ... but they are overdue. I may have sent them to their death.'

'Why these men?'

'Our Diving Bell has been damaged and has dropped to the seabed ... there are no gases being fed into the Bell for the men inside to breathe. They will suffocate in a couple of hours if we can't rescue them. We are currently working on two plans to save them but it depends on Jack Collier and Sandro Calovarlo returning to their Bell.

'The latest news is that the gas pipeline has been shut down, but the crude oil riser is still burning. *North Guard* is cooling the Platform. The site is still too hot for support vessels to contain any escaped oil and collect it. We're ready to spray dispersant as soon as possible.

'I've made arrangements for the mothballed Backup Command and Control system to be made operational and airlifted from Aberdeen to *Monroe Bravo*. In the next hour or so we'll know if the Platform has been saved. If it has, it will take a couple of days to assess the damage caused and what's needed to get it up and running. I'll be returning there as soon as we've finished speaking.'

'No, you're not!' replied Walter T. Brachs forcibly. 'Rick, TransGlobal, the FBI, Homeland Security and the British Government are treating the explosions and fire on *Monroe Bravo* as a terrorist act. I don't want to explain over an open line, but I want you back in Aberdeen, at TransGlobal Headquarters, as soon as possible – like in the next few hours if not sooner. Norton will explain. I know you've got good people on the Platform – give them the chance to move up and do what needs to be done. We'll talk again later.'

Chapter 18

Change of Plan

Tuesday 14th April 2023, 4:40 pm

Rick Johnson returned to the group on the bridge of the *Stavanger*. The discussion paused, and everyone looked at him.

'Walter Brachs, the Chairman and CEO of TransGlobal Oil, wants me in Aberdeen as soon as possible … like in the next few hours. I'm to liaise from there.'

Turning his head in the direction of the officer who had asked him to take the call, Rick added:

'I'm told they can fit one more person on a helicopter that is leaving for Aberdeen in the next few minutes. I've got to take it. I'll back any decision or action you decide to take … I'll phone as soon as I get to Aberdeen.'

Moments later Rick was gone. It seemed no sooner had Rick gone when a crew member strode onto the bridge with a message: Jack and Sandro were inside the Diving Bell, safe and well, the Platform had been shut down. Eagerly, Captain Sorenson, Lucas and Konrad moved from the bridge to the Dive Centre and the radio link to the Diving Bell. Karl, the Gas Technician, was waiting to speak to them. In his helium induced squeaky voice he explained:

'Jack Collier, Sandro Calovarlo and Gunnar Larson are back inside the main Bell. They're having something to eat and drink … they're OK and are resting. I'm giving the microphone to Mr Calovarlo.'

In a voice that was unrecognisable, Sandro confirmed:

'Sandro here. Jack and I followed Rick Johnson's instructions, and we've closed the gas and oil valves. With no more gas and oil escaping, we're assuming the fires will soon be under control and the drama is over. Over.'

The group looked out of the Dive Centre window towards *Monroe Bravo.* It was still shrouded in swirling smoke and steam but whilst some fires still burned, the roaring inferno had disappeared. Smoke was blocking out any afternoon sun but they could see small boats scurrying around. The *North Guard* was pouring hundreds of thousands of litres of sea water onto the Platform. To anyone still alive on *Monroe Bravo* it must have felt like a tropical rain storm – but welcome. Captain Sorenson glanced at Konrad before speaking.

'It's Captain Sorenson here. Great job. We're relieved that you are all OK but there's a problem with the *Monroe Bravo* Diving Bell. I'll let Lucas explain.'

'Sandro, it's Lucas here. There are nine divers, *in sat*, trapped inside the *Monroe Bravo* Bell. They've lost all gas pressure and the reserve oxygen tank is registering zero. We think it's been ruptured by falling debris. They are surviving on the gases inside the Bell, but they'll suffocate in less than two hours. Er … they've no comms or heating. We've explored several options and would welcome your comments and advice on a couple of them. Both involve you, Jack and Gunnar.

'We reckon the quickest and safest is to connect a lifting cable from the *Stavanger* to the *Monroe Bravo* Bell, haul it to the surface, and attach our reserve umbilical. We can supply the gases they need to breathe and can start decompression. All the kit needed is already on our Bell and Gunnar can explain what you and Jack would need to do. That's our plan A.

'The only other possibility we can think of, plan B, is for the three of you to tow the stranded divers, three at a time, between the two

Bells. Talk to Jack and Gunnar and tell me what you think. Over.'

'Give us two minutes.'

Gunnar turned to Jack and Sandro.

'I'm happy with setting up the lift and can tell you what you would need to do. It's not difficult … you just need to be careful and not exert yourselves. Heavy work at ninety metres is not a clever idea even if you are used to it. I can cut the chain on the *Monroe Bravo* Bell. You'd have to ratchet the *Stavanger* cable to me and then clear the *Monroe Bravo* chain. It's all straightforward stuff.'

'What if we hit a snag, have to go to plan B, and tow them? The water is going to be about 4°C outside the Bell. Can we get hold of any wet suits or dry suits? They can't wear the commercial suit without the helmet. They've got to breathe from the spare regulator and the suit would fill with water and drag them down. They're tough guys but cold water and hyperventilation affects all of us.'

'You're right about the cold,' Jack replied, 'but it would be only for three or four minutes. Not long enough for hypothermia but pretty cold. We can't wait for dry suits and fleeces to be flown from Aberdeen. They could all be dead inside two hours.'

'If you end up towing the divers, there are dry clothes, towels and blankets inside our Bell. Once they're inside, I know what to do.' said Karl. 'Each of the divers has a five point harness as part of their dive suit. They can put that on and you can clip them onto you. It'll keep your hands free. You'll need your hands free 'cos their fingers and hands will get cold quickly … they'll lose all feeling in them … so you may have to keep checking their mouthpiece is still in place. I've heard stories of men losing the mouthpiece 'cos they were so cold.'

Karl was silent for a few seconds before he went on.

'If there's no dry suit for them, we'll have to improvise. If they put on a sweater, with a *Rashi* on top, it will trap water next to their body. It'll stop some heat from being flushed away. Again, anything on their legs and feet will help reduce the shock of the icy water and reduce heat lost.'

'So, you think it's feasible?' asked Sandro.

'Not the best way to spend a Tuesday afternoon ... but it'll work.'

Jack looked at Gunnar and asked:

'Do you think the divers will cooperate.'

'They're not stupid. They'll know the main umbilical has failed, that they're on borrowed time ... they'll cooperate but we have no comms. We need to be clear on the plan because we'll be down to hand signals, notes on a slate and a torch.'

The next ten minutes were busy. Jack and Sandro were happy about the procedure to secure shackles to chains. Gunnar demonstrated how the ratchet worked, how it would allow them to draw the heavy chain to the correct position. They also agreed their position around the Diving Bell so they could check for any potential snags or obstructions. Karl checked and rechecked the *Stavanger* Bell. He confirmed everything was operational, fully stocked and ready to go. Captain Sorenson had the *Stavanger* positioned close to the Platform. If they could lift the Diving Bell, the stranded divers had a chance. If it was plan B, and a series of tows, swimming backwards for forwards, it was going to be a challenge.

Jack, Sandro and Gunnar had set up their rebreathers, checked their kit and were ready to go. They had also checked the state of the tide and were not overly concerned. The current was past its peak and there was over one hour to slack water. They would be operating in current but it wouldn't be for long, and getting less all the time.

It was reassuring having Karl and Gunnar in the Bell. Although Karl typically operated the Gas Control System on the surface, he knew what to do inside the Bell. Gunnar had spent years working *in sat*, and his calm manner helped Jack and Sandro relax. Both

Jack and Sandro had been cold when they were closing down the Platform. They didn't want a repeat of that and started to put on layers of clothes that would keep them warm inside the dry suit. The last layer would be the fluffy, all-in-one suit that made them look like bears about to run the London Marathon.

'Careful about how much you put on,' said Gunnar. 'You don't want to be cold but it's going to be heavy work, in current. If we have to tow, it will be hard work for at least thirty minutes. If you get hot, you're going to sweat. Whilst you're active it'll be fine ... but as soon as you stop, you're going to get cold very quickly. I'd suggest just two thin layers under the onesie.'

They were about to crawl through to the Wet Well when there was a message from Lukas.

'Urgent message to Jack, Sandro and Gunnar. Repeat, urgent message to Jack, Sandro and Gunnar, over.'

Karl picked up the radio handset and offered it to Jack.

'Jack here, what's the message?'

'Bad news – the crane that was supporting the *Monroe Bravo* Diving Bell has broken free and fallen away. It may have fallen onto the Diving Bell. There's no way of confirming any damage. Retrieving the Bell may be impossible, over.'

'Message received and understood. Will proceed with caution, over and out.'

Sandro and Gunnar had heard the exchange.

'What yer thinking, boss?' asked Gunnar.

'If it looks as though it's possible to lift the Bell, I say let's try. If it's damaged and flooded ... by the time we get there, it's too late. We'll have to play it by ear.'

Before they crawled through the tunnel and into the Wet Well, Jack repeated the plan in his squeaky voice.

'We've no comms and so it will all be hand signals and notes on a slate. Gunnar will tow the hose and cable for the cutting torch. We'll divide the other equipment between use. We rendezvous outside our Bell and fin gently on a bearing of 45 degrees to the *Monroe Bravo* Bell. It'll be with the current and so I estimate about three minutes or less. There may be lights on, but it may be buried under tons of steel … and ruptured.

'Once we get close to them, we'll need to make an assessment as to whether we proceed with the lift or not. There's no port hole to see inside so we'll only know if it's flooded once we try to enter. If it's flooded, they'll probably be dead – if it's not totally flooded, they may be semi-conscious; we'll see.

'If we decide to attempt the lift, I'll take off my fins, make my way inside and tell them what's happening. That's assuming the Wet Well is still dry and not flooded. If it is … it probably means the main Bell is flooded.'

The dry suits, helmets, fins and rebreathers were all secured in place. In the confines of the Wet Well, it was awkward climbing into the suits and checking the gear. Fins in hand, Gunnar switched on his helmet torch and led the way down the short steps and into the dark water; Jack and Sandro followed.

It seemed unreal in the gloom. Inside the Bell, it had been an intellectual exercise – options to consider, time and gas allowances to judge, level of risk to assess. Now the decision had been made. Gunnar led the way to the foot of the Bell. They grouped around the foot of the ladder and checked their dive computers, dials that glowed in the dark. Gunnar grabbed the line that was attached to the steel lifting cable, pulled it over his shoulder and was ready. He gave a hand signal to say AOK, swivelled in the water and kicked away. He was pointing his left arm into the gloom, grasping his left bicep with his right hand, and checking the bearing as he set off into the darkness. The line curved away above him and was lost in the gloom. The strobe light on his shoulder blinked steadily; it was a beacon for them to follow.

Despite the threat of suffocation to the divers in the Diving Bell,

Jack knew they had to be sensible. It wouldn't help anybody if they blasted through the water and half-way through the rescue were exhausted; he already felt tired. It was a case of conserving energy, finning steadily, keeping the bottom in sight, checking the time and checking the bearing.

With no landmarks, just a dark grey, muddy bottom, the outward leg to the *Monroe Bravo* Bell was disorientating; it was like swimming in a dark grey void. Jack could tell from the particles of sediment around him that they were cruising along faster than the current. The digital watch on the dive computer told him they'd been finning for over two and a half minutes when a dull glow emerged dead ahead. It was the emergency lighting from the Bell. As they got closer, Jack was amazed at the scene. The Diving Bell was huge but the remains of the crane were massive – a mound of mangled steel. At first it looked as though the Bell was buried under the debris. However, as they got closer they could see the remains of the crane had missed the Bell by centimetres. The steel lifting chain was looped over it. Jack shone his torch at the seabed and confirmed only one impression had been made. He flicked his torch to the Bell and searched for damage, but couldn't see any. Miraculously, the crane and jib had missed the Bell.

They finned to the entrance of the Wet Well to discover it was partly blocked by sediment and mud. They fell to their knees and began scooping it away from the entrance so that Jack could get inside; they dug until there was enough space for him to enter and leave. The current wafted the sediment away and they were all set. Jack slipped off his fins, wriggled through the hole, and poked his head inside the Wet Well. It was dry but it didn't mean the main accommodation unit was dry. He crawled along the connecting tunnel, carrying three masks and pairs of stubby fins, and rapped on the watertight door. There was no answer. He knocked again and waited, wondering if the space on the other side of the hatch was flooded and the nine men beyond were all dead. To his relief, the hatch locking wheel turned and the door began to open.

They were alive and it was dry inside.

Jack pulled off his mask and spat out his mouthpiece. Straight away he could feel the hot, humid air on his face and the smell of unwashed bodies. There was a stunned silence before he announced:

'Hi guys. Just to let you know we'll be lifting the Bell to the surface in a few minutes. Anything we need to know?'

Chapter 19

We've got a problem

Tuesday 14th April 2023, 4:50 pm

There were shouts and hollers, questions and tears as the men crowded around him. It took a moment to restore order, but before Jack could explain the plan, one of the divers approached him.

'We've got a problem. When the main umbilical shut down, we switched to the emergency supply. Minutes later, we heard something hit the Bell. Whatever it was it damaged the emergency oxygen supply. We think it's been vented into the sea; we've lost all pressure. The only gases we've got to breathe are the ones in the Bell. There's enough for a couple of hours, max.'

'OK, we know … that's why we're here. We'll have you onboard the *Stavanger* inside the hour. Our guys are ready to connect a reserve umbilical … drama over.'

Jack could sense the collective fear amongst the stranded divers; it gave additional urgency to plan A. He quickly explained the plan and tried to reassure the men as he left. He hoped it wouldn't be the last time he would see them.

Jack made his way through the water-tight hatch, along the tunnel to the Wet Well. Before he stepped down the ladder and wriggled into open water, he wrote a message on his slate:

BELL INTACT & MEN ALIVE. CONFIRM EMERGENCY O_2 SUPPLY LOST!

TWO HOURS BREATHING GASES LEFT IN BELL. <u>MUST</u> RAISE ASAP.

Sandro and Gunnar were waiting for him as he emerged into open water. Jack shone his torch on the slate and showed them the message; they merely nodded and, with grim expressions on their faces, moved away to start raising the Bell. It was mechanical and unemotional as Jack threaded the end of a line through the pulley system and started to haul the steel lifting cable towards the stranded Bell. By the time he had it close enough to attach, he was breathing heavily. Jack realised he'd been too energetic; he had to conserve his energy – he'd need all of it. Gunnar had already cut the existing chain free and Sandro had pulled it clear. Jack was desperately trying to relax and control his breathing. Over exertion at ninety metres could be deadly. He didn't want to add to the drama. When everything was in place, Gunnar unrolled a red Submersible Marker Buoy. He released a small amount of gas into one end of the thin, flexible plastic tube from his mouthpiece and let go. Immediately it began to rise to the surface as the gases inside expanded. Within a few metres, it was racing to the surface with a stream of bubbles behind it. It was the signal to lift the Bell five metres from the seabed.

Gunnar, Jack and Sandro moved away from the Bell and held onto the debris of the crane as they saw the slack on the steel cable taken up and become taut. Puffs of sediment were kicked up and wafted away by the current. Suddenly the Bell lurched as it was dragged a couple of metres away and swayed gently a few metres from the remains of the crane. The problem was over. Gunnar sent up an orange marker buoy to confirm the Bell was free and they were going to check it.

With no time to spare, the three of them descended on the Bell. Torches in hand, they swam around and over it, looking for damage. Sandro finned under the sled and around one side before meeting Gunnar on top. They shared messages on their slates; they judged they were "good to go".

Jack had inspected one end of the Bell and had moved around to the side. He was shining his torch on the large black emergency tank of oxygen that was bolted to the sled. It had bars of metal tube, like bent scaffolding poles, wrapped around it in a protective shield. It hadn't protected it from the two-metre long metal strut that had skewered it. Jack guessed that if you tried to spear the tank a hundred times from the surface you'd be lucky to do it once; but once was enough. As Jack moved his torch, the light reflected off a shiny metal tube that was cable-tied to one of the upright lengths of the bent, scaffolding-type poles. It was between the tank, another box-like section of the Bell, and just accessible. Jack wasn't sure why he finned closer, grabbed one of the protective bars, and pulled himself into the space to take a closer look.

A tingling wave of dread flushed over him as he gazed at the tube. Rick Johnson had told him that four bombs had exploded on the Platform with devastating effect. Was he looking at another bomb? Did a fifth bomb make any sense? Rick had told him that two bombs had destroyed their Command and Control Systems. Two others had ruptured the high pressure gas and crude oil pipe lines. The Platform had only been saved by shutting off the pipelines at the seabed. What if the bombers knew about the shutdown devices on the seabed? What if this was a bomb and designed to destroy the Bell and everyone in it? Jack was no bomb disposal expert – he didn't know the first thing about bombs. "Think, think!" he said to himself.

There were no aerials or antenna on the tube – but perhaps modern devices didn't need aerials to receive a radio signal. What would be the effect of changes in pressure on the device? He didn't know. What he did know was that they needed to find out. It just wasn't worth the risk to move it. Time was short and Jack finned quickly to the rendezvous point above the Bell where Sandro and Gunnar were waiting for him. He unclipped his slate and, shining his torch on its surface, carefully wrote a message:

SUSPECT BOMB BETWEEN O_2 TANK AND BELL

WILL MERELY TELL DIVERS CHANGE IN PLAN.

WILL GET BACK TO THEM ASAP.

WE NEED ADVICE ON POSSIBLE BOMB.
RETURN TO STAVANGER BELL NOW.

Sandro and Gunnar nodded as Jack crossed his arms across his chest as a signal to end the dive.

It took precious minutes to tell the stranded divers of the delay and to return to the *Stavanger* Bell. In a voice distorted by the helium, Jack squeaked:

'Captain, it's Jack here. The divers are alive and well inside the Bell. However, two vitally important pieces of information. One, we may have found another bomb clipped to the *Monroe Bravo* Bell. We urgently need advice about what to do. Can you contact the Army bomb squad and set up a radio link as soon as possible? Two, debris has ruptured the emergency oxygen tank on the *Monroe Bravo* Bell. I can confirm they have only the gases inside to breathe. They will all suffocate in just over one hour unless we get them to the surface or out.'

'Message received and understood, stand by,' Captain Sorenson said as Jack checked the time on his dive computer.

The minutes dragged by in silence. They all knew that every minute took the nine trapped divers towards suffocation. Jack was about to radio Captain Sorenson again when the captain spoke.

'Major Stanford from the 11 Explosive Ordnance Disposal and Search Regiment, British Army's Royal Logistic Corps is waiting to speak to you. He has been briefed about the explosions on board *Monroe Bravo*.'

'Stanford here, what have you got for me?'

'We have nine divers, *in sat,* inside a Diving Bell at ninety metres below the North Sea. They have less than one hour of gases to breathe before they are suffocated.'

Jack was trying to be precise and economical in his language, and sound cool and calm; he wasn't.

'As we were about to lift the Bell to the surface, I spotted a shiny metal tube cable tied to a metal bar between a large emergency oxygen tank and the Bell. It's about half a metre long and about eighty or ninety centimetres diameter. It's solid but one end has a knurled cap. It looks as though the cap will screw off. We've spoken to a dive supervisor and senior staff on the Platform. They all say the Health & Safety Technician, Callum Jeffreys, fitted it and told them it was a sensor. However, we can find no order or worksheet that confirms this. The tube should not be there. I thought it may be a bomb … that's what I've got for you.'

'OK, let's assume it's a bomb. Did you see any marks, numbers, letters … anything written on it?

'No.'

'Did it feel warm?'

'I didn't touch it.'

'Did you see any small holes or slits in the tube or at the ends?'

'No, it looked solid'

'I know about IEDs but not Diving Bells. I'm assuming the tube was put in place before the Diving Bell was submerged.'

'I think that's a fair assumption.'

'I'm also assuming that the Bell would move when it was lowered off a ship, whilst in the water, and when it touched the seabed?'

'Yes.'

'I'm also assuming that whoever attached the device couldn't predict its movement, up and down, in the water? They couldn't predict changes in pressure on the device?'

'That's right; over a period of days and weeks, the Bell would be raised and lowered according to the jobs being completed.'

'I'm told the other bombs went off in a sequence, all within a few minutes of each other. I can't think of a reason why a bomber would delay in exploding a fifth bomb. My assumption would be that the bomb, and it sounds like a bomb, is on a timing device that's failed to trigger.

'A basic principle of bomb-making is KISS – Keep It Simple, Stupid. Bombers very rarely install duplicate systems, multiple triggers ... too much to go wrong. I think it's safe to say the same bomber made all the bombs – the other four went off but not this one. It's a faulty bomb.'

'What happens if it goes off?'

'It all depends on the amount of explosive, the type of explosive, the depth of the bomb in the water and what or who is close by. My estimate would be about two kilograms of explosive. It could be RDX, HMX or C4 and at ninety metres would be devasting to anything close by. The first shock wave would rupture both Diving Bells. At that depth, they would simply implode. The shock wave would kill any diver within a couple of hundred metres – probably more. It would rupture the major organs of the body.

'The explosion would create rapidly expanding, and collapsing, gaseous bubbles. Imagine a party balloon expanding in nano seconds to the size of a tourist air balloon. At one point, the expanding bubble can't be sustained and it will collapse. It will create a shock wave. However, the explosion would be continuing, and the bubble re-forming and expanding again, creating a new shock wave. It's a rapidly diminishing cycle that creates a series of gigantic ripples. The shock waves could immobilise the ship above it. It is like a depth charge going off.

'My advice is not to touch it until we get there. If there's another way of getting the divers to the surface, I'd suggest that you do that.'

The time was now 5:12 pm. The divers were finding it difficult to breathe. The proportion of oxygen inside the Bell was decreasing with every breath.

Chapter 20

Plan B

Tuesday 14th April 2023, 5:12 pm

'OK, it's plan B,' said Jack. 'We can rendezvous outside our Bell, and fin to the other one. I'll go inside and tell them of the change. I'd expect the first three to be ready for transfer inside five minutes. Gunnar, could you lead the way back to the *Stavanger* Bell? As soon as the first man emerges, clip him on and start finning back, bearing 225 degrees. Once you've got him inside, make the return trip for the next one. Remember to vent some air from your kit. The diver is going to be buoyant and will pull you towards the surface – you need to keep just off the bottom. Any questions?'

There were no questions and the three of them made their way back to the Wet Well and into open water. A quick check and they headed off to the stranded Bell. Once there, Jack slipped off his kit and fins, and gave them to Sandro. This time, without the rebreather on his back, it was easy to crawl through the Wet Well tunnel. He rapped on the interconnecting hatch and it was opened almost immediately, the warm fetid gases wafting over him. Conditions had deteriorated since his last visit. He could see the divers gasping for breath.

'I'm really sorry about the delay but we think we've found a bomb attached to the Bell. It's too dangerous to risk lifting it to the surface. Afraid you'll all have to take a short, cold swim to our Bell.'

Jack explained the routine, and ended by saying:

'Remember, no rush … Sandro and Gunnar are waiting for you

outside. They'll offer you their reserve mouthpieces so you'll have your own gas supply. They'll clip a strap onto your harness, and you'll be off. If you can fin, great, just don't stop us finning,' Jack said with a smile. 'You'll be very cold by the time we get to our Bell; we'll help you into the Wet Well. Karl will be waiting with warm towels and blankets, hot food and drinks. It's just a few minutes of a really cold swim – that's it. Let's go.'

It seemed like a long time but it was only a couple of minutes before Jack's legs appeared on the ladder and he floated into open water. It was a relief to breathe from his rebreather as Sandro helped him on with his kit. As Jack pulled on his fins, he held up three fingers and nodded. The first three were coming out now.

Suddenly a pair of stubby fins and skinny legs in pale long-johns emerged at the top of the ladder and dropped under the water. Gunnar offered him the mouthpiece. The diver's eyes looked wild through the mask; his hair waved in the current as he wrapped his arms around his body. He looked sickly pale in the torch light. Gunnar clipped a strap onto the diver's harness and they began to fin away. Jack was so intent on watching Gunnar fin away that he failed to notice another pair of stubby fins and long-johns emerging from the Wet Well. Sandro offered the mouthpiece to the diver and helped him into open water before finning strongly back to the *Monroe Bravo* Bell.

Jack didn't have long to wait for the third diver. He followed the same routine and together they started to fin toward the safety of the Bell just over 50 metres away. For the first few metres, Jack could feel the diver finning furiously; so strongly that at times the diver was towing Jack. However, very quickly the finning subsided and Jack realised the diver was starting to shiver uncontrollably. When Jack gave him the AOK hand signal, all Jack could see in return was a hand, shaking so violently it was impossible to make sense of any message.

Out of the dark a dull light emerged; it was their Bell. As Jack and his passenger got closer, they could see that Gunnar and

Sandro were waiting for them. Their torches created dull balls of light in the darkness. At the steps into the Wet Well, Jack unclipped the strap, positioned himself directly in front of the diver and with the torch between them signalled for him to breathe deeply. There was a nod of the head and he spat out the mouthpiece and allowed Gunnar and Sandro to push him through the water and into the Wet Well where Karl was waiting.

The second trip followed the same pattern. It was uneventful but Jack realised he was getting tired and his hands were cold. The current should have been lessening but it seemed harder to make progress against the particles of sediment flowing towards him on the return leg. Jack, Sandro and Gunnar gave each other the AOK hand signal and set off to the near-deserted Bell for the last time. Jack was glad it was the last trip. As he waited for the last three divers to emerge, he looked at the tangle of steel that had missed the Bell by centimetres. Another metre and it would have been a body recovery operation. The Bell and its various compartments would have shattered like an egg shell at morning breakfast. It wouldn't have been an attractive sight inside. A pair of bare legs emerging brought Jack back to the present. Mouthpiece in, clipped on, finning towards safety ... *two to go ... one to go.*

As Sandro disappeared into the dark, strobe light flashing, Jack wondered why the last diver hadn't emerged. He rapped on the metal ladder with a spare karabiner, but no one answered, no one emerged. In frustration bordering on irritation, Jack pulled himself up the ladder so that he could see into the Wet Well. The last diver was sitting bolt upright on the metal bench, immobile and shivering.

'We've got to go,' shouted Jack, the irritation clear in his voice.

The man didn't move but continued to shiver. It was then that Jack noticed the wide-eyed stare on the face of the diver; he was terrified. Jack pulled himself up the steps into the Wet Well, took off his fins and crawled, still wearing his rebreather, to the man on the bench.

'I'm Jack, Jack Collier, I'm here to help you,' he said as he placed his hand on the man's shoulder; there was no reaction. 'All your buddies have gone; they are on their way to our Bell …most of 'em will be inside by now.'

There was still no reaction, no responce from the diver, and Jack knew they couldn't stay here forever. The air was thick and heavy, Jack was already starting to gasp as he tried to suck oxygen into his lungs.

'It's just a short swim, three or four minutes, and I'll do all of the finning. All you've got to do is hang onto me and breathe through the mouthpiece – easy.'

Jack offered the man his reserve mouthpiece and was about to offer more encouragement when the man made a grab for it, forced it into his mouth and started to breathe. Jack realised he now had a problem. If he tried to reclaim the mouthpiece, he risked damaging it. If they tried to exit together, they risked getting stuck or damaging the kit. In the end, Jack began to crawl backwards towards the ladder and into the water. The diver followed with the breathing hose like a short lead.

It was painfully slow because the diver was reluctant to enter the water but desperate not to let go of the breathing hose. Jack was coaxing the diver down the mini tunnel and making sure the stretched hose wasn't damaged. Jack eventually reached the ladder and started to climb down it. In the emergency lighting Jack could see the breathing hose stretch whilst the diver clamped his teeth onto the mouthpiece. Jack entered open water and paused to refit his fins. When he looked up he saw the diver had followed him, he started to relax. It was a mistake. As the diver reached the bottom rung of the ladder, he suddenly shot forwards. He'd pushed himself off the ladder and knocked Jack off balance. As Jack kicked with his fins, and paddled with his hands the torch slipped from his wrist. Jack was trying to regain his position in the water but the diver had grabbed him. Vice like hands grabbed webbing and straps, the diver's head was buried against Jack's body, and his legs were wrapped around one of Jack's. They tumbled to the seabed with Jack's arms and fins stirring up the sediment. Jack was desperate to regain control but struggled with the weight of the man clamped to his body and restricting his movements. The more Jack tried to free himself, to rise above the seabed, the more they tumbled across it. It was only seconds before Jack realised the diver wasn't fighting him – just holding on to him. He needed to calm the situation and relax. Perhaps if he relaxed the diver would relax. Jack forced himself to be still and allowed himself to roll over the seabed in the current.

Jack felt the strike as the back of his rebreather hit something solid, then his shoulder and his knee. He heard something break but had no idea what it was. He was bouncing against metal bars and plates as the current pushed the tumbling pair along. "We're hitting the crane …the jumble of metal that fell off the Platform," Jack said to himself. It was odd because the overall current should be mild, and getting less, but it was firm. "It's searching for a way around the Diving Bell …that's why it's speeded up," Jack realised. It was pushing them along, bouncing them off metal beams and struts, brackets and plates. Jack cracked his head against something metal. "Shit …I don't need to lose or damage my face mask now!" Jack said to himself as he tried to tuck his head towards his chest. Jack felt he was rolling against a lattice of steel, reached out and grabbed a beam or a strut. He hung onto it with all his strength and tried to be still, tried to control his breathing and tried to control his nerves. In the sudden stillness Jack could feel the diver against him, he could feel the rise and fall of his breathing, but otherwise he was unresponsive; he simply clung on. Slowly Jack looked around and could see a dull glow from the diving Bell in the distance but nothing else. He carefully moved his free arm until it hit another metal strut. A cold shiver ran over Jack's body as he realised, he was inside the tangled mass of steel, the remains of the crane or jib. As he explored the space around him he realised they had tumbled inside the box-like construction of the jib.

"Stay calm and think … stay calm and think!" Jack said to

himself. With his free hand, he searched for the torch; it wasn't on his wrist. It must have slipped off when the diver grabbed him. There was no point in worrying about it now. "The strobe light … when Sandro and Gunnar realise we've not arrived, they will come looking for us. They'll see the strobe light," Jack told himself reassuringly. He turned his head to look over his shoulder but the strobe light wasn't blinking. "Oh no! he thought. It must have been damaged when I collided with part of the crane. I heard something break. It must have been the strobe light."

Jack thought back to what he had seen when he'd approached the *Monroe Bravo* Bell: he'd been more interested in it than the wreckage of the crane. Once he'd established the Bell wasn't damaged, he'd forgotten about the scrap metal. He couldn't judge how far inside the tangled mass they were, but it was far enough for them to be hidden. "We've got to get out of here, but which way is out?" Tumbling in the darkness, he had lost any sense of direction. The dull lights of the Bell were off to his left, which meant ahead was the way out.

Jack reached forward with his free hand, grabbed a metal strut and tried to haul them along. They moved a few centimetres and then seemed to jam. "Gas, will I have enough gas?" he asked himself. "I've been breathing heavier than normal and the diver will have been gulping gas. It may have been just for a few minutes but it all adds up. I've done five journeys of, say five minutes. Even if I double, treble, the time I've still got plenty of gas." For a moment he was relieved, but he was still inside the tangled mass of steel. He reached out again, gained firm hand holds, wriggled and pull them both forwards another few centimetres. He was about to repeat the manoeuvre when he suddenly stopped; *tunnel vision*. He was in danger of focusing solely on one task at the expense of everything else. If he damaged the hose of the reserve, or pulled the mouthpiece out of the diver's mouth, he could end up fighting a drowning man; a man who could drown him as well.

Instead of trying to pull them both along, Jack eased the man towards him. He looked into the man's face but in the darkness he couldn't see anything. Jack now alternated between grabbing a steel strut and pulling himself forwards, and pulling the diver forwards. It was centimetre by centimetre. A few minutes ago, Jack had been cold but now he was sweating inside the dry suit. "Snags …I've got to be careful of snags," he told himself. It would be so easy to puncture his dry suit. There could be a sharp edge or corner, a protruding bolt pressing into the dry suit. Freezing water would flood in, the weight would drag him down, and here would be no way he would be able to haul them out of the trap. They would both drown.

Jack thought of trying to force the diver's hands from his harness or disentangling himself from the diver's legs, but dismissed the idea. "If I force his hand from my harness, he may grab something else. If he pulls out my mouthpiece, I'm in real trouble!" In the darkness, Jack reached out and tried to visualise the position of the jumble of metal around him. There were no snags that he could feel, and there was a way forward big enough for both of them to get through. Another energy-sapping pull and a few more centimetres closer to open water. It became an all-consuming routine: check for snags, decide the way forward, ease the diver forwards, grab a metal strut and pull.

Jack was losing all sense of time. He cursed himself for not checking the time he had arrived at the Diving Bell to transfer the last diver, but guessed it was now three or four minutes since the diver had entered the cold water, maybe even five. The diver would be getting cold. Another ten minutes and he'd be close to hypothermia. Jack couldn't remember if hypothermia would make him compliant. "Would it be possible to release his grip? Would he be 'frozen' in that position?" Jack stopped thinking about it. Check for snags, ease him forward, reach out, grab and pull, then repeat. Jack estimated he must have pulled them well over a metre even two. "How far did we tumble into that maze? We must be getting close to open water. When Sandro returns, he'll see us." Jack suddenly realised that as he was dragging them through the tangled remains of the crane, he was stirring up sediment. It would be all around them, shielding them from view. He rested for a moment.

Sandro and Gunnar had returned. They had finned, a couple of metres apart, with torches searching the area ahead. There was no sign of Jack and the diver. They reached the Bell and found the torch but couldn't understand why it had been discarded or dropped. Gunnar wrote a message on his slate and showed it to Sandro. He was going to check inside. Gunnar slipped off his rebreather and his fins, and ducked inside the Diving Bell. He was back in a few minutes, shaking his head. Sandro gestured that he was going to swim around the Bell. If they hadn't intercepted Jack and the diver on the way to the Bell, and they weren't inside, they had to be somewhere around it. Gunnar gestured that he would swim over the top of it and they would meet at the entrance.

The current was mild at ninety metres but it was dark, and even with a torch the viz was poor. Neither Sandro nor Gunnar had seen any evidence of Jack or the diver by the time they returned to the Bell. The obvious next step was to conduct an area search around it, but it would be just the two of them. There was no way they could get more divers into the water and down to 90 metres.

Sandro looked at his dive computer and wrote a message on his slate. He had more than sixty minutes of gas and was prepared to use all of it looking for Jack. Trying to control his rising panic, he wrote slowly and carefully on his slate.

GRID SEARCH. YOU TAKE NORTH. I WILL TAKE SOUTH.

20 – 30 METRE GRID. RETURN HERE IN 30 MINUTES.

Gunnar gave Sandro the AOK hand signal, checked his dive computer, turned in the water, and kicked to start his grid search. Sandro did the same and set off due west on the first leg of his grid. He was sweeping the torch left and right as he tried to estimate how far he could see, how far between the legs of his grid.

Although Jack felt hot, his hands and fingers were cold and he was getting tired. He'd struggled to complete the last pull and wondered how many more he could do. As he rested, he looked ahead. There was a dull light moving in the distance. It must be Sandro. He was coming to find them. As he looked, he realised the light was moving left to right, not closer. He'd no voice comms, no torch. He fumbled with a karabiner on his jacket and almost dropped it, his fingers were so cold.

Tap, tap, tap ... tap ... tap ... tap, tap, tap, tap

Jack tapped out SOS on the metal beam he was holding.

Tap, tap, tap ... tap ... tap ... tap, tap, tap, tap

But the torch was disappearing into the gloom. With all the force he could muster, Jack knocked out the morse code again.

Tap, tap, tap ... tap ... tap ... tap, tap, tap, tap

If Sandro swam away now, he may never return. He'd drown, with this diver clinging onto him.

The light was suddenly brighter and then dull, brighter then dull. Jack could tell that Sandro was waving his torch from side to side as he searched for them. He continued to rap out SOS on the metal beam. As Sandro got closer, Jack continued to send out his SOS and realised he was close to exhaustion. Sandro was suddenly above him, shining the torch to one side and giving him the AOK sign. He started to write on his slate.

AOK ... HOW MUCH GAS?
STAY PUT ... WILL GET GUNNAR ... GET YOU OUT
BACK IN FEW MINUTES

Jack offered his dive computer towards Sandro so he could check how much gas they had left. Sandro put his hand on Jack's shoulder and squeezed. It would be OK. Sandro's problem now was to find Gunnar. He finned quickly back to the Bell, kicked due north and started counting his kicks. "Steady and strong ... regulation kicks ... I want to be in the middle of his track when he returns." Sandro didn't have to wait long. He stopped, pointed the torch to the seabed, and waited until Gunnar was by his side. He'd written:

FOUND THEM – TRAPPED INSIDE CRANE WRECKAGE

The time was now 5:42 pm. One last push to haul Jack and the diver out of the mangled wreckage of the crane and get them to safety.

Chapter 21

Reluctant hero

Tuesday 4th April 2023, 5:42 pm

Gunnar and Sandro finned back to where Jack and the diver were trapped. They were close to a way out but several sharp metal edges, like claws, were barring the way. It looked like a fish trap – easy for the fish to get in, hard to get out. Sandro wondered how they had managed to get inside without being impaled. Gunnar unclipped a scuba strap from his harness, looped it around his wrist, and pulled with the other hand. He was suggesting they tow Jack and the diver out by wrapping straps around Jack's wrists and pulling. He then mimed him pulling and Sandro guiding them out of the maze. It made sense, and Jack signalled AOK and nodded.

Sandro looped his long scuba strap around Jack's wrist and threaded it through the tangle, while Gunnar did the same on Jack's other wrist. As Gunnar took up the slack and jammed his fins firmly between two struts, Sandro placed a gloved hand on a protruding piece of steel and started to pull. It wasn't pretty, but it worked. Within a couple of minutes, they had Jack and the diver in open water. Between them, they started the tow back to the *Stavanger* Bell, and safety. This time there was no economical finning, no thought of conserving energy. It was a full out drive to get back to the Bell as quickly as possible. Both Gunnar and Sandro were breathing heavily by the time they arrived.

Gunnar rapped on the side of the Bell to alert Karl, and they started the awkward process of getting the diver inside the Wet

Well. He was deathly white, and his ears, lips and nose, fingers and toes were blue. He had stopped shivering; he was hypothermic, but alive. Jack was simply exhausted, glad of help to get into the Wet Well and take off his kit. As Sandro pulled off Jack's dry suit, he asked:

'What happened? How did you get inside the remains of that crane?'

Jack took a couple of deep breaths before he replied, his head bowed in exhaustion.

'He didn't come out like the others ... I went back into the Bell and had to talk him into leaving. I could see he was scared but we had no option as it was getting difficult to breathe inside. As we started to leave the Bell, he grabbed the reserve, stuck it in his mouth and wouldn't let it go. I should have left him, but I couldn't.

'I had to crawl out feet first, with him breathing through the reserve ... it was a nightmare. Once we got into open water, he lunged at me and grabbed me. It was so sudden. We tumbled on the seabed and must have rolled into the remains of the crane. I've no idea how we managed to roll inside without being caught up or impaled. When I think of it, I'm amazed we survived.

'I just couldn't get him to release me and was scared he might grab something else ... like the mouthpiece. I tried to haul us out ... towards the light from the Bell. I was about at the end of my strength when you came along. Thanks for getting us out,' Jack smiled.

'I think I still owe you,' was all Sandro said before they started to crawl into the accommodation area.

Jack was grateful for the warmth inside the Bell, and encouraged by the welcome he and Sandro received. Gunnar was already in the middle of a group of divers who were all slapping his back, shaking his hand, just glad to be alive. They turned their attention to Sandro and Jack, but could see Jack was exhausted. Karl was fussing over the last diver to be rescued, putting warm pads on his chest and stomach to warm him gradually. As a small mountain of blankets were draped over the casualty, Jack noticed the diver was shivering; he'd survive.

Jack looked around for somewhere to sit but realised the Bell was overcrowded; it would be like this for days until they'd been decompressed. He waved and shouted: 'I need a piss,' and disappeared to the heads; it was a ploy to be alone. He sat in the tiny cubical and slowly regained his composure. His mind returned to the rescue and what he could have done differently. "I should have had a back-up torch, a long hose on the reserve." He had fitted a long reserve hose onto his regulator when he was training open water divers at university. He'd cut it back to avoid snags and entanglement when diving commercially. "Should we have waited in open water until all three divers were out? Not really, they would have been submitted to the freezing water for another couple of minutes." He reviewed how he'd prepared and what he'd done. In the end, he accepted that he knew the diver was scared but there was no option, they had to go. He also knew he wouldn't have cut him loose.

*

Hundreds of kilometres away in the OSCT Office, Penny was fielding call after call, email after email, and integrating fresh data into the incident timeline. On a white board was a situation update which included the number of dead and injured. She had just instructed a UK Border Force Cutter to stop and board a boat that was ignoring the fifteen-mile exclusion zone when Tommy stopped by her desk. His expression and body language signalled unwelcome news. She completed the call and turned to him.

'I've just had an update from the MV *Stavanger*. We're told that Jack Collier and Sandro Calovarlo have successfully shut down the Platform. They dived to the base and turned off a series of valves.'

This was great news and for an instant Penny couldn't understand why Tommy was looking so solemn. A tingling, cold wave washed over her as she realised bad news was to follow.

'It seems Jack, Sandro and a guy called Gunnar, volunteered to tow stranded divers from one Bell to another before they suffocated. Jack and one diver are missing.'

Penny was stunned by the announcement. This must be a mistake. Jack and Sandro were just visiting *Monroe Bravo,* they weren't meant to be diving to the seabed below it; they wouldn't even have their diving equipment with them.

'It's a mistake … Jack and Sandro are just visiting … why would they be diving?'

'I don't know … but from what I can gather, breathing gases to the commercial divers were cut off as a result of the fires and explosions, and they couldn't raise the Bell. There were no other divers in the vicinity and so Jack and Sandro volunteered. I've asked for an update as soon as they have any more information. I know this is a shock … what do you want to do?'

Penny stood in silence for a moment before she replied.

'There's nothing I can do, but carry on with my job … but thanks for telling me, I know it couldn't have been easy.'

*

The euphoria of the escape from the doomed Bell to the safety of another Bell, wore off. Messages were sent to family members, the divers organised themselves into bunks and places to rest, eat and sleep as they resigned themselves to several more days before they could exit. Jack, Sandro and Gunnar retreated to the equipment store. It was tiny with about enough room for two people to sit and one to lay down. When all the divers had made phone calls it was Jack's turn. He didn't want to disturb Penny at work and so left a message on her answering machine in her apartment. She knew he was on *Monroe Bravo* and would have heard the news.

The senior bellman worked out a rota for eating, sleeping and resting, with regular updates to the *Stavanger* Dive Centre. The fires of *Monroe Bravo* were out, the Platform was being cooled, and damage assessment was underway. There was nothing they could do now but eat, sleep, relax, and be patient. It was now 6:20 pm on Tuesday 4th April 2023. It would take almost four days to decompress safely. They wouldn't be able to exit the Bell until Saturday afternoon.

Chapter 22

Message to Houston

Tuesday 4th April 2023, 5:42 pm

Less than one hour after climbing onboard a helicopter on the *Stavanger*, Rick was at the TransGlobal helicopter terminal in Aberdeen. One of the doctors checked his injuries during the flight. He'd cracked or broken a couple of ribs, painful but not life threatening. The sight of other injured men and women on stretchers, with medics holding drips as they were transferred to ambulances, was strangely reassuring. TransGlobal Oil were doing everything they could to respond. He would have preferred to be on *Monroe Bravo* but consoled himself by thinking he may be able to help in a different way; he hoped so.

The sense of urgency was reinforced by the short, high-speed drive, and the crowd of people and photographers milling around the entrance to TransGlobal Oil headquarters. The limousine simply cruised past them to a service entrance at the rear.

He'd been to Headquarters numerous times but never had doors opened for him, elevators standing open and Flynn's PA leading him briskly to the VP's office. Even the "clip, clip, clip" of her heels on the floor gave urgency to the meeting with Norton T. Flynn. The PA hardly broke stride as she knocked once on the door, opened it and stood aside; Rick just kept walking. Rick had never been in the Flynn's office. All his meetings had been in the Board Room or seminar rooms. In contrast to the utilitarian décor in the rooms he recognised, Flynn's office looked as though it had been transported from Houston, Texas. It was grand to the point of being opulent.

The knock at the door, and its opening, had prompted Norton to rise from his desk. They met in the middle of the room.

'Glad you could make it here so quickly. I know you'd rather be on the Platform but we need you here. But before we start, I've an apology to make. At the time you tried to phone me about the fire on *Monroe Bravo*, I had my phone switched off. I know I shouldn't have done that, and I'm truly sorry for putting you and others in danger. Whatever sanction I receive, I will accept – no matter what it is. It was a stupid error of judgement and I'm sorry.'

Norton Flynn looked crestfallen for a few moments before recovering.

'However, we've got things to do now. I'll worry about the future later. What I'm about to tell you is strictly confidential; it can go no further. From your account of the explosions and fire, we believe what happened was a terrorist attack on *Monroe Bravo*. So far, no group has admitted responsibility. The FBI and British Government are urgently trying to discover who is responsible. The loss of life and injuries to our people is tragic. We're currently treating those with minor injuries on board the *North Guard*, and evacuating the seriously injured and burnt to Aberdeen. I've got a team contacting the relatives and next of kin of everyone on the Platform. We are keeping them up to date. We'll do the right thing by them. I've also been in touch with the standby ship; they're keeping us up to date.

'There are other potential losses. The shares in TransGlobal Oil are dropping like a stone. Every minute, we're losing millions of dollars. Once we announce the Platform has been saved…'

'What do you mean … the Platform has been saved? When I left, only the gas pipeline had been shut down, the crude oil riser was still aflame. I assumed it hadn't been possible to shut it down.'

'I heard about an hour ago from the *Stavanger*. Both pipelines have been shut down. The two divers who used EPLAST are now trying to rescue nine stranded divers in our Diving Bell … but one of our divers and Jack Collier are missing.'

'What? Jack Collier and Sandro Calovarlo have been trying to rescue our divers and now one of them is missing along with the diver he was trying to save? Do you mean they're dead?'

'We don't know if one or both of them are dead. The message said Jack failed to return with the last of the nine divers to the *Stavanger* Bell. They are searching for them. That's all I know.'

Rick was silent as he pondered the implications and realised there was nothing he could do, but others would be trying their best to find them. He nodded to Norton, inviting him to continue.

'As I was saying, as soon as we announce the gas and oil pipelines have been closed down, and the Platform has been saved, we're confident the share price will bounce back. If it doesn't, the forthcoming weeks and months could see thousands of jobs lost in the industry, and billions of dollars lost in tax revenue. The fire could have had devasting consequences. By shutting down the Platform, you didn't just save an installation, the people still on it, but thousands of jobs and government services here in the UK and in the US.'

'I just encouraged two total strangers to risk their lives to save our company. They not only shut down the gas and oil pipelines, but risked their lives to save our divers trapped on the seabed. If they haven't saved Jack Collier and our diver by now … they're both dead.'

Norton let out a long sigh. The expression on his face turned grim; but he continued.

'The reason Walter wanted you here so quickly is that he's got two things to ask, things he didn't want to discuss over a phone line that could be intercepted. It's all explained in this official email for you from Walter, here in the file.'

Norton tapped the plain manila file on the table in front of them.

'There's a copy to me. Firstly, he's asking you to coordinate the assembly of a recovery plan and lead teams to get *Monroe Bravo* back in production as quickly as possible. We both know that's going to be a challenge, but Walter is promising you'll have anything, and anybody you need, to do it. He hopes you will accept. He also knows you've already initiated action.

'In the email he asks that you tell me what and who you need. The TransGlobal Oil Board have given me unlimited resources. The entire Scotland office is going to be at your disposal as well as anything you need from the States. However, there's something else.

'Over the next seventy two hours, the Board want you to join me as a representative of TransGlobal Oil in reports to the media. The Board would like the first news report to be broadcast on the BBC News, live, as breaking news this evening. However, what we say has be to be carefully choreographed. I've got a crib sheet here that lists what we can say and what we mustn't say at each scheduled interview – we can get to the detail later. Let me give you some background and an overview of what's happening.

'At the request of the US Government, the UK Government have imposed a seventy-two-hour blackout on news coming from inside a fifteen mile exclusion zone around the Platform. The mobile phone companies have imposed a mobile phone blackout, and marine radio traffic has been restricted to emergency only. They want to deprive the terrorists of news that you have shut down the Platform. As I said, US Homeland Security and the FBI are working with the UK Secret Service to find the culprits.

'In the interview, I'll field any questions about the exclusion zone and security.

'At the moment, the belief is that the fire on *Monroe Bravo* is out of control and we are looking at another *Piper Alpha* and *Deepwater Horizon,* total destruction of the Platform, with millions of barrels of crude oil gushing into the North Sea for months. Millions of cubic litres of gas polluting the atmosphere. There's already speculation and debate about everything from gas shortages to rationing fuel, pollution of fish stocks in the North Sea to impact on tax revenues and social services – it's a madhouse out there. You saw the reporters and photographers around reception.

'You will answer the questions about the fire. Do not tell the media that the Platform has been shut down. There are phrases in the crib sheet that avoid a direct answer and suggest we have people working on it.

'The UK Government doubt they can keep the shut-down a secret for long. They reckon seventy two hours is the maximum. It gives the authorities three days to find out who was behind the bombing. There's something else.

'The price of TransGlobal oil shares is in free-fall. They've already lost over one-third of their value, and the graph is going straight down. In seventy two hours, with no good news, the prediction is that it may be as low as twenty percent of the price yesterday. We're talking tens of billions of dollars and thousands of jobs lost … but seventy two hours may give investigators time to find out who bombed the Platform and who was seeking to benefit from it. Again, I'll field questions about the share price, impact on the company and so on.

'In seventy two hours, the UK and US governments want you to announce *Monroe Bravo* has been saved, it's been shut down, and will resume operation in a matter of months. We want you to announce that it was shut down within minutes of the bombing and that pollution has been minimal and is in the process of being cleaned up. We want you to stress the loss of life resulting from the fire act. We want you to the be caring face of TransGlobal Oil; I'll be the money man.

'As soon as you make that announcement, the share price will soar and the terrorists will dive for cover.

'It all starts with us giving a live TV interview in the next thirty minutes. Here's what we've been asked to say … Oh, by the way, the interviewer will be Lucy Rottmuller: *Mad Dog* Rottmuller.'

'Who? I don't recall hearing her name. Why *Mad Dog* Rottmuller?'

'She's an investigative journalist with a mixed reputation. I'm told she can be charming and considerate or obnoxious and aggressive; she's unpredictable. She's often accused of coming to an interview with her own agenda, an agenda that has little to do with its intended focus. I'm told a characteristic of her interviews is latching onto some issue and not letting go – typically forcing the interviewee onto the defensive, ending up saying something they shouldn't. I'm told she's not well liked within the business but the public love her.'

'Great, we're going to be grilled on TV for hours by some obsessive journalist.'

'Not for hours, just minutes. The broadcast interview is scheduled to be three minutes and twenty seconds. Walter insisted on a live, breaking news interview here, in our headquarters, so it couldn't go on for hours, be edited and give a potentially distorted version of what we said transmitted. She has been told that after three minutes twenty, we walk off the set.'

Norton glanced at his wrist watch and announced:

'There's a BBC crew in the Board Room getting set up. I said we'd aim to be there in, er, fifteen minutes.'

Chapter 23

Lucy 'Mad Dog' Rottmuller

Tuesday 4th April 2023, 6:05 pm

Preparation for the interview with Lucy Rottmuller was incredibly short for such an important announcement. However, as Rick and Norton rehearsed their answers to expected questions, they were aware there would be unexpected questions. Rick was preoccupied with the tasks he must get underway whilst the Platform was being cooled and damage assessed.

Norton had recommended the Board Room for the interview. At just past six o'clock, Rick and Norton approached the room and were surprised to see it transformed into a mini studio and how many people were present. A corner had been set up with three chairs. There were spot lights shining onto dull white screens to illuminate the scene, cables draped across the table and around the edges of the room. There was a portable camera on a tripod with two women and two men in a huddle close by. It looked like a briefing of those who would be involved in transmitting the interview.

One of the women, holding a clip board to her chest, broke away and approached them.

'Hi, I'm Lucy's assistant. She'll be here in a minute. While we're waiting, can we make-up dust your face? We can then get you settled in your seats.'

Rick had given interviews before but had never been invited to have make-up applied. The assistant picked up on his reaction immediately.

'The lights tend to reflect off faces. A light dusting with powder will make your face look normal … it'll take seconds. If you take a seat, I'll get it sorted.'

From nowhere a young woman appeared with what looked like a large travel bag. She wrapped a towel around Rick's chest and shoulders but wondered why she bothered. The guy was in a soiled, orange boiler suit and she could smell sweat, smoke, burnt plastic and something else. As she looked more closely, she could see black smudges around his hairline, nostrils, eyes, ears and mouth. "He's just come from the burning oil rig," she said to herself and revised her earlier judgement.

She moistened small pads and quickly wiped away the soot and grime. She didn't carry spare first aid plasters and so the blackened plaster would have to stay. A quick dusting of his face with a soft brush, a comb through his hair, a smile and she pulled the towel free. She was quicker with Norton, and left them sitting in silence; they were not kept waiting long. Lucy simply burst into the Board Room, clip-board in hand, and made a bee-line for Norton and Rick. Big smile, beautiful teeth and flashing eyes was Rick's first impression. Next was the slightly grating tone as she thanked them for giving the interview at such short notice.

'Our slot will be slipped into the news, as breaking news. I'd like to start by asking Dr Johnson to describe what happened on *Monroe Bravo* this afternoon and what you're currently doing. I'm sure you're aware there has been a lot of speculation about the incident and I'm hoping you can give our viewers the facts.'

Lucy turned to Norton, gave him the million dollar smile, and said she would be asking him about what TransGlobal Oil would be doing to support the families of those who had been killed and injured, and about plans to mitigate pollution into the North Sea.

'We've only got three minutes twenty – so I'd be grateful if you could be as succinct as possible.'

She turned to a man standing by the camera operator who gave a three finger gesture, which Rick guessed meant three minutes to the breaking news item. He was looking at a TV monitor on the table when Lucy spoke to them again.

'In a couple of minutes, the presenter will conclude an item, announce breaking news, and hand over to me. I'll make a brief statement and then turn to Rick with my first question. Is that OK?'

Rick returned to gazing at the TV monitor when he noticed a sudden movement off to his left. A massive image of *Monroe Bravo* on fire had been projected onto a screen behind them. He was suddenly taken back to the Platform, the searing heat and choking smoke, the explosions and cries of men. The sound of Lucy's voice broke the spell and focused his attention.

Elsewhere, a background of *Monroe Bravo* ablaze, and a TV presenter looking directly at viewers, had the attention of everyone crowding around the TV monitor in the OSCT, with Penny front centre.

'At three o'clock this afternoon a series of explosions ripped through the *Monroe Bravo* Oil & Gas Platform in the North Sea. It's feared that dozens of men and women working on the Platform have been killed and injured.

'A photograph, taken within minutes of the first explosion from a supply ship, shows the Platform ablaze, with the fire out of control. It is feared that millions of gallons of crude oil are gushing into the North Sea, polluting the waters, oil that will end up on Scottish and Scandinavian beaches.

'I have with me Dr Rick Johnson, Off-Shore Installation Manager of *Monroe Bravo,* and Norton Flynn, TransGlobal Oil Vice President, Scotland.'

It was a dramatic introduction with an equally dramatic backdrop. Lucy turned to Rick to ask her expected question. There was something about her body language and facial expression that suggested it wasn't going to be the benign, opening question she had described.

'Dr Johnson, you are the Off-Shore Installation Manager on *Monroe Bravo,* a similar position to a captain on a ship. Why did you desert your post and abandon the Platform within minutes of the first explosion? Surely your place was *on* the Platform, not off it?'

So, Lucy 'Mad Dog' Rottmuller was going for the sensational, adopting her 'obnoxious and aggressive' stance.

'Ms Rottmuller, I did not desert the Platform, nor did I abandon my post. When the first warning light appeared on my computer screen, I started to go to an installation where I could check on the problem. I was less than thirty metres away when the installation exploded, killing everyone inside, and sending shrapnel in all directions. Had I not been shielded by a building, I would have been killed – along with my friends and colleagues.'

Lucy started to talk across Rick but he raised his hand, indicating that he be allowed to respond.

'Ms Rottmuller, you asked me a question, made a serious allegation, please allow me to reply,' Rick said with a smile that looked almost genuine.

'As Off-Shore Installation Manager, my first responsibility is to the safety of all the crew. I immediately contacted Chief Ridley, our Fire Chief, and checked on his actions. There will be a time log on my phone, and his, to show this was within seconds of the explosion. I also phoned our two other Platform Controllers to check that our emergency procedures were being followed.'

Lucy again started to talk over Rick in an attempt to regain the initiative. Rick again raised his hand and continued. He was aware he was talking over the interviewer but was determined to answer the question.

'Ms Rottmuller, Ms Rottmuller, prior to the interview you asked if I would explain to your viewers what happened on the Platform today and what I was doing about it. I'm trying to explain.

'The closest installation where I could liaise directly with key emergency staff was the Dive Centre. On route to it, there was another explosion that ruptured a gas pipeline, less than one hundred metres away. The temperature around that fuel rupture would rise rapidly to over two thousand degrees centigrade. It would incinerate and melt anything in its vicinity, including part of the accommodation block containing my friends and a crane supporting our Diving Bell. It was also generating massive amounts of choking black smoke. At this time, I phoned Norton Flynn to alert him to the situation, and Walter Brachs in Houston, Texas – the TransGlobal Oil Chairman.'

Rick sensed a stillness in the studio and scanned the faces of the technicians, the Floor Manager and others in the studio. Even Lucy was listening.

'The Dive Centre had lost communication with our Command & Control Centre. Fire and smoke were swirling around the Centre. A dozen klaxons were blaring, the plastic windows facing the inferno were starting to melt, the ceiling panels were melting and dripping onto us, choking smoke was pouring into the Dive Centre. Through the melting plastic windows I could see the pipes supplying the divers below with breathing gases were on fire, and would fail any second.'

Rick paused as he looked at Lucy Rottmuller.

'You asked me what I did? I gave instructions to two visitors to the Platform as to how they could dive to the seabed and try and close valves to shut the Platform down. One of these divers is currently missing. He probably went to his death.'

Penny didn't hear anything else for seconds as the enormity of what the man on the TV had just said. *One of these divers is currently missing ... He probably went to his death.* One of these divers was Jack ... and he hadn't replied to her text. Tommy Steel had been watching Penny and moved to her side, put his arm around her shoulders and gave her a reassuring squeeze.

'Assume the best not the worst ... let's wait until we know,' he said.

Rick was clearly emotional but, maintaining the set expression on his face, he continued.

'The Dive Centre was on fire. Bubbles in the plastic windows were bursting ... smoke and heat was pouring in; we had to leave. I'd checked my plan of the Platform and found a route that would take us to lower levels, away from the heat and smoke. There was another explosion, close by, and hot crude oil was spraying over everything. It was running over tanks and ducting, dripping off rails and onto decks below. We had to leave.'

Rick turned to face Lucy. He was oblivious of anyone else in the makeshift studio.

'Crude oil will ignite at about two hundred and fifty degrees centigrade. The volatile constituents much lower. It was just a matter of time before the gases ignited and the whole surrounding area was ingulfed in flames.

'As we battled through the thick smoke and heat, the soles of the boots my friends were wearing were starting to melt. I could see their footprints smoking, their jackets were starting to smoulder. Crude oil, like heavy rain, was falling all around us and coating every surface, the volatile constituents were bursting into flame. We managed to reach the base of the Platform and were eventually taken to a standby ship.'

Rick turned away from Lucy and towards the camera as he finished his explanation.

'Whilst we waited for rescue, I phoned one of my Platform controllers to tell him I was being forced off the Platform. I was told he and his team had checked the accommodation, recreation and dining areas and were evacuating workers.

'When I was on the ship, I phoned the TransGlobal Oil Chairman, about 3:30 pm, with an update and to say I was returning to the Platform immediately. I was ordered to travel to

Aberdeen to meet with you. I repeat, I did not desert my post, I did not abandon the Platform.'

Lucy and the whole studio team had been captivated by Rick's account. The final remark from Rick broke the spell. Lucy realised she had lost the initiative and was desperate to regain it. She turned to Norton Flynn.

'Vice President Flynn, we understand there is a significant loss of life on *Monroe Bravo*, perhaps exceeding the 167 who died on the *Piper Alpha* disaster in the North Sea several years ago. We understand the fire is out of control, and both gas and oil are gushing from the Platform. It also sounds reminiscent of the *Deepwater Horizon* where oil gushed into the Gulf of Mexico for months.

'At the start of the day, TransGlobal was trading at 107.78. When the London Stock Exchange closed, it was at 56.24; it had lost almost half of its value. We are told the stock market is driven by performance and confidence. I am told that unless good news emerges from *Monroe Bravo,* your share price will continue to fall to a level where it is unrecoverable. You're not giving our viewers any good news. I suspect investors are unimpressed by the performance of TransGlobal Oil and have little or no confidence in it.'

Rick was taken aback by the venom in Lucy Rottmuller's tone but Norton seemed unruffled. He'd noted the time the interview had taken so far and guessed the Floor Manager wouldn't want it to run on. If the breaking news item over-ran, it would have consequences for the rest of the news programme.

'Ms Rottmuller, TransGlobal Oil did not become one of the most successful companies in the world by luck. It's performance has been scrutinised for years and investors have demonstrated their confidence by long term investment.'

Norton could see the manager giving Lucy Rottmuller the hand signal to wind up the item. Norton was happy to continue and run the clock down even further.

'May I suggest that your viewers judge TransGlobal Oil by our actions surrounding *Monroe Bravo* and not from sensationalised statements? Perhaps we could return, in say seventy two hours, and provide a full account of what we know about this incident and our actions?'

Lucy could see the manager giving her exaggerated 'cut-throat' gestures to end the interview. She turned to the camera and ended the item in seconds.

Rick had no wish to talk to Lucy Rottmuller and concentrated on removing his microphone and handing it to the assistant. He noticed Norton had stood up, moved towards Lucy, and the two were talking. He'd no wish to be part of the conversation and stood with the assistant until they'd finished. Rick and Norton walked in silence back to Norton's office. Once they were inside, Norton was animated.

'You were tremendous!' he said as he punched the air with his fist. 'You refused to be cowed by her comments and gave nothing away. Your account was mesmerising and will ensure everyone will be watching in seventy two hours. It's given us breathing space.'

'We've got to go through all this again?'

'Afraid so. The seventy two-hour news blackout will be over, hopefully enough time to assemble the good news the market wants to hear. In three days, 'Mad Dog' Rottmuller will be straining at the leash for news and we'll give it to her.'

Chapter 24

Towards a new life

Tuesday 4th April 2023, 10:15 am

Cal walked confidently from the hotel room, through reception, down an escalator and into the melee of travellers either leaving the airport in Amsterdam or catching a connecting flight. It was odd. Wearing his own suit, his own clothes and his Omega watch gave him a confidence he didn't have before. He looked up at the electronic board listing all the flight transfers and noted the gate for the flight to Tehran; thirty minutes to boarding. As he approached the gate, he recognised Nazarene and his daughter. His daughter was sitting astride a small pull-along bag that looked like a turtle; it must be new because he'd never seen it before. Neither Nazarene nor his daughter recognised him at first. Dressed in a suit, with designer stubble and slicked back hair and glasses, he looked different. Nazarene would never expect a kiss in public; she was a devoted Muslim and such a public display of affection would never happen. However, his daughter jumped off the turtle, ran to him and then stopped. She realised something had changed. She stroked his face and said, 'No hair.'

    Callum tried to concentrate on what Nazarene was saying as she updated him on what had been happening. However, he was tense and feared the authorities were waiting to stop him as he tried to board the plane. No one did and as he stretched out on the business class seat, he started to relax. All that he had strived for over the years was coming to fruition and a new life awaited.

The MI6 agent glanced up at the monitor displaying the list of carousels to which baggage would be directed from incoming flights. Bags from the Amsterdam flight would be arriving on carousel number two. He casually walked away from it and mingled with other travellers waiting for their bags; there was no rush. As travellers started to congregate around carousel number two, he turned to face the approaching travellers. He spotted Nazarene Jeffrey and her daughter almost immediately. She was dragging a pull-along with one hand and struggling with two large bags in the other. Her daughter was sitting on a mini suitcase, which looked like a cartoon turtle, and was being pulled being pulled by the target, Callum Jeffrey. The asset didn't recognise him at first. In the photograph he'd received Callum Jeffrey had a short beard, medium length hair with a side parting. The Callum Jeffrey walking towards him had designer stubble, slicked back hair, glasses and was wearing a suit. He looked like a businessman not an oil rig worker.

The agent waited until Nazarene and her daughter had found a place to sit and Callum moved towards the carousel. "Change of plan," the agent said to himself. The target was going to retrieve the baggage; he'd just make sure the tracker was stuck in place. The agent merely shadowed the target, making sure two or three people were between them. "Left-handed or right-handed?" the agent asked himself, and then knew. Callum Jeffrey was adjusting the time on his expensive looking wrist watch. It was on his left wrist, so he was probably right-handed. It was an important detail. As soon as the target moved to collect his suitcase, he would make sure he was on his shoulder. Whilst the agent had been waiting, he'd unpeeled the backing from the tracker and stuck the two ends onto his palm, with the sticky band facing outwards. He'd practised the move several times before today. He let Callum Jeffrey grab his suitcase, pivot, and drag the bag off the carousel. The asset smiled broadly as he steadied the bag with one hand and stuck the tracker in place with the other. It took a split second to place his palm on the end of the suitcase and smooth it in place; job done. The agent remained in the same place for one or two minutes as though waiting for his bag before drifting away. It was unlikely that anyone would recognise or even remember him.

Colonel Hussein Zand and an armed soldier were waiting for Khalid in the arrival hall. As soon as Zand recognised Khalid, he stepped forward and embraced him, kissing him on both cheeks.

'Welcome home, brother, the hero returns,' he announced with a broad smile on his face whilst merely acknowledging Nazarene. 'You must be tired after the long flight and after such a momentous day. You also have a busy day tomorrow, but there has been a slight change to the arrangements for you. Your new home in the Elahi Jeh district is ready for you, but there have been three cases of diphtheria nearby. As a result, you will be staying in a city hotel for a few days until we are certain your home is safe.'

Little had been said about where Khalid and his family would be living on their return to Tehran. However, Khalid knew that the Elahi Jeh district was the most affluent and prestigious part of the city in which to live. Until now, he hadn't really thought a great deal about his new home but was now eager to see it.

'We've also arranged for you to have a vaccination against diphtheria tonight at a private clinic. It will takes moments and ensure you are safe. This soldier will take your luggage to the hotel; it will be in your room and waiting for you. I'll drive you to the clinic now, and then back to the hotel. Please, let's go.'

Hussein and Khalid led the way, Nazarene and their daughter walking behind. The soldier disappeared with the luggage, including the turtle case. A large black Mercedes, guarded by another armed soldier, was parked directly outside the arrivals area. Callum was certain that cars were not allowed to park so close, but guessed Colonel Zand could arrange it. The soldier saluted and opened the passenger door as Hussein approached.

'Sit with me in the front,' said Hussein as he took Khalid's arm and directed him around the front of the car.

He left Nazarene and their daughter to climb into the rear seats. Hussein was obviously in no rush to move the car from such a busy part of the airport. He took a mobile phone from his pocket, tapped the screen, gave the phone the Khalid, and announced:

'This photograph of *Monroe Bravo* on fire is circulating around the world. It will no doubt be replaced by just a burning pool of oil on the surface of the sea,' he added.

Khalid didn't know what to say. He'd lived and worked on the Platform for a long time. He knew most of the people who worked on it. Many of them would be dead or severely burnt, but it would be a decisive blow against the West. Today, he had avenged the murder of his family. He gave the mobile phone back to Colonel Zand, said nothing, and gazed at the busy traffic around the airport.

'The clinic isn't very far,' explained Zand. 'It's on the western outskirts of the city, about thirty minutes' drive. Another twenty minutes and we will have you at the hotel.'

They drove in silence for a few minutes before Colonel Zand began to explain the arrangements for tomorrow.

'There are a lot of people who want to speak to you tomorrow. I'm afraid it will be a busy day. However, I'll make sure you are back to the hotel to have supper with your wife and child.'

The car slowed and turned off the main road into a short drive. It curved through lawns and trees and stopped in front of a single storey building.

'We're here, and they're expecting us,' announced Zand as he opened the car door, walking around the front to wait for Khalid and his family to join him.

The spacious, portico style entrance was well lit and Khalid could see through large double glass doors into a modern reception area. Two people dressed in pale green jackets and trousers were waiting for them. It wasn't until Khalid got close that he realised one person was a man and the other was a woman.

'Mrs Jaffra,' said Colonel Zand. 'Would you and your daughter go with this nurse? Khalid, this attendant will take you to the doctor. I will wait for you here.'

Khalid followed the attendant from reception, along a corridor and around a corner to a small waiting area with chairs. The attendant opened a door and invited Khalid inside; a doctor in a long white coat was waiting for him. Khalid began to take off his jacket but was stopped. 'No need to take off your jacket. Just pull back your jacket sleeve,' said the doctor as he prepared the syringe.

Khalid was confused. He'd worked in countries as diverse as Mexico and Nigeria, Kuwait and Norway, and received dozens of vaccinations before and whilst working there. They had always been intra-muscular and never intravenous.

'What sort of injection is this?'

The doctor was taken aback, surprised that his action was being questioned.

'Er, it's just the routine vaccination.'

'Why is it intravenous rather than intra-muscular? I've had dozens of vaccinations and never intravenous.'

The doctor returned the syringe to the stainless steel tray and announced.

'I'll fetch my friend, he's an expert. He will explain.'

Khalid had a dull headache, he was tired, irritable, and just wanted to get to bed and sleep. He'd been tense for the last couple of days and didn't need this hassle. He decided he wasn't going to have the vaccination. He'd argue the implication with Colonel Zand tomorrow rather than tonight. He was about to leave when the doctor returned with two orderlies, the one that had brought him to the room and another one.

'I've spoken to my friend and we've decided …'

The two orderlies had moved past the doctor to stand either

side of Khalid. Before the doctor could finish what he was saying, one of the orderlies grabbed Khalid, pulled him off balance, and kicked away his legs. As he fell to the ground, the orderly pinned one of his arms to his chest and cupped his hand over Khalid's mouth. The other orderly fell on top of Khalid, wrapped his arms around his legs, and used his weight to stop him moving. The doctor calmly turned away and retrieved the syringe, held it up to the light, and made sure it was primed. Strangely, he then held the syringe between his lips, kneeled on Khalid's stomach and yanked the suit sleeve and shirt back to expose Khalid's forearm. A few moments of wrestling on the ground had Khalid's forearm exposed and the doctor stroking it for a vein. A controlled incision into the vein, a slow press of the plunger and the 'vaccination' was administered. But it wasn't a vaccine for diphtheria: it was a powerful sedative that was already starting to work. The men holding Khalid could feel him start to relax; he stopped struggling and his breathing slowed. He would be dead in twenty seconds.

One of the orderlies left the room and returned moments later with a trolley. Together they lifted Khalid onto it, draped a white sheet over him and wheeled him away. He was joined by his wife and daughter, also on trolleys and under white sheets. They were wheeled down deserted corridors, through doors, until they reached an almost bare room with an open metal shutter and a waiting white panelled van. It had taken less than five minutes for Khalid and his family to be transferred from the black Mercedes to the white hearse; their next destination was the crematorium.

The white panelled van drove slowly through the deserted suburbs. No rapid acceleration, no heavy braking, just a sedate journey to a final destination. The van negotiated the cremation site, arrived at a discrete bay, and backed into the secluded place where loved ones were received. Two men and a soldier were waiting for the delivery. The men certainly didn't look like medical professionals. Lined and craggy unshaven faces, grey boiler suits and heavy boots. They'd brought their own trolleys and simply waited while the orderlies transferred the bodies onto them. Not a word was spoken. The van disappeared into the night, and the three loaded trolleys were taken inside the deserted building.

It was a short distance to the actual incinerators; modern, efficient, German built. As one of the attendants, Yaser, manoeuvred the trolley to an incinerator door, the other, Asad, pulled out a packet of American cigarettes and offered one to the soldier. It was a practised move. Despite a national obsession against everything American, their cigarettes were valued. It took only moments to distract the soldier's attention, for him to select a cigarette, have it lit and take the first puff. In those moments, the shroud had been removed and the arms of the corpse crossed across his chest. Deft movements had revealed the expensive looking watch and removed it. It was a bonus that they looked for on these "special" jobs.

They had two twin incinerators at the facility. Khalid and Nazarene were cremated side by side, their daughter and all their luggage a few metres away.

'How long?' asked the soldier as the attendants pressed the buttons to start the cremation process.

'About one and a half hours to incinerate the bodies, another two hours to cool down, and a few minutes to collect the ashes and anything that may be left.'

'I've been ordered to wait,' explained the soldier.

They waited into the small hours of the morning until the incinerators were cool enough to open. When he looked inside, the soldier was surprised that nothing was left.

'At the end, the bars are vibrated to release the last of the ash … want to check it?'

The soldier didn't answer and simply walked away. He could report that he had done his duty. Yaser and Asad then began to sieve the ashes, another perk of the job. There would be dull 'droplets' of gold and silver in the ashes – especially from this 'special' job. Asad had seen the gold rings on the woman's fingers.

Gold chains around her neck and bangles or her wrist. He wasn't to know that most of her gold jewellery had been inside one of the bags she had clutched to her chest throughout the flight. The man had a gold wedding ring, he may have gold teeth. Even the girl had gold studs in her ears. They weren't disappointed. As the fine ash flowed through the sieve, the beads of precious metal remained behind. Yaser rubbed the droplets between grubby palms before revealing the shiny metal. It would be added to the growing pile of precious metal and eventually sold to their friendly jeweller.

'Good night tonight,' said Yaser as he removed the Omega Seamaster from his pocket. 'What do you think it's worth?'

'Don't know, but easy to find out. Do you think the jeweller would be interested?'

'We can soon find out. We've got enough silver and gold to make a visit worthwhile.'

Chapter 25

Lost contact

Wednesday 5th April 2023, 10:12 pm

Harry Preece and Tommy Steel were alone in the Office for Security and Counter Terrorism, London. Penny had left a few minutes ago, but Harry and Tommy were waiting for news about the tracker. Earlier, the agent in Tehran had sent a brief, innocuous text message which indicated the tracker had been attached. His job was done and he had disappeared into the crowd and into the night. For the team following the tracker, their job was just starting. They had eased away from the parking area and made their way to the airport exit. On a mobile phone, a red, flashing dot had crawled slowly across a map of Tehran as the baggage was driven from the airport. On a second phone, the technician had announced:

'They're away from the airport but not heading for the city centre hotels or the Army barracks. Looks as though they are skirting the suburbs.'

They had stayed more than eight hundred metres behind the target vehicle as they monitored its journey. As the technician changed the scale on the map, he could see the individual roads that the car was travelling upon. As the target vehicle slowed, the technician had given an update:

'The car is turning into … Gulistan Crematorium in the west of the city – odd place to visit at this time of night.'

Moments later, he confirmed:

'Signal stationary … can't see them staying at the crematorium.'

Fifteen minutes later, the signal from the tracker was lost and London was informed.

When the message was relayed from the embassy in Tehran, the reaction was predictable.

'How can they lose the signal?' asked Superintendent Steel. 'I thought you said it was state of the art, and would stick like glue to the suitcase!'

'It *is* state of the art, the tracker *does* stick like glue, and I don't know why the signal was lost,' Harry said with annoyance.

It was clear that Harry was not a happy person. He'd persuaded Tommy and Penny to accept his plan, and it had now gone belly up. They now had no idea where Callum Jeffrey was and whom he was meeting. The chance of linking individuals to the bombing of *Monroe Bravo* was getting less likely by the minute. The only option now was old-fashioned, passive surveillance, waiting for Callum Jeffrey to cross the path of an observer. They'd stake out his relatives and Nazarene's family, the mosque and military offices. With about nine million people in Tehran, and another sixteen million in the greater metropolitan area, it was a daunting task.

To make matters worse, the US Homeland Security team would be landing in a few hours. Tomorrow morning they'd be setting up and expect a briefing. He'd have to tell them that the tracking of their main lead had disappeared. He could visualise the expression and body language that would greet him.

Harry's expectations were partially confirmed when he strolled into the Coordination Office next morning. As he opened the office door, the smell of freshly brewed coffee and American accents wafted over him. He walked towards the noise, and could see Penny and Tommy were already chatting to the arrivals. He raised his hand, waved at the group and said 'Hi.' A look-a-like Robert

Redford had been sitting on the corner of a desk and stood up as Harry walked in. Deliberately, he placed his mug of coffee on the desk and walked towards Harry, hands outstretched, and a big smile on his face.

'The famous Harry Preece ... good to meet you ...' smiled Special Agent Gene Dilks as he grabbed Harry's hand in both of his and began to pump it up and down. 'My boss sends his regards and said I had to buy you a drink ... wanna start with a mug of coffee?'

Harry returned the smile and asked, 'Is the old sod as paranoid as ever?'

'You bet ... wait till you see the pile of kit he insisted we bring ... half of it is still in the basement. Let me introduce you to Pamela Edwards, she's Penny's equivalent in Washington.'

Pamela was short, slim, with cropped black hair. The pale green military style trouser suit made it look as though she had just got off the plane from the Middle East. Her tanned face reinforced the impression, but wasn't accompanied by a warm smile. Indeed, Pamela Edwards had a permanent scowl which changed little when introduced to Harry.

Gene called out to the third member of the team, Davie Perry. He looked like a caricature of an IT geek in jeans and trainers, T-shirt and back-to-front baseball cap. Davie squinted through large round glasses as though inspecting who or what was before him before he offered a handshake.

'Davie will be spending most of his time sitting in front of the hardware. Reckon he'd prefer to sleep next to it if we let him. Our two other team members are in the basement unpacking the rest of the kit; it'll take them all day.'

Davie Perry smiled weakly and returned to his keyboard and screens. The banter continued for a few moments until Chief Superintendent Steel brought them back to the present.

As they sat round the table, Steel led the briefing and summarised the mass of information pouring into the Office for

Security and Counter Terrorism. Tommy called up CCTV footage of Callum Jeffreys passing through Aberdeen Airport and Schiphol. Careful examination of the footage had spotted a possible male accomplice, and Dutch police were urgently trying to find him. One of CS Steel's team had conducted further investigations into Callum's visits to the local mosque while he was a student at Loughborough University. His analysis of discussions in and around the mosque suggested the Iman may have been his contact. The idea, which had earlier been dismissed, was suddenly a possibility when Tommy disclosed that the Iman had flown from East Midlands Airport to London, transferred to Heathrow and on to Tehran.

Gene commented at the end of the briefing.

'Thanks for the update and copy of your latest report to Commander Short. At the moment, I can't see what else you could have done. It was certainly worth pursuing the possible suspect you'd identified, and it's a shame about the tracker, but I'd have made the same call. Those trackers are virtually bomb proof, but shit happens. You didn't want to spook him with close surveillance, and the chance to identify and roll up a network was too good to miss.

'Agent Davies will be consulting with our HQ and collecting the latest intel they have. As soon as we have anything, we'll let you know.'

The briefing meeting broke up. The US Homeland Security Team continued to fill desks with equipment. Tommy, Harry and Penny waded through email after email, and responded to one phone call after another. The team continued to assemble an impressive array of supportive evidence around the bombing, but they were no closer to apprehending a culprit. Tommy Steel's comment about the investigation becoming a grind was turning out to be true. They were all slowing down – especially the US Homeland Security Team. At six o'clock, Pamela announced she was heading for the hotel. She'd already been on the go for over twenty four hours; Tommy and Harry left an hour or so later, and Penny wasn't far behind. She'd wait until she was back in the apartment before she phoned Jack. She also dreaded the thought of seeing a message light blinking on the answer phone.

Chapter 26

Stavanger … we've got a problem

Wednesday 5th April 2023, 8:45 pm

Life inside the *Stavanger* Diving Bell soon fell into a pattern. The divers were all professionals, resilient, and grateful to be alive. The eight-hour shift system continued and whilst a third of the men slept, the others ate, chatted, rested, and ticked off the days until they could exit the Bell. The busiest person was Karl who was constantly checking gas concentrations and pressures. Accommodating additional people inside the Bell had a major effect on the gas supplies needed, and the internal temperature: more gas needed to breathe, more warm bodies.

Most of the men simply slipped their minds into neutral and relaxed. They read, played video games, watched films, listened to music, thought about the next three weeks on shore, and assumed there would be a job waiting for them on *Monroe Bravo*. One person was thinking and acting very differently: Alex, the diver who believed he had been abandoned by the other divers, stranded on the stricken *Monroe Bravo* Bell, and left to die. He was simmering with anger at what he saw as an attempt to drown him or kill him by hypothermia. However, he prided himself on his toughness. He was a survivor, getting stronger every day, and planning his revenge. Until then, he simply lay still, closed his eyes, and tried not to attract any attention. He'd wake when it was food time, and exaggerate his stumbling journey to the heads, but otherwise kept to himself. He either ignored comments directed to him or gave one word replies. He knew they'd all tried to kill him even though they pretended to be concerned about him. He would show them.

Alex had palmed a serrated steak knife from the discarded plate on the diver's bunk next to him and hidden it under his pillow. No one had noticed, so no one was looking for the missing knife. It was now a case of planning his move and deciding how to strike. Mentally, he rehearsed what he needed to do. He could ease the blanket over him so that in one movement he could throw back the covers. It would then be a case of simply swinging his arms and legs off the mattress, dropping into a crouch and springing into action. It would be all over before Collier knew what had happened. He'd watched Collier twice as he spoke to someone on board the stand-by ship on the surface. He'd strolled into the accommodation section as though he owned it – arrogant bastard. He always turned his back on the others as he chatted, as though what he was saying was confidential. That would be the moment to strike. He knew one of the main arteries, the carotid artery, ran from just below the ear and into the chest. The serrated steak knife was sharp and strong. Mentally he'd practised the sequence again and again. Spring to his feet, move behind Collier, and stab him in the middle of his neck. He'd aim just beyond his ear and drag the knife back with all his force. One blow, just one blow would do it; revenge would be sweet. He just had to be patient, he just had to wait for the right moment, but it would be soon.

'This time tomorrow we'll be getting ready to exit the Bell,' said Jack.

'Not a moment too soon,' replied Sandro. 'I don't know how these guys do it time after time, month after month. I get bored and struggle to maintain concentration when hanging onto a line for a few hours. Waiting around for days is difficult. It'll be interesting to see what the Platform looks like after the fire. Bet it's a mess.'

'There'll be people swarming all over it, trying to get it back into production as soon as possible. We need to get back into production as soon as possible. In fact, I'll check with Lukas on the arrangements to get us back to Aberdeen and on to Manchester. I'll also check with Lesley about any messages on tenders. I'll be back in a moment.'

Jack ducked through the water-tight hatch, into the main accommodation module and towards the communication console. It seemed most of the men were awake. Some were still lying on their bunks but others were sitting around chatting or reading. He gave them a smile and a wave before turning away to pick up the telephone and press the 'connect' switch. A moment later, it was answered by Lukas.

'Hi, Jack here ...'

Jack never saw or heard the movement behind him. One moment, Alex was motionless on his bunk, the next he'd thrown off his cover and was swinging his legs to the floor. He had to duck because the underside of the bunk above was low. As he tried to spring to his feet and lunge at Jack, he slipped and fell to the deck. He hadn't fully recovered from the hypothermia and had lost some coordination. The sound of metal falling onto the deck suddenly had everyone's attention, except Jack's.

Alex scrambled for the knife and regained his balance. With eyes focused on Jack's exposed neck, he launched himself from the deck. He flung his arm back, twisted his shoulder as he prepared to deliver the fatal blow. With the knife arched towards its target, he uttered a guttural scream that seemed to start in his stomach and rise like lava in an exploding volcano.

From nowhere, Sandro appeared. Simultaneously, he grabbed the wrist holding the knife with both hands and shoulder charged Alex. The two of them barged into Jack and all three tumbled to the deck. The tranquil scene inside the Bell was instantly transformed into pandemonium. Alex was fighting to free his hand and screaming incoherently. Sandro was shouting, 'Drop the knife, drop the knife!' as he tried to shield himself from the blows raining down on him. Jack had been knocked against the bulkhead, banging his head and dropping the phone. When he realised what was happening, he grabbed the diver's flailing arm and dropped to the deck to help Sandro subdue him, shouting for help at the same time.

Two nearby divers grabbed the thrashing legs and a third twisted the knife from Alex's hand. It took all of them to subdue him. As Jack glanced at the knife, he could see that the blade had snapped off close to the hilt but there was a short, stubby part of the blade remaining. It could still cause severe damage and he was glad it had been twisted from the attacker's grasp. The men were managing to control Alex's kicking and writhing, but he was now trying to bite Jack.

'Sandro, hold his head … try to stop him biting! Where's the medic? Do you have anything to calm him down?'

It took five men to get Alex under control. They were lying across his legs, kneeling on his arms and holding his head. He was still bucking and writhing, screaming and trying to bite anything close. One of the divers, a medic, returned with a medical bag. As he unpacked items from the bag onto the deck, he unfolded a sheaf of papers and checked the entries.

'He's listed as weighing sixty eight kilos … that will tell me how many millilitres of the sedative to inject to calm him down.'

The medic seemed remarkably calm as he pushed the hypodermic syringe through the plastic membrane on the cap of the phial and drew fluid into it. He was concentrating hard as he held the syringe up to the light, flicked to dispel any bubbles, and pressed the plunger to register the dose he was about to inject.

'I've only done this a couple of times, and practised on a manikin, but I know what to do. Jack, you've got to hold his arm as still as you can so I can inject into a vein.'

Jack moved his weight slightly so that one knee was on Alex's shoulder, the other on his upper arm, and the rest of his weight on the bare forearm. The medic moistened a piece of gauze with antiseptic and, transferring his weight on the diver's arm, slid the needle into and along the bulging vein. He pressed the plunger, and the sedative slowly entered Alex's bloodstream.

'Hang onto him. It'll only take a few seconds, and we can all relax.'

The effect on Alex was as expected. One moment he was cursing, shouting and trying to break free, the next he visibly relaxed, the tension disappeared, and he became quiet and compliant.

'OK, let's get him back into his bunk. He's going to be under sedation for a couple of hours. After that we'll have to wait and see.'

In the confines of the Bell, it was awkward but they lifted Alex from the deck and onto his bunk. The medic called to one of the other divers.

'Can you get me four of the heavy cable ties from the store? I'm going to put bandages around his wrists and ankles and then cable tie him to the bunk. We can't afford a repeat of that performance when the sedative wears off.'

Jack picked up the handle of the steak knife and the blade. He was looking at them and the deep scratch on the bulkhead wall when Sandro approached.

'Thanks for saving my life, or at least serious injury,' said Jack. 'Have a look at what the knife did to the paint work. It would have made a bigger mess of my back.'

'I don't think he was aiming for your back. I'd say he was aiming for your neck.'

The medic finished wrapping bandages around Alex's ankles and wrists before cable tying him to the bunk. He then walked through to the equipment store where Jack and Sandro were sitting.

'I've been watching Alex ever since he was brought into the Bell. At first I was worried about hypothermia, but he recovered well. His temperature, breathing and pulse rate returned to normal well within twelve hours. But he behaved strangely. I began to notice that he acted as though he was asleep or resting. When anyone spoke to him, he either ignored them or gave one-word answers. At meal times he was suddenly awake, ate the food, and seemed to go to sleep straight away. A few times I saw him staring vacantly at the underside of the bunk. Once I saw him looking at you when you were making a phone call. If looks could kill, you'd be dead.

'I knew I couldn't watch him all the time and so the Bellmen and me took it in turns. It happened to be my turn on this shift. Just as well your mate Sandro was close 'cos it all happened so fast.

I'm not a doctor but I don't think the effects of hypothermia would result in this sort of outburst. I'd say it's something psychological, maybe linked to having to abandon the *Monroe Bravo* Bell, but I don't know. I'm going to contact the doctor on *North Guard* and ask for advice. The problem is we've got hours of decompression before we can exit the Bell. We really don't want to rush the decompression and endanger all of us. Equally, if there's something I can do for Alex, I need to do it. We also need to report this to the authorities. If Alex has had some sort of breakdown, he needs treatment before he can return to diving … *if* he ever returns.'

Chapter 27

Breakthrough

Wednesday 5th April 2023, 9:55 pm

Penny was weary and anxious. It had been another long, tiring thirteen-hour day, and the lack of news about Jack sapped her resolve. All she wanted to do was get back to the apartment, hear from Jack, get something to eat, have a shower, and get to bed. Rush-hour had been over hours ago and so it was a simple walk to the tube station, a short ride to her stop and a short walk to the apartment.

    As she approached the front door of her apartment, her anxiety became trepidation. She punched in the security code, opened the door, and sleep-walked towards the answer phone. She saw it blinking; the small blue light was like a homing beacon. Was this good news or confirmation of the fears she'd pushed to the back of her mind for the last few hours? It was as though someone else was reaching out towards the phone and pressing the 'play' button.

    It was Jack; she recognised him immediately despite the helium induced, comical voice, and was overwhelmed. Her throat squeezed tight and tears ran down her cheeks as she listened.

    'Hi, Jack here … wanted to let you know Sandro and I are OK. There have been explosions and fires on *Monroe Bravo* … but I suppose you've heard. We managed to close a couple of valves to shut the Platform down, and have been towing divers from their Diving Bell to ours … job done. Afraid we are now stuck in this Bell until everyone decompresses … see you as soon as we get out and back to Manchester. Oh, you can phone the *Stavanger* and they will transfer the call to me. Bye.'

There was no hesitation. Penny phoned the *Stavanger* straight away and after a short delay was connected.

'Jack Collier here ...'

Penny didn't let him say anymore before she interrupted. The words gusted out.

'You're safe, you're alive ... I had a message to say you and a diver were missing ... I've been so worried. I thought you were dead. Why didn't you phone me to say you were OK?'

Jack could hear the emotion, the challenge in Penny's voice, and realised how upset she was. He tried to explain.

'Visitors aren't allowed to take mobile phones onto the Platform ... I had to leave my phone behind. I thought I'd only be gone for an hour or so. The first opportunity I had to leave a message was when I'd towed the last diver to the Bell.'

Jack could hear Penny sobbing and realised he should have left a message when he first entered the Bell, not after his return.

'I'm really sorry ...and I'm stuck in this Bell for the next three to four days, decompressing. I'll be back in Salford by the weekend ... can we meet up then?'

Penny should have felt happy; no, more than happy. She should have felt wonderful, ecstatic, bouncing for joy. She wasn't and she couldn't explain why. What she did know was that it had been an extraordinary day. The pressure of coping with the terrorist incident, plus the anguish of thinking Jack was lost and alone in the depths of the North Sea, had been all consuming. It was as though an emotional switch had been thrown. From being anxious and worried Penny was now angry and resentful. "He could have made more of an effort," Penny said to herself. He knew she would be worried and now she was hurt. The hurt expressed itself in a brusque tone when she replied and cut the conversation short.

'I'll be working over the weekend … bye'.

Penny didn't remember putting the phone down or slumping into a chair. As she sat there, she felt emotionally and physical drained; her thoughts were in turmoil. She was relieved that Jack was safe, but couldn't help thinking of him lost and alone in the depths of the North Sea. She felt as though she had been punished and she was now punishing Jack. As the minutes passed, she realised she had been unreasonable. She shouldn't have reacted in the way she did, but the twinge of resentment persisted. She would sleep on it and phone him tomorrow. Decision made, she suddenly felt ravenous. A quick check of the freezer revealed it would be lasagne tonight. There was still some green salad left but she'd have to wash it and pick out the bits that were edible. The remains of a bottle of white wine were enough for a small glass.

As she waited for the microwave to ping, she flopped onto the sofa, sipped the wine, started to relax, and switched on the TV. There was a discussion about the impact of the *Monroe Bravo* fire on the environment. Penny wasn't really listening to the interview but suddenly an idea crashed into her consciousness as she ate. Ships were delivering food and drink, spares and supplies all the time to *Monroe Bravo*. If Callum Jeffrey was indeed the bomber, could the devices have been sent to him directly on the Platform? They had previously assumed the bomber took the devices on board, but so far found no evidence. All they'd discovered so far suggested Callum wasn't particularly successful at concealing his movements … checking anything sent to him was worth a try.

The ping of the microwave, her weariness and resentment were forgotten as she speed-dialled the lead Inspector in her team.

'Senior Inspector Watkins, how can I help you?'

'Douglas, it's Penny here. Can you get colleagues to check if any parcels or packages, anything at all, were delivered to Callum

Jeffrey on board *Monroe Bravo*? Start with the last month and go back, say, three months. There should be a record of any deliveries in TransGlobal Oil offices.

'Will do, ma'am, but the offices are closed. I'll instigate this first thing ...'

'No, you'll do it tonight. I'm going to contact Norton Flynn, TransGlobal Oil Vice President, now. He will get back to you with contact names of people and places. I want to start the check tonight ... I'm going to get TransGlobal staff back to their offices in the next hour. Is that understood?'

'Yes, ma'am, I'm on to it.'

It took a few minutes for Norton to come to the phone – and he wasn't very pleased at being interrupted. However, when Penny reminded him this was not only a murder enquiry but a terrorist attack on an TransGlobal Oil installation, he was more cooperative. Offices would be opened, staff would be brought in, and the checks would start straight away.

Penny devoured the piping hot lasagne but decided against the sorry looking salad. She'd sat down with her glass of wine and started to watch a TV programme but couldn't remember falling asleep. She was woken by the sound of her phone.

'Pendleton Price ...' Penny announced, half asleep.

'You were right,' Senior Inspector Watkins blurted out enthusiastically. 'Once we started, it took only minutes to discover a crate weighing 34 kilograms containing remote sensing devices was delivered to Callum Jeffrey on *Monroe Bravo* three weeks ago. It was just after he arrived at the start of his three week hitch. The crate was allegedly sent by CamSensors Limited. It's a Cambridge based, high-tech company which specialises in such equipment.

'But here's the thing. We got the owners of CamSensors out of bed. They got staff to check and they say they have no knowledge of any such order. No remote sensing equipment was ordered by TransGlobal Oil for *Monroe Bravo*; nothing has been delivered.

We are currently checking courier services and TransGlobal records – but nothing so far.'

Penny was now wide awake and energised.

'Great work ... well done, Doug. This could be a breakthrough. Could you continue checking TransGlobal Oil records and try to trace who delivered the crate and where it came from?'

Penny looked at her watch and realised it was almost six o'clock in the morning. She needed to get back to the office.

'Could you give me an update in, say, ninety minutes, at 7:30 am? I'll be back in the office then. Thanks, Doug, splendid work.'

Penny seemed remarkably refreshed – even though she'd spent the night on the sofa. She was in the office well before 7:30 am and going through the messages waiting for her; nothing was of significance. At precisely 7:30 am her phone rang; it was Senior Inspector Watkins with an update.

'We've double checked with CamSensors and can confirm they never received an order, never sent anything to *Monroe Bravo*. The delivery company tell us that the crate was dropped off at their collection point in Cambridge. The crate was correctly addressed and the customer paid cash for delivery to Aberdeen. This is unusual but they accept cash transactions. There's no CCTV but we'll continue checking with the rest of the staff when they come in to work this morning.

'We've also checked at the TransGlobal dispatch centre in Aberdeen, the centre through which all goods destined for *Monroe Bravo* are processed. Here's the thing: they have an order, and paper work, for remote sensing equipment from CamSensor in Cambridge. The order is approved and signed by Norton T. Flynn. I'm sending you a copy of the order but I have not spoken to Flynn about it. What do you want me to do?'

'What you've done has been excellent – thank you. Can you send your report asap, but do not contact Norton Flynn; I'll do that. Can you try to identify the person or persons who dropped off the crate? They would be in a car or van, they wouldn't be carrying a crate weighing 34 kilograms from a bus stop. There may be CCTV in the area. If we have an ID, we may be able to link the person to a car. See what you can do – and thanks again.'

Penny had just ended the call when Tommy Steel walked in. If he was surprised to see Penny, it didn't show.

'Just had a phone call from one of my teams. A crate weighing 34 kilograms was delivered to Callum Jeffrey on *Monroe Bravo* three weeks ago. The consignment was from a high-tech company in Cambridge called CamSensors. It was supposed to contain remote sensing equipment, but CamSensors deny any knowledge of it. The crate was delivered to a courier collection centre, all in order, paid in cash. We're trying to trace the person or persons who delivered it.'

Tommy sat back in his chair, aware that this information must have been collected overnight.

'The TransGlobal dispatch centre in Aberdeen received the parcel and checked the paperwork ... the order was placed and approved by Norton T. Flynn. I'm printing it out now.'

'Who initiated this line of enquiry?'

'I did ... last night,' replied Penny, self-consciously.

'This doesn't necessarily mean Norton is part of the plot to bomb *Monroe Bravo* – but we need to chase it up straight away. I suggest we contact Flynn and arrange a meeting today. I don't want to do it by phone, better in person. Can you fix two seats on the first possible flight to Aberdeen? I'll organise a car to take us to Heathrow, blue lights flashing, and set up a meeting with Flynn.'

'Sure, I can do that ... but there's something else. If you were a bomber's accomplice, would you sign the order for a crate of bombs to be delivered to the Platform? The guy is not stupid. He's a career executive, near the top of the tree, well paid. It's my guess that when we check him out, we'll find someone used his name.'

'It wouldn't be the first time criminals, terrorists, have used influential people as a front to cover their activities.'

'Someone close to him ... like his girlfriend. He had his phone switched off when the bombs went off,' Penny reminded him. 'That's a major breach of TransGlobal rules. I'll get my team to check out CCTV at the hotel. We may be able to get facial recognition and link her to a passport. They can do it whilst we're on our way to Aberdeen.'

The recent news and build-up in frustration over the last few days had left Chief Inspector Steel on a short fuse. When his phone call was eventually transferred to Norton Flynn, he picked up similar frustration from Flynn.

'What is it now?' said Flynn, clearly annoyed at the call. 'Your colleague, er... Deputy Director Price, phoned me late last night. I was running around the office, dragging people in until the early hours ... I've had about three hours sleep and I've a lot to do.'

'Mr Flynn, Deputy Director Pendleton Price and I are en route to Aberdeen to interview you. We expect to be at your Aberdeen office before noon.'

'That's not possible ... I've a busy day today and can't waste my time talking to you ...'

'In that case, sir, I will be arriving in your office before noon to arrest you under Section 38B (1) and (2) of the Terrorism Act 2000. You will be held in a police cell until such time as you can be transported to London and interviewed under caution. You may wish to contact your legal representative and have that person with you at the time of your arrest.'

'What? This is *crazy*!'

'Do you wish me to repeat what I have just said? The choice is yours. You can either make yourself available for interview around noon today, or face arrest. What would you like to do?'

'I will be in my office at noon ... I'll be asking a TransGlobal Oil legal representative to be present.'

'Thank you for your cooperation,' said Steel. 'I look forward to seeing you at noon.'

A high-speed drive to Heathrow Airport, blue lights and siren sounding, and a sprint through check-in and security, and they were on the flight to Aberdeen.

Chapter 28

Conspiracy to undertake an act of terrorism

Thursday 6th April 2023 11:40 am

Staff in reception were not aware that Chief Superintendent Steel and Deputy Director Pendleton Price had a meeting with Norton Flynn. However, a quick phone call, and Norton's PA arrived to escort them to his office. Norton introduced the TransGlobal Oil legal representative and they moved to a nearby table to sit down.

'Thank you for agreeing to meet with us,' said CS Steel, but with no gratitude in his voice. 'We believe that the Senior Health & Safety Officer on board *Monroe Bravo*, Callum Jeffrey, was involved in the bombing of the Platform. Indeed, we believe it was Callum who placed the devices.

After arriving at your transport terminal in Aberdeen on 4th April, he flew to Amsterdam, attempted to change his appearance, and flew on to Tehran. His wife and child met up with him in Amsterdam and travelled with him. We are in the process of locating him. Of course, if this does prove to be a terrorist act, and Iranian nationals are involved, it may be …er, difficult, to secure their full cooperation.

'We have discovered that a crate weighing 34 Kilograms was mailed to Jeffreys and delivered to him via your Aberdeen dispatch centre. Documentation indicated the crate contained remote sensing equipment – supplied by CamSensors in Cambridge. CamSensors deny any order was placed and deny any equipment was mailed to Jeffrey. We have documentation, order numbers, invoices and signatures linking a TransGlobal Oil employee to this fictitious order. That person is identified as Norton T. Flynn.'

Steel removed documents from his briefcase and gave them to Norton. Steel turned to Norton's legal representative.

'I have a series of questions I'd like to pose to Norton Flynn.'

'Is my client under arrest?' asked the legal representative.

'No. However, if Mr Flynn would like to be arrested, transferred to a police cell, and interviewed under caution in London, I'm happy to oblige.'

He then turned to Flynn.

'Did you place this order?' he asked.

'No, I know nothing about it ... I don't place orders ... that's down to procurement. The board make decisions about significant expenditure, approve specific requests, and delegate detailed purchases to heads of department. A request and argument would be made about buying remote sensing equipment, depending on the cost and the benefits. The board may be involved in discussion, but I don't recall anything about CamSensors and such equipment.'

'At the end of this interview, I intend to designate your office a crime scene. My officers will seize your files, confiscate your computer, and check all documentation that has entered and left this office in the last three months. Do you understand?'

Norton Flynn looked totally bewildered, and simply nodded his head.

'Did you sign this authorisation?' asked Steel as he handed Flynn a single sheet of paper. 'It names you as the authorising person and appears to have your signature on it.'

'It looks like my signature but it must be a fake. I never signed such an order ... I don't sign such orders.'

Penny was watching Norton's reaction carefully. If he was lying, he was very convincing. She recalled the discussion with Tommy about the possibility of Flynn being used, and that at the time of the explosion on *Monroe Bravo* Norton was in a local hotel with an unknown woman. Penny asked her question.

'At the time of the explosion on *Monroe Bravo*, you were in a hotel room with a woman who was not your wife. What's her name?'

'What has this got to do with anything!'

'It has to do with what we believe is a terrorist attack on a TransGlobal Oil installation and the murder of your employees. Please answer the question.'

Norton lowered his head and eyes as he replied.

'Her name is Sonya Aslan ... she's a post-graduate student from Turkey, at Aberdeen University.'

'Which faculty ... which department?'

'Er ... History, I don't know what department ... she's on a course and doing research into Assyrian Reliefs. I really don't see what this has to do with the bombing of *Monroe Bravo*! Why are you invading my private life?'

'We believe that an Iranian national, Callum Jeffrey, also known as Khalid Jaffra, planted the bombs on your Platform. If you didn't sign the fictitious order for remote sensing equipment, perhaps someone close to you did.'

The TransGlobal Oil legal representative, who had said little so far, leaned across and whispered something into Norton's ear; Norton nodded.

'When did the relationship with Sonya Aslan start?'

'It began about a year ago. I was presenting an award to a student as part of the university graduation celebrations. TransGlobal Oil gives a cash reward to the most outstanding student in petrochemical engineering; we typically head hunt the winning student. There's a wine and nibbles event afterwards … I met her then.'

'Can you recall how the meeting took place? Who initiated the contact, how did your initial contact with her … er, develop?'

'I accidently bumped into her and spilled her drink … I was simply being polite by getting her another one and briefly started chatting before I left. I really didn't know anyone there … I'd done my job and was planning to leave after showing my face for a few minutes.'

Norton stopped talking and looked as though he was trying to recall what happened.

'I remember her saying she'd just arrived in Aberdeen and was about to start her course … she was chatty … an attractive young woman who seemed to be enjoying my company. She was asking me what I did. I suppose I was flattered. She was a raven-haired beauty.'

Penny didn't interrupt. She let Norton explain, in his own words, how the relationship started.

'I think she mentioned something about wanting to find her way around Aberdeen, seeing some of the sights before she became absorbed by her course and research. I offered to show her around.

'It started with the odd weekend drive around the area, places of interest like Balmoral, local castles, whisky distilleries; it soon became every weekend.'

Norton paused as though reflecting on how his relationship with Sonya developed. He leaned forwards in his chair, rested his arms on the table, and held his head in his hands. He stayed in this position for a few seconds before sitting upright and continuing.

'We'd taken a drive around Loch Ness. It was freezing and there was snow on the hill tops and on the ground. We were approaching that stretch where there are several hotels overlooking the Loch. Sonya suggested we stop for afternoon tea

– she'd never had afternoon tea and had been told the hotel ahead served it.

'I remember we'd had tea, sandwiches and cake next to a log fire. The place was almost deserted. We'd finished the tea, and were about to leave, when Sonya said she'd booked a room at the hotel … that's when the relationship really started.'

There was complete silence around the table following the admission. It was Steel who broke the silence.

'Mr Flynn, thank you for being so honest with us. We make no judgement about your private life … but I do need to explore your relationship with Sonya Aslan a little further. Could Sonya have gained access to TransGlobal Oil headed note paper, your email address and signature?'

Norton didn't reply immediately. His facial expression was grim when he replied.

'It's possible. We met in my office, after work, a couple of times.'

'How many times?' asked Steel.

'I can't remember – half a dozen, maybe more.'

'When you were in your office, were you always together? Were there any times when Sonya was alone?'

Norton pointed to an office door. It looked like an interconnecting door to another room or corridor.

'Yes, there's a bathroom through there. I'd have a shower before I went home. I'd be in the bathroom for five or ten minutes. I sent Sonya emails from my private email. She'd have my email address. There'd be letters and headed note paper on and around my desk … letters with my signature on them.'

'When did you last see or speak to Sonya?'

'It's been a few days. I tried to phone her yesterday and this morning but all I got was a message saying the number was unobtainable.'

Penny turned to CS Steel who nodded as she left the room.

'Deputy Director Pendleton Price is initiating a check on Sonya Aslan. She will be back in a few moments. Whilst she is away, what else can you tell me about Sonya?'

Meanwhile, Penny phoned the head of her team, Senior Inspector Douglas Watkins.

'Inspector Watkins, can I help you?'

'It's Pendleton Price here ... there's been a development that we need to chase up urgently. There's a chance we may have found an accomplice.'

'I was about to phone you. We got pictures of the woman at the airport hotel, from the CCTV. Sonya Aslan entered the UK on a Turkish passport ... but she's not Turkish. The spooks checked her picture against their data base. They've got a positive match; her real name is Shirin Mousari, an Iranian national. She left the UK on the morning of the first explosion on *Monroe Bravo*; flight to Amsterdam and on to Tehran.'

It looked like the hunch was paying dividends.

'OK, I need you to do several things. Contact the vice chancellor's office at Aberdeen University. If the Vice Chancellor is not immediately available, talk to the deputy vice chancellor or the most senior staff member. Tell him or her there may be a terrorist masquerading as a post-graduate student in the university, and we need their urgent cooperation, stress *urgent*. Don't tell him she's left the country.

'Explain that we need a digital photograph of Sonya Aslan. They'll probably want an official request. Argue about protecting student data or whatever, I'll see to that. Tell him that Chief Superintendent Steel and I will be in his office in the next 30 minutes. They'll have her photo for student records, student services, the library ... Get a copy to Border Force headquarters, through facial recognition, and compare to her passport photograph and the one from the hotel asap.

'Finally, inform the vice chancellor that we need to interview her tutor as soon as possible and see any records held on Sonya Aslan. Preferably on our arrival in his office.'

'I'm on to it,' was all Watkins said.

Penny next phoned Harry and brought him up to date. He agreed to liaise with Inspector Watkins and check out Sonya Aslan, aka Shirin Mousari.

CS Steel was about to ask another question when Penny returned to the room and interrupted the interview.

'Chief Inspector, can I have a quick word … outside?'

Penny quickly brought Tommy up to date with the latest news; things were progressing. As soon as they returned to their seats, CS Steel continued.

'We believe Sonya Aslan's real name is Shirin Mousari. She is not Turkish but an Iranian national. On the morning of the explosions on *Monroe Bravo*, she flew to Amsterdam and on to Tehran. We are currently investigating her background and whereabouts.'

Norton was stunned into silence.

'Mr Flynn, I'm not going to arrest you at this time. It may be you have been unwittingly involved in a terrorist plot. However, I am ordering you to hand over your passport to the police officer waiting outside. I am also expecting your full cooperation over the coming days.'

Penny continued.

'UK Border Force Officers will have your photograph. Should you attempt to leave the country, you will be arrested.'

They left Norton's office leaving a police officer securing the scene. With siren blaring and lights flashing, they were whisked from quayside TransGlobal Oil Headquarters to the tranquil grounds of Aberdeen University.

Chapter 29

Lover, sleeper, or agent?

Thursday 6th April 2023, 1:40 pm

The Vice-Chancellor had been decisive. By the time Steel and Pendleton Price arrived in his office, he'd assembled all that had been asked of him. He had a file containing everything that was known about Sonya Aslan on his desk and Dr Mike Stewart, Sonya's tutor, was in an adjacent room. Stewart had been told by the VC to cancel his lecture, to come to his office immediately, and bring any and all information about Sonya Aslan with him. Mike Stewart had never been summoned to the VC's office before … he didn't know of anyone who had been summoned.

It didn't take long to skim through the file: letter of application and research proposal, confirmation of funding and accommodation address, assignment grades and tutor comments. Steel and Pendleton Price joined Dr Stewart in the adjacent office. Penny initiated the conversation.

'Dr Stewart, I want to apologise for the disruption we've caused to you and your students this afternoon. All I can tell you at this time is that we are investigating a terrorist attack and we need your help.'

Penny could see the tension in Dr Stewart evaporate as he visibly relaxed in his chair.

'How can I help you?'

'What can you tell us about one of your students, Ms Sonya Aslan?'

Dr Stewart gave a wry smile, crossed his legs, and leaned back in his chair.

'Ms Aslan applied for a place on our master's degree programme. It has a taught, research methods component in the winter term, and research and dissertation components in the spring and summer terms. She's likely to fail the course.'

Stewart waited for a reaction to his pronouncement.

'Could you elaborate?'

'Ms Aslan allegedly obtained a first-class degree in history from the Sabanci University in Turkey. It's a well-respected university in Istanbul. Her references and research proposal were excellent.'

The academic in Dr Stewart couldn't resist a comment on the proposal itself.

'Although the study of Assyrian Reliefs is a well-worn path, her study could offer new insights into the diminishing effects of symbolism on power structures after the death of King Ashurbanipal around 631 BC ...'

Penny interrupted.

'At the moment, we are more interested in Ms Aslan as a person, her behaviour, relationship with other students.'

'I was coming to that,' Stewart remarked testily. 'It was clear to me in the first few weeks of the research methods course that Ms Aslan was not a scholar. She struggled with both the concepts and the detail involved in various research methods. The group of students is small and it's difficult to hide – even though Ms Aslan tried hard to hide. I suspect other students helped her with the assignments, but she performed very badly on the end of term exam. I would have failed her but, er ... these overseas post-graduate students pay a lot of money to study with us. I was, er, persuaded to be more generous than I should.'

Chief Superintendent Steel was an experienced officer. He'd interviewed hundreds of suspects and could tell when they were telling lies or not telling the truth. He sensed an awkwardness, an embarrassment in Dr Stewart.

'Dr Stewart, before you finalised the end of term examination results, did Ms Aslan, ... did she make an, er, appeal to you?'

Steel and Stewart held each other's stare for a couple of seconds. Steel was playing a hunch.

'Yes, Ms Aslan offered ...er, sexual favours if I increased her grade from a fail to a bare pass. I informed the Dean immediately, and he agreed to remark her script and recommended a bare pass. I did not take up her offer and no other action was taken. I'm sure she will fail the end of course exam.'

'Thank you Dr Stewart for being so honest. You are giving us what could be vital information. Is there anything else you can tell us about Ms Aslan?'

'Yes. I said her proposal was excellent but I don't think she wrote it. In seminars and tutorials, it became clear that her knowledge of Assyrian Reliefs was rudimentary, familiarity with key references absent, knowledge of the period non-existent. I wondered what she was doing at the university.'

'Dr Stewart, what you have told us is extremely important. Could I ask you to give a statement to the police officer standing outside? Simply repeat what you have just told me, plus anything else you can recall.'

As Steel and Pendleton Price made another high-speed return to Aberdeen Airport and back to London, Tommy voiced what they were both thinking.

'Too early for conclusions but it's looking like Ms Aslan, Ms Mousari, is not who she says she is. I'd put my money on an Iranian sleeper or agent. Harry, Homeland Security, and Interpol will give us more over the next few hours and days.

'We also need to trace the characters who delivered the crate to the courier and on to the TransGlobal Oil depot. However, it's looking like anyone involved in the bombing has already left the country.'

It was late afternoon by the time Tommy and Penny returned to the office. Everyone was keen to hear the outcome of the trip, and Steel provided the summary.

'It seems the TransGlobal Oil Vice President was having a relationship with who he believed was a Turkish post-graduate called Sonya Aslan. It seems clear from the comments by her tutor that she was masquerading as a student. Her real name is Shirin Mousari. She's an Iranian national, and returned to Tehran, via Amsterdam, on the morning of the bombing. It's starting to look like Norton Flynn was targeted to obtain his private email address, headed note paper, and copy of his signature to get the bombs on board *Monroe Bravo*.'

'Unfortunately, it looks like Shirin Mousari is back in Tehran … our "raven-haired beauty" has disappeared,' Penny added.

Gene suddenly put up his hand to stop Penny's comments and looked across the table to his colleagues.

'Penny, did you just make that phrase up, "raven-haired beauty", or was it mentioned in connection with, er, Shirin Mousari?'

'It's how Norton Flynn described her, it's how he referred to her.'

'Where have I heard that description before?'

Gene tapped his fingers on the table top and tried to think. Penny merely continued.

'It's not an uncommon phrase. It's usually associated with Lord Byron's poem, 'She Walks in Beauty', but he never used the phrase "raven-haired beauty". He talks about "every raven tress".'

Gene smiled broadly and almost laughed.

'I'm impressed! But it wasn't linked to a poem; it was linked to something else. Davie, can you run the phase through the operational data base and see what it flags?'

Davie disappeared for a few minutes. His fingers danced across the keyboard, the printer clattered, and he collected several sheets of paper. He read quickly, highlighting several sections. His expression didn't change as he walked back to his chair and read from the sheets.

'Just one hit on the database. The Levinson Case – just over eighteen months ago in Israel. Colonel Ezra Levinson was a US military adviser, attached to the Israeli Air Force in Haifa. He committed suicide and left a suicide note saying, and I quote: "I would rather die than betray my country". His death was judged to be suicide and the letter authentic. It was never established which country he was referring to; he was Jewish and his family had originated from Israel.

'The subsequent investigation believed he was in a relationship with an unknown woman. There were numerous occasions when the Israelis were unable to account for his whereabouts. He made regular unaccompanied trips between Haifa and Tel Aviv and numerous weekends away from the base. The investigators found two poor-quality photos of Ezra with a woman. A witness was located who claims he saw them together. He never saw her face but described her as a "raven-haired beauty". When pressed, he explained that he didn't need to see her face to know she was beautiful. He said it was all about the way she stood, the way she moved … he could tell she was beautiful. She was never traced.'

'It's worth shot. We can run the photo of Shirin Mousari through Israeli immigration, and see if she arrived in Israel and, if so, when she left. She may be back in Tehran – but she may travel somewhere else in the future. If she does, we have her,' smiled Gene.

Later that afternoon, Gene strode into the central office.

'Got a hit! Shirin Mousari, aka Sonya Aslan, aka Maria Carla Mendez, entered Israel on a Spanish passport seven months before the death of Colonel Levinson. There's no record of her leaving Israel during this time. However, she left Israel for Paris two days after the death of Levinson. It's too much of a coincidence. The Israelis are currently checking her movements during the period.'

A few minutes later, Davie walked into the central office waving a sheet of paper.

'Guess what! We believe she is currently in the US, on another Spanish passport, under the name of Gloria Joy Morella. She could have only been in Iran for hours before flying back to Amsterdam and on to Washington. We'll have traced her in a couple of hours.'

Chapter 30

The analyst

Thursday 6ᵗʰ April 2023, 6:00 pm

There was a knock on the door and a large elderly woman entered the office. She was carrying a laptop, a thick file, and a handful of cables.

'Randall, you can put your laptop on the lectern. You'll see the sockets for power and projection cables.'

Tommy pointed her in the direction of the electronic console and moved to his usual position at the table. As soon as Randall had set up her machine, she joined the table and sat next to him.

'This is Randall, head of our Forensic Accounting Team,' said Steel. 'Her colleagues on the Middle-East desk have been working through mountains of data.'

Tommy introduced the US Homeland Security Team and Penny before asking:

'What have you got for us?'

'I may have something for you, or rather our analysts may have something for you.'

Penny looked at Randall and realised she wasn't old. It was her choice of frumpy clothes; hairstyle and old-fashioned glasses that made her look old. However, her voice and manner were confident and precise, albeit pedantic.

'I lead a group of analysts who look for financial anomalies in the accounts of governments in the Middle-East, where accounts of income, expenditure and assets don't add up. We draw upon published accounts, data we obtain from third parties, as well as other estimates and extrapolations.

'It's not unusual to find anomalies that are simply mistakes; mistakes that are eventually corrected. We also find evidence of fraud, embezzlement, and misappropriation at all levels. When the incident on *Monroe Bravo* was brought to our attention, we looked again at Middle-Eastern governments and companies linked to the petroleum industries.'

Penny was starting to get irritated. Insights into the work of the UK Government was fascinating but she wanted something concrete, something that would progress the investigation.

'We've been aware for some time of the regular transfer of funds from the Iranian Ministry of Economic Affairs and Finance to the Islam Revolutionary Guard Corps, the IRGC. We've also detected that a proportion of these funds have been surreptitiously redirected to the Quds Force; it's a substantial amount.'

Turning to Penny, and in a patronising tone, she explained.

'The Quds Force is an independent group, loosely attached to the IRGC. They are engaged in unconventional warfare and small scale military operations. The Force is headed by Colonel Hussein Zand and a small team of military personnel, government ministers and clerics.

'The funds – and we're talking about tens of millions of dollars each year – are transferred through a dozen different channels, but we tracked them,' she said with a self-congratulatory smile.

'Whilst we found some evidence of these monies funding direct Quds Force activity, we traced a substantial amount to stock brokers in several Middle-Eastern countries, Saudi Arabia, Dubai, Qatar, UAE and Kuwait. These proxy companies bought TransGlobal Oil shares. Over approximately sixteen years, they have amassed 4.7% of all shares.

'We thought the leaders of the Quds Force were creating a

substantial retirement fund for themselves – until the last few days. When the Saudi Arabian Stock market opened on Wednesday 5th April, the coordinated sell off of TransGlobal shares began. It wasn't wholesale selling, but rather strategic selling. When the rate of selling began to slow, and the stock started to stabilise, Quds Force brokers sold off another block of shares to keep the price falling.

'Our estimate is that the group of brokers, who originally bought TransGlobal Oil stock, are close to liquidating their entire investment. TransGlobal Oil is currently worth just over one-third of the price listed prior to the fire on *Monroe Bravo*. Unless there is good news about *Monroe Bravo*, it is unlikely the company will survive and Quds Force will have delivered a major economic blow to the West.

'Furthermore, Iranian oil and oil companies are now worth more, significantly more, than they were two days ago. We estimate that the short-term financial gains to Iran are likely to be greater than the losses incurred during the sell off.'

'So, what can we do about it?' asked Penny.

'Well, we've started to do a couple of things,' Randall replied. 'We've drafted a letter to the Saudi Stock Exchange, alerting them to suspicious trading activity on TransGlobal Oil shares. We've assembled evidence and argued that a collection of brokers have collaborated to drive down the price of TransGlobal Oil. We've argued that these companies should be suspended from any further trading until the charges have been examined.'

'That doesn't sound like dramatic action,' said Penny.

'Accepted ... but it depends on another action we're proposing,' Randall replied. 'I'm confident that the Saudi Stock Exchange will act immediately to protect its reputation; it will suspend the companies we list. There's no love lost between the Iranians and the Saudis. This is why I'm confident the brokers will be suspended. This means that Quds Force will not have brokers ready to act on their behalf. If news from *Monroe Bravo* is positive and it sparks – oh, sorry, about the pun – a run on TransGlobal Oil shares, there will be a delay in their purchase of shares at rock-bottom prices. That delay could be highly significant.

'For example, if US and UK banks were poised to loan significant amounts of money to TransGlobal Oil, they could purchase shares immediately a positive announcement is made, purchases made at rock-bottom prices. Within hours, the share price would soar and the company would not only recoup their losses, but own more of their company than they did before. In fact, we predict that TransGlobal Oil shares could go even higher than they were before the fire on *Monroe Bravo*. The stock market is driven by confidence. The fire on the oil rig was a disaster, but if they weather the terrorist attack and are back in production in months, it will be a major boost to them. It's a company with this sort of resilience that investors like.

But it's all about timing. The timing of any announcement about the damage to *Monroe Bravo* and the subsequent timing of share purchases. Unless the Quds Force has ready access to significant funds, and brokers, they will miss the opportunity. They will have lost billions of dollars. It's the sort of event that ruins careers … or worse.'

There was silence around the room. Penny was aware that share prices could fluctuate dramatically but had never witnessed these dealings and manoeuvring first-hand.

'This is above our pay grade,' announced CS Steel. 'We need to pass this on immediately to Commander Short for a decision to be made elsewhere.'

Elsewhere, senior government ministers and senior executives from TransGlobal Oil were in discussion. They had also received a briefing from Randall. It was the TransGlobal Vice President, Norton T. Flynn, who summarised the discussion and the actions to be taken.

'So, we're agreed: another twenty four hours to keep the news of the Platform being saved out of the media and to set up the sting. The barrels of oil that are still burning are creating lots of smoke, but it can't fool satellite surveillance with thermal imaging and smoke penetrating sensors. We've been informed that certain countries are changing the orbit of satellites but it will take another twenty four hours to get them repositioned.

'If the Platform hadn't been shut down within minutes, the whole thing would be at the bottom of the North Sea by now. That's what the bombers expected. That's what we want them to keep thinking. American and UK teams are currently trying to trace the bombers; they know the timeline and what to do.'

Chapter 31

An unusual decision

Wednesday 5th April 2023, 8:40 pm

It didn't take long to discover the Omega Seamaster Chronograph was a very special watch. It was in good condition and even second-hand it was worth between three and four thousand US dollars. That afternoon, they had arranged to meet with their Indian jeweller. It was early evening, and the shop had been closed for hours. There were still lights in the narrow alleyway but most of the shops were closed. Yaser and Asad stopped outside the shop and looked around before knocking. They didn't want anyone to see them entering but they were expected. The jeweller released several heavy bolts and unbarred the door to let his visitors slip into the darkened shop. He re-locked everything before leading them from the small shop through an even smaller workshop packed with tools, and into a bright, cosy and elaborately furnished room. It was a complete contrast to the modest shop and tired looking displays. The jeweller deliberately toned down his public image and didn't cater for passing trade. He had discerning customers who all wanted bespoke jewellery that was an investment rather than a luxury.

It was a familiar routine. They exchanged greetings of welcome, embraced each other, sat around an elaborately inlaid wooden table and enquired into the health of their families. The jeweller's wife brought a large tea tray into the room, set it down on the table, and left without saying a word. The jeweller poured the strong, reddish-brown tea into shaped glasses, placed it before his guests and waited. Yaser loved the strong Persian tea. He picked up a sugar cube, placed it between his teeth, and sipped the hot tea through it; delicious. Asad wasn't keen and diluted the tea with hot water and took one sip; he wouldn't drink any more.

Once the ritual was over, it was down to business. Two small plastic bags containing beads of silver and gold were placed on the table top. The jeweller placed an empty plastic bag on the digital scale and zeroed it. In the past, he'd checked that each bead was gold – but tonight there was too much gold. He took a gamble and simply transferred the beads into the bag, checked the weight, and showed it to his guests.

'Eighty-five point two grams at seventeen point two dollars per gram.'

The jeweller tapped the calculator and announced:

'That's one thousand, four hundred and thirty-four dollars; I'll give you fourteen hundred and fifty.'

'Agreed,' said Yaser and Asad, broad smiles spreading across their faces.

The jeweller weighed the silver beads, rounded up the price, and gave them a total. He left the room and returned a few minutes later with a bundle of cash which he counted out in front of them. Just as the jeweller was expecting them to leave, Yaser took the Omega Seamaster Chronograph from his pocket and placed it on the table.

'Would you be interested in buying this?'

The jeweller hardly moved as he looked at the watch for several seconds before picking it up.

'Come,' he said as he led them to his small workshop, switched on lights, sat at his workbench, and placed a loop in his eye socket.

He inspected the watch closely and then fitted it into a small, cushioned vice. With a tiny screwdriver, he removed the back cover of the watch and inspected the inside before putting it back together, handing it back to Yaser and leading them back to his living room.

'It's original, good condition but I don't deal in watches ... it would be too expensive, too specialised for my customers. The only places selling this sort of watch are the dealers in the city centre.'

Yaser and Asad were disappointed. This was the first time the jeweller had ever declined to buy anything from them. They knew it was an expensive watch and were desperate to sell it.

'How much is it worth?' asked Yaser.

'I can tell you what it's worth but that's different to what you're likely to get for it. Whoever buys it may have to hang onto it for months, if not years. If there's doubt over the, er ... previous owner, dealers will be reluctant to buy it. If someone lost such a watch, or it was stolen, they'd report it to the police – dealers would be alerted to it – so be careful.'

This was not the news they were expecting.

'Would you offer us a price?' asked Yaser.

The jeweller paused and looked again at the watch on the table.

'I'll be honest with you. If this watch was on sale in a city centre shop, the price would be at least three thousand US dollars. I do not wish to insult you and could only pay a fraction of that. Even then, it's only because you're my friend.'

'How much will you offer?'

The jeweller shook his head and gave a deep sigh.

'I really do not want it, but as a friend I'll give you one thousand dollars. I will have to find a buyer outside the country, probably Turkey, and I will eventually hope to make a few hundred dollars. It's the best I can do ... but it's your decision.'

They agreed the sale and left with their money. In truth, they were delighted with the one thousand dollars for the watch; it was all an unexpected bonus. The jeweller was also delighted. He had a supply of silver and gold at bargain basement prices, and a watch that he could pass on to a contact for a handsome profit. He'd make a phone call and get rid of the watch as soon as possible, maybe even tonight. It wasn't wise to hold on to dubious items of jewellery. If the Omega was reported as stolen, and found in his shop, it would be unpleasant and costly – better to move it on quickly.

What the jeweller didn't know was that his contact, or rather informant, worked for the British Embassy in Tehran. His contact was a petty crook who bought and sold stolen goods. He didn't actually steal anything himself, far too dangerous; he simply made a profit on everything he bought and sold from other thieves. He also passed on snippets of information, gossip and rumour about Iranian business people and clerics, politicians and military officers. The informant was part of an extensive network that supplied isolated pieces of information to the Iranian desk, or rather the large open plan office at MI6 headquarters in England. Over time, they put the isolated pieces of information together until a picture emerged. They advised on what action could be taken to ensure a business person, under pressure, signed a deal or not. Whether an ambitious politician could be bribed or not.

It was an unusual decision on the part of the informant. He seldom passed on stolen items to his contact. Occasionally, the return of a sentimental item that had been stolen could be repaid with a favour or snippet of information. Today he had the chance to make a quick thousand dollars and ingratiate himself with his contact. It was the odd remark from the jeweller that made his decision. He had said the watch had been "saved from the incinerator". It was a remark he'd heard before amongst his fellow criminals. If you were "saved from the incinerator", you avoided a premature death at the hands of the authorities. If he had information that the watch had been saved, but not the owner, it may be worth money from his contact; it was.

Within hours of the watch being resold, a photograph of it, and an accompanying note, was in an encrypted email to London. The watch would follow in the diplomatic bag. An analyst on the Iranian desk checked the serial number of the watch, revealed the name of the original owner, when the watch was last serviced, and the address of the latest owner. When the brief report was routinely run through a search programme, part of a continuous digital trawl against existing data bases, it generated a red flag on Harry Preece's desk.

'Guys, I've got something. Callum Jeffrey owned a fancy watch that was, quote, "saved from the incinerator" in Tehran two days ago. I'm guessing that the body attached to the watch wasn't – but we need to find out.'

'Are you sure it's his watch?' asked Penny.

'Yep. The watch and serial number are authentic. Intel is that a jeweller sold the watch to one of our undercover agents within hours of Khalid's luggage disappearing. I need to find out who the informant bought it from and how it was, er … acquired.

'This is our first strong lead since we lost contact on the trace. I'll be on the first plane to Tehran.'

'We need you here,' argued Steel.

'To do what?' challenged Harry. 'I've been sitting on my arse for two days doing nothing. Nothing is coming through, and I'll only be gone a couple of days. Between you, you can check what's coming through from my end.'

Harry was suddenly animated. He was blasting off top-level messages to his opposite number in the Iranian Embassy, fielding the replies, and sending more. In just under an hour, he announced:

'Just off to pick up a bag and get the Tube to Heathrow. Back in a couple of days.'

Chapter 32

TV updates

Friday 7th April 2023, 4:20 pm

Rick Johnson and Norton Flynn were feeling relaxed and confident as they were driven from TransGlobal Oil Headquarters to the BBC studios in Aberdeen. They had just finished a video meeting with Walter Brachs and TransGlobal lawyers in Houston, Texas. They had typewritten notes that summarised all that was currently known about the explosions on *Monroe Bravo*, or rather all that TransGlobal were prepared to release. Walter had confirmed the news blackout surrounding the Platform would end shortly after five o'clock that evening – at the same time as the planned recording for the BBC News item with Lucy Rottmuller. As they waited in reception, Norton turned to Rick.

'I'm pleased you agreed to take control of the repairs to *Monroe Bravo* and get it operational as soon as possible. I'm confident you'll do a great job … and I'll do everything I can to get you what you need. When we've finished here, you can concentrate on it.'

Rick nodded. It was going to be a massive and pressurised effort, coordinating a dozen or more teams in a carefully choreographed but evolving plan.

'As soon as the Platform is recommissioned and operational, Walter wants me back in Houston. It may be a one way trip. I'll probably be out of a job.'

Rick looked up, confused.

'Why would you be out of a job?'

However, as soon as Rick asked the question, he knew the answer. Although he was Off-Shore Installation Manager, it was Norton who had the ultimate responsibility for everything that was transferred from the mainland onto the Platform; Rick and his team merely accepted it. The systems and procedures Norton oversaw had allowed the bombs to be placed. The buck stopped with him.

Norton flicked out a finger.

'One, I switched my phone off at a critical time – big mistake. Two, I fabricated a meeting to get me out of the office – not good. And three, I met with a lover who's likely to be an Iranian agent.'

Norton gave a wry smile as he shook his head.

'The UK Border Force officer told me they think it was a woman called Shirin Mousari who arranged for the bombs to be delivered to the Platform. She's now back in Iran. It may have been unknowing, but I helped the terrorists circumvent the very security procedures I'd put in place and was charged to maintain. It all makes me look like a fool.'

Rick looked at the man by his side and realised the pressure he was under.

'I make no judgement on your private life ... but you're not a fool. We all make mistakes – I've made plenty. What we need to do now is put on a grandstand performance, and over the next couple of months demonstrate we're assets, not liabilities.'

The arrival of the PA for Lucy Rottmuller stopped any further conversation. They took their seats as requested, let make-up dust them, and sat waiting for Lucy to record the news item. Lucy wasn't in the room and arrived just minutes before the agreed time for the recording.

'Sorry I'm late ... last minute things to check,' said Lucy breathlessly. 'I'd like to start with a question to you, Norton, about the actions you've been taking to bring the fires on *Monroe Bravo*, and escape of gas and oil, under control.'

Lucy looked down at her notes before turning to Rick.

'I'd then like to switch to Rick and ask about the death toll and state of the Platform. Is that OK?'

Rick nodded and wondered if Lucy Rottmuller would be charming or obnoxious. Interestingly, no mention had been made about how long the interview would last. Both Rick and Norton guessed this meant Lucy was being given as much time as she needed to assemble material for the edited news item. It would be an extended interview. They sat expectantly with the backdrop of *Monroe Bravo* on fire behind them as the Floor Manager gave Lucy the five, four, three, two, one hand signal. Suddenly, Lucy was looking into the camera lens and reading the auto cue.

'Just over seventy two hours ago, a series of explosions ripped through *Monroe Bravo*, a mega oil and gas Platform off the coast of Scotland. Dozens of men and women were killed in the explosions and fires. Millions of cubic feet of gas were released into the atmosphere and millions of barrels of crude oil into the North Sea.'

The expression on Lucy's face reflected the ongoing, grim scenario taking place less than two hundred kilometres from TransGlobal Headquarters.

'Viewers will recall that three days ago I interviewed Norton Flynn, Vice President, Scotland, about the disaster. He agreed to talk to us again and provide an update on what TransGlobal Oil have been doing in the last seventy two hours.'

Lucy turned to Norton, smiled, and asked her question.

'Mr Flynn, the pollution caused by the explosions and fires on *Monroe Bravo* has been described as a humanitarian and ecological disaster, to rival similar disasters such as the destruction of the *Piper Alpha* Platform in the North Sea and *Deepwater Horizon* in the Gulf of Mexico.'

Lucy let the accusation hang between them for a few seconds before she continued.

'A fifteen-mile exclusion zone has been imposed around the Platform, along with a news blackout. Only certain officials, and no reporters, have been allowed inside the zone. What are you hiding?'

Flynn looked totally unruffled by the charge as he replied.

'Ms Rottmuller, we are not hiding anything. When the first explosion occurred, a whole sequence of actions were implemented. Attempts were made to shut down the Platform. Firefighting vessels manoeuvred close to it, and began to contain and put out the fires. Fast Rescue Craft rescued people from the Platform and searched for people in the water. In subsequent hours, search rescue teams were flown in from Aberdeen. Our own teams searched the wreckage for the injured.

'Support vessels began to contain and collect the oil spill. It was a major search and rescue, damage limitation, pollution control, and clean-up operation. Under such circumstances, we did not want spectators around the Platform, for their own safety, and potentially hindering our work.'

Lucy knew that this was a rehearsed answer, designed to placate. She wanted detail and would give the VP a little more rope to hang himself before she launched into her prepared accusations.

'So, tell us what is happening. How many people have been killed or are missing? Are the fires still raging? Are millions of gallons of crude oil still pouring into the North Sea?'

Norton paused as though deciding which of the questions to answer first.

'I can tell you that less than sixty minutes after the first explosion on *Monroe Bravo,* the Platform was shut down. After this time, no gas or oil escaped into the atmosphere or into the North Sea. All fires have been extinguished and an assessment of damage to the Platform is underway.'

Lucy couldn't disguise the look of surprise at the news. She'd been late getting to the studio because she was checking the news outlets for any updates, any information about the disaster.

Norton continued.

'I'm informed that forty two men and women have been killed, or are missing. The search is continuing on and around the Platform for survivors. A number of staff have suffered burns and have been flown to specialist units for treatment.

'TransGlobal Oil are in touch with the relatives of those who have been killed, injured, or who are missing. We are providing counselling support and have already made an interim compensation payment to their next of kin. We are committed to rapid and generous compensation to all our staff.

'Alongside the search and rescue of those on the Platform, and in the water, support vessels began collecting any oil that had escaped. I understand this phase of the clean-up operation is being scaled back as the vast majority of the oil has been collected and any residual oil dispersed. Pollution has been kept to a minimum. I personally guarantee no oil from *Monroe Bravo* will be washed up on Scottish beaches or those of any nearby country.'

This was not the answer Lucy was expecting. Norton's comments were in danger of defusing the entire interview. She couldn't allow that, and responded aggressively.

'Have you discovered what caused the explosions? Was it cost-cutting measures, sloppy procedures, poor communication, or something else that caused them?'

The aggressive tone wasn't lost on Norton, but he was prepared.

'The UK Health & Safety Executive, the Marine Accident Investigation Branch, the police and security services along with forensic scientists are currently investigating the explosions on *Monroe Bravo*. May I suggest that we wait for their findings rather than speculate? I'm sure they will be more than happy to explain their findings and conclusions.

'I understand Commander Short, Head of the Office for Security and Counter-Terrorism at New Scotland Yard, will be making a statement shortly.'

Norton could see Lucy's reaction. The mere mention of the word "terrorism" had her full attention. The statement could be a major revelation; it could be journalistic dynamite.

'Are you saying the explosions were a result of terrorism?'

'No, I'm not saying that. I'm merely alerting you to a forthcoming statement. The authorities are investigating the death of over forty people on *Monroe Bravo*. They will be exploring all possibilities. You should direct your questions about terrorism to them, and not to me.'

Despite the request, Lucy couldn't help herself, and blasted question after question at Norton. He simply shrugged his shoulders and repeated that she should direct the questions to Commander Short, not him. Lucy was furious. She'd been out-manoeuvred, and didn't like it. This was her story; she had a TransGlobal Vice President and the Off-Shore Installation Manager in front of her, and another reporter could get the scoop. She flicked through her notes, and moved to a different line of questioning.

'Before the disaster, *Monroe Bravo* was supplying about fifteen percent of UK crude oil production and almost twenty percent of natural gas. We've seen oil and gas prices rocket, and concern over shortages mount. What is TransGlobal Oil doing to alleviate these concerns?'

Norton smiled and sat back in his chair.

'You are correct: oil and gas prices *did* rise on the news of the explosions on *Monroe Bravo*. However, this was an emotional rather than a considered response. The United Kingdom has massive, strategic reserves of oil and gas that it can draw upon until such time as *Monroe Bravo* is back in full production. There will be some minor disruption but certainly no shortage of either gas or oil. Furthermore, the announcement tonight that the Platform has been safety shut down, and will be back in production shortly, will, I believe, reassure the market.'

This wasn't going well and she could sense it. She turned to Rick.

'Dr Johnson, you've had seventy two hours to reflect on your actions before abandoning the burning Platform. When we last spoke, you admitted that you ordered two divers to undertake a suicide mission, and one of them was missing. Has the person been found? Have you spoken to his relatives?'

Rick heard the intake of breath from someone in the studio.

'Ms Rottmuller, if you check the recording of our previous interview, I explained that I did not abandon the Platform but was driven from it by the heat and cascading, burning oil. The clothes that two colleagues and I were wearing were smouldering in the heat. The soles of our boots were melting on the steel deck. Despite my wish to return to the Platform, I was ordered to Aberdeen to meet with you.'

Lucy was suddenly relishing the interview. She thought she had Johnson on the defensive, and could pursue the line of questioning. She'd let him continue for a moment and dig himself deeper into a hole.

'When I arrived at the Dive Centre to coordinate the response to the emergency, the area around it was ablaze. The surrounding temperatures were so great that the jib of the crane holding the Diving Bell had failed; it was melting. The Bell had dropped to the seabed. The plastic windows in the Dive Centre were melting, the roof was on fire with toxic smoke billowing in.

'The main umbilical supplying oxygen and helium to the divers below was on fire; the tanks of oxygen would explode at any minute – boosting the flames. The ruptured gas pipeline was like a massive oxy-acetylene blow torch. It was melting steel structures close to it. Parts of the Platform were about to fall off into the sea.

The Bell was directly beneath this carnage. I judged that the divers below would soon be dead – but their actions could save their colleagues and friends ... and the Platform itself.'

The emotion in Rick's voice permeated the studio. Lucy was only half listening. She was trying to judge the point at which to interject and drive Johnson into a corner, into an admission.

'With no gases to breathe, the divers would suffocate in a few hours. We had no way of winching the Bell to the surface. There was no way they could swim to the surface. If they tried to do so, the rapid decompression would kill them. At any moment, the rest of the crane could topple from the Platform onto the Bell below.

'If the two visitors, Jack Collier and Sandro Calovarlo, could turn off certain valves there was a chance we could save the Platform and those on it. I made a calculated decision to direct them under it and I stand by my decision.'

Lucy couldn't let the moment pass, but broke the golden rule: "Never ask a question that you don't know the answer to." Or, "Never make a statement that can be immediately rebutted."

'So, your *calculated decision* resulted in the death of one of these divers?'

The Floor Manager was checking the time but knew they had another ten to fifteen minutes before they would have to stop and edit the interview for the six o'clock news. This was dramatic stuff; he knew the viewers would be hooked and would want to hear the rest. He held his breath as Rick Johnson paused momentarily to control his obvious emotion.

'Jack Collier and Sandro Calovarlo were instrumental in saving the Platform and countless lives. They shut off the oil and gas pipelines. Then, with a fellow diver, Gunnar Larson, they made repeated trips in dark and freezing water to the stricken Diving Bell to tow three divers at a time to safety. All nine divers were rescued. It was during the last rescue that Jack Collier, and a diver he was rescuing, were trapped inside fallen debris. Sandro and Gunnar rescued them.'

Rick glanced at his watch before he continued.

'All of the divers are fit and well. They are currently completing their decompression sequence from ninety metres to sea level. Once our medical staff have checked them out, they will be returning to Aberdeen.'

It was the obvious point to stop. Lucy Rottmuller had more than enough material for her two minute slot and so the Floor Manager signalled to her to wrap it up. For one of the few times in her career, Lucy had been out-manoeuvred, and she knew it. She uttered an insincere "thank you" and ended the interview.

However, Norton wasn't finished. He caught Lucy's attention.

'Miss Rottmuller, if you would like to interview Jack Collier and Sandro Calovarlo, they are due to arrive in Aberdeen some time on Saturday or Sunday. I'm sure an interview with them could be arranged either here or in Manchester. It may serve to provide a heart-warming story after such tragedy.'

The London Stock Market was closed when Norton made his dramatic announcement but it was lunch time at the New York Stock Exchange. In New York, there had been the usual frenetic action during the morning and traders were enjoying a well-earned lunch. A few were monitoring the news feeds but an unannounced item on a BBC radio programme wasn't even noticed by most traders. However, it was eagerly awaited by others. Days of careful planning, the transfer of significant funds to brokers, and timing, were about to come to fruition.

As soon as Flynn had announced *Monroe Bravo* had been shut down within minutes of the first explosion, there would be no more oil flowing into the North Sea, the fires were out, and the Platform would be back in production in the near future, the buying started. In minutes, TransGlobal Oil bought millions of shares at bargain basement prices; they exhausted their available funds. The massive purchase by TransGlobal Oil kick-started the buying spree. The price of their oil shares began to soar, and prompted others to join the frenzy. It couldn't last and eventually the price began to slacken. It eventually halted eighteen points above the price immediately prior to the first explosion. In minutes, TransGlobal Oil had not only regained their losses and increased their holdings, but were now worth significantly more than before lunch in New York. It had been a major killing in the market, just on the edge of legality but unlikely to be challenged.

Chapter 33

Our man in Tehran

Saturday 8th April 2023, 7:30 am

It was an uneventful flight to Tehran, and Harry's plane was one of the early ones to land. Just carry-on luggage and a diplomatic passport ensured a quick and smooth transit through the airport and an early meeting at the Embassy. His colleagues had already been briefed and started to trace key people. The Cultural Attaché, Third Secretary and Vice-Consul were waiting for Harry. As he walked in, the smiling Attaché greeted him.

'Hi, Harry … long time no see. Good of you to bring us a load of crap.'

The title of Cultural Attaché was merely another name for the resident MI6 agent based in the Embassy. Harry had worked with him several times and they had a good rapport.

'I managed to get hold of one of my informants last night,' announced the third secretary. 'He's a petty crook, a fence, but has provided useful information in the past. If he hadn't been offered the watch, we'd never have this lead.'

Harry cut the self-congratulations short and merely asked where he got it from.

'He bought it from an Indian jeweller … a shop in Keshan Street, an alley just off Afshar Square … it's a couple of kilometres away from the city centre.'

'Will the shop and alley be busy this morning?' asked Harry.

'The alley is always busy … but the shop isn't. Intel is that it looks run down but caters for private clients who have money and want gold jewellery designed to order.'

'What do you think about him being paid a visit this morning?' asked Harry forcibly. 'Who he bought the watch from, name, how to find him – or her.'

'Be better tonight, less people around,' replied the Vice-Consul.

'I'd prefer not to wait. Do you have a couple of guys who could, er, encourage the jeweller to tell us what we need to know this morning?'

The three Embassy staff looked at each other. Relations between the Embassy and the Iranian Government were strained at the best of times. They were sure that the Iranian Immigration Department would have noted Harry Preece, his diplomatic passport, and his drive to the Embassy; they knew by now that Harry was MI6 and not an innocent visitor.

'If you really can't wait, we do have a couple of men whom we can brief and who will get any information our jeweller friend may have. We can give them a plausible back story in case of trouble – but I wouldn't expect any.'

It took longer to lose the car following them than to brief two brothers working at a scrap yard. It was stressed: they just wanted to know the name or names of those who sold the jeweller the watch. It would be a 'one and only attempt' and so they must be sure the jeweller is telling the truth. They must also be quick. Within the hour, and by late morning the two brothers parked in Afshar Square and made their way to the shop. They paused by the window to inspect the display, which was not very encouraging, but it did confirm there were no shoppers inside.

One of them pushed open the drab shop door, a Bell rattled, and he strode to the counter, his brother following. The jeweller slid off his seat and approached the counter with a big smile.

'*As-salamu alaykum* … peace be upon you. How can I help

you?'

The man didn't return the smile, didn't change his expression, just placed a colour photograph of an Omega Seamaster Chronograph on the counter.

'I want to know who you bought this watch from, and where I can find them. If you tell me the truth, we will thank you and leave you in peace.'

The man paused for merely a second or two, and, before the jeweller could answer, spoke in a flat monotone, a voice without feeling.

'If you refuse to answer, my brother will begin to hurt you – but he won't hurt your hands or your eyes. If you tell us lies, and we have to return, my brother will crush your fingers and put out your eyes. The person who sold you the watch was a thief. What do we do to thieves?' asked the man, inviting a reply with a movement of his head.

'We cut off four fingers of the right hand,' mumbled the jeweller.

'If the person is your friend, I will not cut off the fingers,' he promised.

The jeweller didn't even pause. He could sense the menace that flowed from the brothers.

'They work at the crematorium, the private Gulistan Crematorium in the west of the city …Yaser and Asad. They're not thieves – they rescue items the families have discarded,' he said unconvincingly.

'Where do they live?'

'I don't know … they've never told me, I've never asked, I've never visited … I just buy things from them from time to time.'

'What do they look like?'

'Workers … grey boiler suits … rough hands and old faces.'

'Remember, this is your one and only chance to tell me what I need to know. If we have to return, it will be very unpleasant.'

'I've told you all I know. I paid them US1,000 dollars for the watch. I bought it off Yaser and Asad. They will be working the incinerators today. I think they will finish work at four o'clock.

The man smiled and as he turned away said, '*Ruz-e xubi dâšte bâši ...* have a good day.'

*

'It sounds plausible,' said Harry. 'The informant said the jeweller mentioned the phrase "saved from the incinerator". It's possible that these crematorium attendants stripped the bodies before they were incinerated.'

'Possible but unlikely,' the Vice Consul corrected. 'In a conventional cremation the family prepares the body. They may leave some jewellery on the body but it would be unusual. If it was an irregular cremation, we believe soldiers or officials would be witnesses. If they wanted to remove all evidence of Callum Jeffrey and his family, the fail-safe would be to incinerate everything.'

Harry nodded. He didn't want to share information about the tracker and how they had lost contact in less than one hour after the suitcase left the airport.

'OK, let's pick up Yaser and Asad this afternoon.'

Harry no longer marvelled over the wizardry of GCHQ in Cheltenham. In just over one hour, three encrypted sheets arrived at the Embassy. Two of them gave basic information on Yaser and Asad, full names, dates of birth, last known address and, most importantly, a photograph. It also provided a map of the crematorium and route they would follow to get home. The consensus was they would catch separate buses after a short walk from the crematorium. The other was an update on information relating to Callum Jeffrey with photos of his wife and daughter.

It was clear the brothers had done this sort of work before and took an active role in deciding the best places to intercept Yaser and Asad. It was decided two separate venues were best. The brothers had 'acquired' an ancient, cream coloured, Peugeot 404 station wagon. The number plates were from some wreck being dismembered in their scrap yard. One brother drove, Harry sat in front, the Cultural Attaché sat in the rear with the other brother. The plan was as simple as it was audacious. There were few workers at the crematorium and Yaser would have to take the long path around the back of the building towards the road. He would part company with Asad and then walk eight hundred metres or so along the road to the junction and bus stop. He would never reach it. The old Peugeot crawled a hundred metres behind Yaser until there was no one close by. The car accelerated and stopped just in front of him. The front and rear side doors opened and both the brothers got out. Yaser wasn't a young man and no match for two, young strong men. They had left the doors open and bundled Yaser into the car. It had taken seconds.

'What do you want, what do you want?' shouted Yaser in fright.

A solid blow to the ribs from a brother cut short the cry and replaced it with a groan. 'Shut your mouth,' was one of the few phrases Harry knew in Farsi but he delivered it with confidence. The brother in the rear cable-tied Yaser's hands and put a small sack over his head. As Harry turned to look at him, he saw Yaser trembling. It wasn't far to the lockup unit, but the brother drove them around in circles for a good twenty minutes. Eventually they arrived at the shuttered garage. The brother in the rear got out, unlocked and opened the garage shutter and closed it as soon as the station wagon was inside.

'Out,' he shouted at Yaser who struggled to get out of the car with his hands tied together. As the two brother roughly handled Yaser from the garage to the workshop the others followed. They sat Yaser in an old tubular steel and canvas chair, tied his body to the back and his arms to the arms of the chair. Harry could hear Yaser snivelling and began to say, 'I've done nothing.' A brother whispered something in his ear and the mumbling stopped.

Harry nodded and the sack was pulled off Yaser's head. A brother crouched in front of Yaser, his face only centimetres away. In a low growl, and in Farsi, he said:

'You rob the dead. While my brother's body was still warm, you stole from him! You stole from my family.'

'No, no, I'm just a worker ... my job is to place the dead inside the incinerator ... that's all I do ... I promise,' Yaser pleaded.

'You know the punishment for stealing, don't you?' asked the brother.

Yaser said nothing, but sweat was running down his face. His eyes were wide and appealing. The brother produced a wicked looking knife from nowhere.

'I'll remind you what we do to thieves ... we cut off four fingers from the right hand,' he said and laid the blade across Yaser's fingers. 'Unfortunately, this knife is sharp and will cut them off quickly ... better I use a blunt knife so I have to saw each one off,' he sneered.

Yaser started to speak and had just said, 'I didn't steal ...' when the brother slapped him across the face. Harry produced the colour photograph of the Omega Seamaster Chronograph and put it directly in front of Yaser's face.

'You stole this from the body of my brother, didn't you?' asked the brother.

The menace was so great in the words and tone it did not have to be shouted. Yaser simply sagged in the chair and sobbed as he nodded his head. The Third Secretary was a fluent Farsi speaker and playing the role of the 'good cop'. In a much softer tone and non-threatening he explained that he had some questions for Yaser. If he answered them truthfully, he would be taken back to the place he was picked up – unharmed. However, if he lied, he would lose four fingers from his right hand and be dumped by the side of the road - did he understand? He did.

The information then poured out of Yaser. He identified the 'special' as Callum Jeffrey, his wife Nazarene, and their daughter. He confirmed that all their luggage had been cremated at the same time, and that he and Asad had only taken the watch, and he was truly sorry. He admitted that there had been other 'specials' and the routine was always the same. They arrived in a white panelled van; the orderlies were from a private clinic: the Tukumani Clinic. As an afterthought, Yaser, who was very eager to please, announced that the army officer in charge was a colonel. The attaché had photographs of all the senior army officers on his phone. Colonel Hussein Zand, of the Quds Force, was quickly identified as the person involved in the murders of Callum Jeffrey, his wife and child. A few hours later, Harry and the team met with Asad in his small apartment. He was just as cooperative as his friend, and confirmed all that had been said.

Chapter 34

Meeting with Colonel Zand

Saturday 8th April 2023, 7:30 pm

The wizards working inside GCHQ Cheltenham had somehow sent a text message to Colonel Zand, from a name and number he would recognise, so that he would open it. The text message was not from whom he expected. It simply said:

Balthasar Restaurant

Miramar Hotel

7:30 pm, Saturday 8th April 2023

Do not be late

Harry Preece

Harry had reserved a table in an alcove from where he could see other diners entering. He was drinking a cup of coffee, and there was a thick manila envelope on the table in front of him. It had been a busy day; extracting information from the Indian jeweller, the two attendants at the crematorium, reading all the intel from Steel and Pendleton Price, and reviewing surveillance photos and video. If the meeting with Zand went well, it would be a very satisfactory day.

Harry saw Hussein Zand as he paused by the restaurant reception desk and talked, briefly, to the Maître D'hôtel. He had changed little since their last meeting. Harry wasn't surprised that Zand was now a colonel with twin rows of medal ribbon. When

Harry had been in Iran before, Zand had a code name. It was *Machiavelli,* and very apt – "the end justified the means". Zand had worked for Iranian Military Intelligence in both Syria and Yemen where Iran had taken an active part in the civil wars. When prisoners or civilians were interrogated, Zand was at the forefront, obtaining the information needed. Harry guessed his methods got him the medals and the promotion.

Zand had put on a little weight since their last meeting but it was well disguised by the tailor-made uniform. He strutted across the dining room as though he was on parade and in his best uniform. Harry noted that he was armed and seemed to ooze an arrogance. The same old Zand.

'So, Major Harry Preece returns to Iran! You know I can have you arrested and shot –like that!' and he clicked his fingers.

'No, you can't. I'm travelling on a diplomatic passport; the British Ambassador is dining with one of your ministers next door and there are half a dozen embassy staff in the building. It wouldn't be in your interest to draw undue attention to yourself.'

In a change of approach, Colonel Zand said:

'Do British soldiers no longer stand in the presence of a superior officer?'

'I don't regard you as a superior officer and I'm not in uniform. If you sit down, I have some information for you, and you have a decision to make.'

Colonel Zand sat down at the table and flicked an imaginary crumb from his place setting. He gave the surroundings a look of disdain – as though he was sitting by a hawker's stall in a back street. As he waited for Harry to speak, he signalled to the Maître D'hôtel, and slowly took a silver cigarette case from his pocket, selected a cigarette, and waited for the Maître D'hôtel to offer him a light. He never even turned to look at the man offering the light, or to thank him.

'You have some information for me?' said Zand as he blew

smoke across the table.

'Yes, we know it was Callum Jeffrey, also known as Khalid Jaffra, who planted the explosive devices on *Monroe Bravo*. The explosions killed 42 men and women – many of whom regarded this terrorist as a friend and colleague.'

Colonel Zand's face was impassive.

'We also know that Jeffrey travelled to Amsterdam, met with his wife and daughter, and travelled with them to Tehran on Tuesday 4th April, the day of the bombing.

'Within an hour of arrival, you had him and his family murdered at the Tukumani Clinic and incinerated at the Gulistan Crematorium.'

Zand made a flippant hand gesture as though to signal that these were petty details below his concern.

'The British Government would like to thank you for removing this terrorist from circulation. However, we believe Nazarene, his wife, knew nothing of his actions. We had no quarrel with Nazarene or her daughter. It would be interesting to learn what clerics within the Islamic Republic of Iran think about murdering citizens without trial. Oh yes, we have the names of witnesses to these deaths and the incineration of their bodies.'

Colonel Zand seemed irritable rather than concerned as he shifted in his chair.

'Is that all the information you have for me? If so, it is of little interest and I'll be leaving.'

'Oh, I have more information for you, I certainly do,' smiled Harry. 'We have known for several years that your small group of ministers, politicians, clerics and army officers have been misappropriating funds provided by your central government, and intended for the IRGC, to the Quds Force. You've been secretly buying TransGlobal Oil shares through brokers in Saudi Arabia, Dubai, Qatar, UAE and Kuwait.

'When Jeffrey exploded the bombs on *Monroe Bravo*, you instructed the brokers to sell off the shares, at critical times, to depress the share price. You were happy to sell shares, even at rock-bottom prices, if it served to destroy this oil company.'

Harry made an elaborate move to check the time on his watch.

'A few minutes ago, the Saudi Arabian Stock Market suspended your brokers. The Saudis have not only been alerted to the misappropriation of funds to buy shares, but abnormal share dealing related to the sale of TransGlobal Oil shares. The Saudis were extremely keen to cooperate. I understand your brokers have been arrested and are likely to face serious charges that may result in large fines and even imprisonment.

'It's really unfortunate because there was an announcement a few minutes ago, by TransGlobal Oil, that the fires on the *Monroe Bravo* Platform have been extinguished and it will be back in full production shortly. They expect the share price to soar to a level above what it was before the explosion. I also understand that TransGlobal Oil is buying millions of shares at rock-bottom prices. The company will be richer and stronger than before the bombing.'

Colonel Zand's face had lost any expression of arrogance. He was no longer lounging in the chair but sitting upright.

'The action also means that the money from the sale of your TransGlobal Oil shares will be frozen – for years. I suspect your government will be extremely unhappy about losing so much money. Oh, by the way, my friends have left a paper trail. It will appear that you diverted funds intended to buy TransGlobal Oil shares into a private account in Switzerland. The documents will be easy to find and the money is in your named account.'

'You forget, I have powerful friends, friends who will denounce these accusations as a Western conspiracy.'

'I'm sure you do have powerful friends; it's just a case of whether they will stand by you when all of this is in the newspapers and on the TV ... but let's move on.'

Harry picked up the thick manila envelope and handed it to Zand.

'I have a present for you ... please, open it ... it won't explode.'

Colonel Zand opened the envelope and took out the bundle of photos and documents. His eyes opened slightly at the sight of what was before him.

'We've known for some time that you've been visiting the wife of one of your fellow officers ... I think the first few night-time photos capture the evening light beautifully, your car number plate, and your distinctive profile. The quality of these cameras is so good these days you can enlarge the image massively. It will even show your name badge and row of medal ribbons.'

Zand dropped the bundle of photographs on the table as though they were of little interest.

'I've only included the last 30 days but we have the rest. If you turn to the colour coded chart, you'll see we noted the dates and times of each visit, and when you sent her husband off to some base or encampment, and when he was on active duty out of the city. There's a list of the cell phone calls and texts between your numbers. You've obviously been in close and regular contact with her.

'The other pictures are a selection of stills from video cameras we installed in certain rooms in the house; they're motion activated. I have to tell you, there's a lot of motion when you visit the home of your fellow officer. Your lady friend appears to be both inventive and athletic. I didn't have time to watch all of the footage, but here's a memory stick that has several hours of action on it.'

Harry removed a memory stick from his pocket and placed it on the table in front of Zand.

'It's all fake.'

'Hussein, we both know it's not fake. There are identifying

features on both your body and that of your lover. It will be easy for any investigator to confirm your movements, those of her husband, and the authenticity of the photos.

Both Harry and Hussein were silent for a few moments before Harry continued.

'I can imagine what will happen. Your fellow officer will drag his wife to the home of her parents. He'll denounce her as an adulterer, disown her, and leave her destitute. If she can get out of the country quickly, she may escape being stoned to death.'

Harry's body language and facial expression suggested he was unsure what would happen next.

'I'm told your colleague's family is orthodox Shi'a Muslim. It's my guess he'll tell his family of his shame … there'll be demands to satisfy family honour and he'll come looking for you.

'I doubt it would be a single bullet in the back of your head. I think he would want to make you suffer, as he is suffering. It could be hours, days, or weeks, but I think he'll want you to be aware that he is going to kill you. Quite honestly, I don't care if her husband shoots you, the mob stone you to death or they hang you … but I've been ordered to make you an offer.

'You can deny everything and take your chances, or you can answer a few questions. If you answer truthfully, all the photos and videos will be given to you – no copies. We'll tell you where the cameras are hidden, and your lover and her husband will never know.'

Over the last few minutes, Hussein Zand had been reeling in shock. He knew British and American security services would be investigating the fire on *Monroe Bravo* but never thought for a moment they would be so quick to discover how it had happened. He didn't understand the detail of the share buying and selling, but what Preece was saying sounded plausible. He was in no doubt about the reaction amongst some of his army colleagues, politicians and clerics: righteous indignation.

Zand was thinking rapidly. He may be able to pre-empt some of the charges against him, but it would be damage limitation. Compared to the death and destruction on *Monroe Bravo*, his affair with a married woman was minor. However, her husband's honour and his family would demand retribution – it would be difficult to survive.

'What are your questions?'

'We want to know the names and positions of the group that designed and manufactured the bombs that exploded on *Monroe Bravo*. Once we have verified them, all the photos and documents will be returned to you. The paper trail to your Swiss bank account will be deleted, and the witnesses to the murder and incineration of the Jaffra family will not be called to testify.'

'How can I trust you?

'You can't … but it's the best offer you're going to get. Of course, we'll check your information. If we think you haven't included everybody, or have substituted people, we'll release the information.

'I'm catching the late evening flight back to Amsterdam and on to London. I'm rather hoping you decide to die a martyr. If the embassy don't hear from you by eleven o'clock tomorrow, they will start the release of the information I've mentioned. Your fellow officer is back in town; he'll be the first to know.

'Well, I think that's all. I'm sure you've a lot to think about. I'll leave you to it.'

Harry got up and left Colonel Zand sitting at the table. A car was waiting for him outside the hotel. It would whisk him back to the Embassy for a debriefing, and then on to the airport.

Chapter 35

Knight in shining armour

Saturday 8th April 2023, 8:55 pm

'That's me done for the day. All I want now is a burger, a beer, and to hit the sack. I'll start again tomorrow,' Gene announced to an almost empty office.

Pamela, Tommy and the technicians had left almost one hour ago, and Harry was on his way back from Tehran. Penny realised she was also weary, and not being productive. She'd also call it a day and start again tomorrow.

'They've booked you into the Dunsmore Hotel in Bayswater,' said Penny. 'It's not far from my apartment. If we walk to the Westminster Tube station, we can catch a Tube on the Circle Line to our stop. The Dunsmore is a five to ten minute walk along Bayswater Road, due west. My apartment is five minutes' walk due east. Not sure if there are any burger bars – but I'm sure you'll find something.'

As Gene and Penny shut down their computers, Davie announced:

'I'll be here another hour or so. I want to catch the latest feed from Washington. Five o'clock in Washington will be ten o'clock here.'

There had been a shower of rain that had left a fresh and earthy smell behind as Penny and Gene walked towards Westminster. There were a few people about, some who were obviously tourists. The office workers had cleared the streets hours ago and it was too early for the theatre crowds. It was easy to negotiate the Tube station barriers, make their way to the platform where they had only a couple of minutes to wait for the train. It was whilst they were waiting for the west bound train that Gene announced:

'Last time I was in London was twelve years ago. I was a rookie, part of the detachment protecting President Obama ... first time outside the States. I thought it was so exciting. I still get the buzz from working on an incident, but savour the times we neutralise a threat before anything happens. It'll be interesting to discover if anything could have been done to stop the bombing of Monroe Bravo.'

The sound of the train approaching and the blast of wind as it pushed air ahead of it and onto the platform stopped any conversation. As the train slowed, they could see that it was almost empty, so no rush for a seat. They sat opposite a weary looking, middle-aged woman. She was holding a full shopping bag on her lap, almost resting her sleepy head on top of it. There was a slight delay before the train moved on. Suddenly, there was the sound of commotion on the platform. Three youths burst onto the train shouting, waving their arms, and pushing each other. One sprang through the doors, grabbed the steel handrail, and swung around it like an energetic pole dancer. He landed with his feet on the seat next to the woman with the shopping bag. Penny could see the shock and look of apprehension on her face. The other two youths were yelling as they jumped from seat to seat as though they were small trampolines.

As she tried to sink into her seat, the woman spilled her shopping bag, and a couple of apples tumbled out onto the seat beside her. The youth, who had just jumped off the seat to one across the aisle, picked them up. In a poor imitation of a circus act, he tried to juggle the two apples and failed. In frustration, he scouped up an apple from the floor and tossed it at his friend. It was caught and tossed back with a mindless yell.

Gene's arm shot out and caught the apple. The sharp smack as he caught it, and the sight of a suited man standing before them silenced the rowdy and now expectant trio. They had been looking for trouble, encouraging it, and now they thought they'd found it. The youth who had originally thrown the apple was closest to Gene. The other two were just behind him in the narrow aisle. Gene turned to the nearest youth, his arm outstretched as though offering the apple to him. A look of smug satisfaction swept across the youth's face. It was as though the 'ball boy' was doing what he was supposed to do – returning it to the main man. However, as the youth moved to take it, Gene flexed his hand and crushed the apple to a pulp. With his eyes fixed on the youth in front of him, he minced the remaining bits between his fingers.

Still maintaining his focus on the youth, and in a smooth, athletic action, Gene reached down and picked up the other apple from the seat. He tossed it in the air as though inviting the youth to collect it; he didn't, but Gene did. In his other hand, he crushed the apple to a pulp, moved towards the three youths, and whispered something to them. It was then that Penny noticed the difference in sizes: Gene was tall and muscular, a whole head above any of the youths and twenty to thirty kilos heavier than any of them. They backed away as the train slowed for the next stop and they left the train.

Gene was wiping his hands on a handkerchief as he approached the woman with the shopping bag.

'I'm sorry about your apples, ma'am. Can I offer to pay for them?'

In embarrassment, he added:

'I've only got American dollars.'

'I think I should be paying you ... thanks for what you did ... it was very brave.'

Gene smiled and returned to his seat as the train continued its journey towards its next stop.

'Very impressive ... you must have an amazingly strong grip. I've never seen an apple crushed like that.'

'Party trick ... it's really all in the technique, not the strength. I just wanted to calm the situation.'

'What did you say to them?'

Gene gave a little laugh.

'I told them I'd crush their balls to pulp if they didn't behave.'

Penny laughed too before her tone changed.

'Gene, those young men could have had knives.'

'And I've had years of training and lots of practice disarming men with knives. There was never a problem.'

Penny and Gene made their way from the train to the exit. Penny asked one of transport workers near the barrier if there was a shop selling hamburgers nearby, or a fast food place.

'Not this time of night, love. The sandwich bars open in the morning til mid-afternoon. There's a kebab house opposite, but that's about all. Fast food is more towards the centre,' he added before returning to a passenger who had lost his ticket.

Penny could smell the kebab house before she saw it. As they walked out of the exit to the Tube station, it was directly opposite.

'Well, maybe not a burger but do you want to try a kebab?'

They walked across the road, stood by the shop window, and looked in. A mis-shaped column of roasting meat was slowly turning on a spit. Gene recognised the unmistakeable smell of burnt fat and watched as it slowly dripped off the end of the meat roll. A server was slicing thin slivers of meat into a metal scoup. He watched as the server shovelled the pieces of meat inside a large bread bun, dumped a spoonful of other cooked food into it before a sauce was squirted over the top. It smothered everything.

'I think I've just lost my appetite.'

'I don't remember seeing any other fast food places between

here and my apartment. There may be one towards your hotel ... I'm not sure. I'm more than happy to make you a cheese sandwich. It's not very exciting but it won't be dripping in oil and fat.'

In Washington, an invitation to a woman's apartment, and an offer to make a sandwich, suggested more than a sandwich was on offer. Gene's tiredness disappeared and his ardour was aroused. As they walked to Penny's apartment, they talked about Gene's last visit to the UK.

'It was briefing, work, eat and sleep ... certainly no sightseeing. A bit like this trip. I guess as soon as this is over, I'll be off to somewhere else in the world.'

Gene hoped he was making it clear that if anything happened, it would be a one-night stand. There would be no complications. Penny negotiated the front door security keypad, and they walked into the apartment.

'Wow, what a smart apartment ... and so neat.'

The walls were painted white. There were several paintings on them, lit by small lights in brass fittings. Honey-coloured carpets and large light brown leather chairs and sofas blended into the lounge. Soft downlighters and table lamps completed a fresh but cosy room.

'My father is a great negotiator and my mum has good taste. He found it and my mum had it redecorated and furnished; I just have to pay the mortgage. Choose a CD and I'll get us a sandwich.'

When Penny returned with two plates, a beer in a tankard and a glass of wine, Gene was sitting on the sofa, head back, listening to Ella Fitzgerald. She put the beer, glass of wine and sandwich on a side table, and sank into one of the big leather chairs opposite Gene. He took a sip of the beer, and began to negotiate the next hurdle. He looked across at Penny and asked:

'Tommy told me that one of the guys who shut down the oil pipeline, spotted the bomb, and towed divers to safety is your friend. He must be quite a guy,'

'He is. Sandro, another friend, was with him, and one of the other divers helped tow the stranded divers to safety.'

'It's still pretty amazing. I had to do some diving as part of my training. Great in warm, clear blue water ... scared the shit out of me in the cold and dark. It was one of the reasons I transferred to land based security. Shame I won't have the chance to meet him. Tell him next time he's in Washington to call in.'

Penny had been thinking about Jack at times throughout the day, and how she had left the relationship between them. She now realised the abrupt way she had ended the conversation had been churlish. Jack and Sandro had been under tremendous pressure ... *she'd* been under pressure ... but she'd made no allowance. She would phone Jack tonight.

'I suppose it's only when you think you've lost someone that you realise how much they mean to you. I thought I'd lost Jack when he was declared missing.'

Gene's ardour disappeared as he realised Penny's invitation had just been kind and considerate. He finished his sandwich and beer, thanked her, and set off on his way back to his hotel.

Chapter 36

Praise and promotion

Sunday 9th April 2023, 7:15 am

Penny was in the office early. The intensity caused by the initial explosions and fires on *Monroe Bravo* had passed, but there were several avenues that were being explored by her teams. She'd waded through the voicemails, noted any action, added the information to the timeline, her report, and opened her email. The first email, with an attachment, was from Captain Stanford, the Army Bomb Disposal Officer. He'd sent it late last night. It was a report on the unexploded bomb that had been retrieved from the *Monroe Bravo* Diving Bell. The good news was that the report was written in simple English and easy to understand. The disturbing content described the destructive force of the device and the intended effect.

Stanford explained that the device contained two and a half kilograms of military grade explosive. It was a big bomb and if detonated at ninety metres, three things would have happened. Firstly, shock waves would have instantly destroyed the Diving Bell and thus any chance of shutting down the Platform at the seabed. Secondly, it would have destroyed two or three of the closest Platform legs, severely damaged two or three others, and weakened those remaining. Thirdly, the shock waves would have severely damaged any ship directly above. Penny focused on the effect on the Platform.

By destroying two or three legs, the unsupported part of the Platform would either have broken away and fallen into the sea, or, more likely, have sagged towards the sea and pulled the nearby structure with it. This would have exerted enormous pressure on the rest of the Platform. Stanford speculated that the effect of the fires would have weakened the structure even further and resulted in the whole Platform being dragged from its base and to the bottom of the North Sea. He also thought this would have happened in hours rather than days. It would have been catastrophic, with dozens of lives lost and millions of gallons of oil and gas venting into the sea and air around the Platform.

There was a sound in the corridor outside the office. Penny suddenly realised that she had stopped concentrating. She was thinking about Jack, and what would have happened if the bomb had gone off whilst he was close. She then recalled her reaction to hearing Jack was missing during the rescue of the stranded divers, and realised how much he meant to her. She was so glad she had phoned him last night.

Penny's attention was again distracted for a moment by the American voices next door. It sounded like Gene and Davie had just arrived, and were talking. She heard their coffee machine being set up, and returned to Stanford's report. In the next section, she read how a faulty electronic component, costing less than a single barrel of oil, had caused the device not to detonate. Penny sat silently for a moment, thankful that the full horrors of the planned explosions had not occurred. It was only when she read on that she noted an odd remark. It read: "Device operational and ready for deployment".

Penny was about to turn to the next email, the one from Harry Preece, when Tommy Steel walked through the door, carrying two paper cups of coffee and two paper bags.

'It was "buy one get one free" – couldn't resist.'

Then, confidingly, he added:

'I find the American coffee too strong. Any major developments?'

Penny gave him the summary of Captain Stanford's report and explained Harry had sent a report from Tehran which she was about to read. Tommy didn't walk away.

'Are you OK? You look a bit down ... I bet you haven't had any breakfast ... just as well I brought the coffee and a bun,' he said with a smile.

Tommy was observant. He'd spotted that she wasn't behaving normally. It's what made him a good copper.

'Just been talking to Alice. She appreciates all the work we've been doing and expects the intensity of the *Monroe Bravo* investigation to ease next week. If you want a break, you could leave on Friday afternoon, and be back in the office Monday afternoon. Just let me know what you want to do. If there's another emergency, you can always come back. I've no plans to go anywhere, so I'll be around.'

Penny returned to her emails and opened the attachment from Harry that he'd sent from the embassy in Tehran. It was a succinct account of tracing the watch to Callum Jeffrey, his death and that of his wife and child, their cremation, and the involvement of Colonel Hussein Zand. It ended with an explanation of how he hoped to get the names and contact details of the bombers from him. A final note in the email explained that Colonel Zand had been given an eleven o'clock deadline, Tehran time, to supply the names. Harry hoped to be in the office by this deadline.

Just as Penny looked up to see what time it was, Harry walked through the door. If you didn't know he'd been working in Tehran for a couple of days and just got off a long flight, you wouldn't have guessed. He looked like the same, relaxed Harry. It was only the stubble on his chin that told a different story.

Hi, I'm back,' Harry announced. Tommy got to his feet.

Gene and the others must have heard Harry's arrival because they all walked through the door and into the Coordination Room. With outstretched arms, Gene strode towards him saying:

'Harry, you've done it again ... what a man!'

Harry couldn't escape the hug from Gene, and Penny could tell he felt awkward and slightly embarrassed; Harry wasn't a hugger – at least not with men.

'OK, tell us about it,' said Gene as Tommy and the others joined the group around the large table.

'Get me a cup of your coffee and I'll bring you up to speed,' was all Harry said as he sat down heavily in a chair.

Over the next few minutes, Harry elaborated on the brief report he'd submitted from Tehran. He was fulsome in his praise for staff at the embassy and how their painstaking surveillance of Colonel Hussein Zand had paid dividends. This morning, whilst traveling from the airport to the office, he'd heard that Zand had supplied the names and contact details of the bombers.

'Do you believe him?' asked Gene.

'I don't believe anybody until I've got rock solid evidence. Between us we can check out the names and confirm if they really are the bombers – it will take a little time. Once confirmed, I guess they'll be terminated.'

'…. and Zand?' asked Gene.

'To be decided. Despite what I told him, it's likely the husband of his lover will get a copy of the videos and stills. My guess is that within forty eight hours Zand will be dead.'

It was Penny who reacted immediately to his off-hand comment.

'That would be a mistake! Instead of having him murdered, we should be getting him promoted to Brigadier, getting him another row of medals. He's already a traitor, he's crossed the line ... he's made a major decision to survive, so we should be using him to get more information out of him rather having him killed.'

'Elaborate,' was all Tommy said.

'Harry told us that Zand is smart, ruthless, ambitious and vain

… we should be exploiting these traits rather than getting him replaced by someone who may be even worse. We've got levers on Zand … maybe none with his successor.'

The random ideas that had been rattling around in her head suddenly crystalised.

'Here's an alternative, but I'll need your help in refining it.'

Penny breathed deeply, and started on her alternative.

'We provide Zand with a collection of case files of real or invented Quds Force operations; a mixture of those that could be judged to have been successful and those that were a disaster. We'd need to ensure they are credible and survive detailed scrutiny. With Zand's cooperation, we can amend and add to these to create an impressive dossier. We then get Zand to request a meeting with the IRGC chief of staff … not sure how easy or difficult this would be. Perhaps Zand says the meeting relates to an issue of national importance; it's highly confidential. He's probably never requested such a meeting before. Assuming he is in good standing, the chances are the meeting will be granted.

'At the meeting Zand announces that he believes there is a traitor somewhere inside Army Chief of Staff Headquarters. It will be a bombshell that will get the Chief of Staff's attention. Zand then announces he has had these suspicions for months, if not longer.'

Penny paused for a moment before adding:

'The time scale he mentions will depend on the case files assembled and what Zand can confirm. He then explains that many Quds missions have been intercepted, personnel killed, equipment destroyed, and operations disrupted. He also mentions other army operations that have gone badly. We know of some – like the drones to Russia being impounded, but he will know of others. We may be able to provide other examples that the Iranians have tried to keep secret. As a result, he says he has disobeyed orders.

'As soon as Zand says he has disobeyed orders, the chief of staff will really sit up and pay attention. Zand then goes on to explain that for some operations he has continued to forward details to headquarters but for others he hasn't, he's kept them a secret. He knew this was wrong but needed confirmation of a traitor. He says he's also laid traps for the traitor by forwarding sensitive information to Army HQ and checked up who had access and what action was taken.

'He can describe two or three operations that Quds planned, but which ended in failure. He can make it sound as though the Americans, the Israelis, the Brits must have been tipped off. He'll argue there's no other explanation. He then goes on to describe two or three operations that were unknown to Headquarters. He could include the bombing of *Monroe Bravo* but at the moment we don't know if he passed on that information. We can decide what to reveal about the fifth bomb. He could say if was just bad luck that it didn't explode, or suggest we were tipped off.

'He could say he was ordered to divulge the name of his agent, Shirin Mousari, to the person he suspected as the traitor. He says she was extremely effective and undetected for years, but within days of her existence being known she was detained in the US. We can help Zand create a convincing case that suggests a traitor is present.'

The ideas were now flowing like a torrent, with Penny becoming increasingly animated. She continued.

'Zand could mention a forthcoming operation to, say, blow up an Israeli Army barracks in Tel Aviv or some other place. If the Israelis are offered future intel from Zand, I suspect they would allow an explosion inside a barracks, empty of course, and then let the two-way propaganda run for days. If Zand predicts an explosion at an Israeli barracks, it reinforces his credibility.'

Penny paused again but no one interrupted her.

'I'd need to confirm, but I think the Head of Iranian Military

Intelligence is part of the Chief of Staff Headquarters. We know that Zand is a former Intelligence Officer. We could generate misinformation to discredit whoever is Head of Military Intelligence, and work towards Zand replacing him. When pressed to name the suspected traitor, he could identify the Head of Military Intelligence. If we can provide Zand with credible information, he's on his way to Brigadier and another medal. We play on his ambition and vanity, and get him firmly entrenched in Army Headquarters. We get inside information for, months if not years.'

There was silence around the table as the enormity of what Penny was suggesting was considered. It was Harry who responded first.

'Penny's right … it would be a mistake to eliminate Zand. He's far more useful alive than dead.'

Harry took a deep breath and looked up before continuing.

'Afraid I made a classic error … I allowed myself to be driven by revenge rather than reason. I wanted Zand dead and didn't want to think beyond that. He's responsible for the death of a close friend in Yemen, and I wanted to avenge his death. However, as a traitor and informer, he's sentenced to a living death. He'll never know when his cover is about to be blown and when the knock at the door will signal the end.'

'Gene, what are your thoughts?' asked Tommy.

Gene was self-assured as he looked around the table.

'Thank you, Chief Superintendent. Washington has anticipated the question and shared their thinking with me. They note Zand's rapid promotion and what he's done to get it – not a pretty story. They believe that the bombing of *Monroe Bravo* represents an escalation in his actions and will have emboldened him, as well as the IRGC and Quds Force. Our analysts are of the opinion that even though the Platform was not completely destroyed, and Quds Force suffered massive financial losses, they will regard it as a victory and a spur to future activity.

'Their recommendation is to terminate Colonel Hussein Zand at the earliest opportunity. It is believed it will disrupt the Quds Force and send a strong message to Iranian leaders.'

Penny was the first the react.

'If we are considering courses of action, I can suggest an obvious one. We orchestrate a visit by members of the Iranian Military, including Zand, to a country that has an extradition treaty with the UK or USA. He could be detained, charged, extradited and put on trial. If we do have the evidence to convict him, he will be convicted.'

Tommy turned to Penny.

'I agree with your sentiments. The track record and threat of Zand is not in doubt. Whilst I suspect the Police Commissioner will be reluctant to agree to Zand's assassination, he could be overruled.

'In terms of bringing him to court … I think it would be difficult to plan such an extradition. As far as I am aware, there are dozens of countries that have extradition treaties with the UK and USA. However, I think it's highly unlikely Zand would expose himself to detention in any of these countries. Harry, any thoughts?'

Harry paused to consider what to say.

'The direct and immediate threat to Zand may have paid off. It depends if the names he gave are in fact the bombers. He's smart enough and ruthless enough to play for time until he can neutralise the threat. We'll know soon enough if the captain and his wife disappear.

'If the extradition option is to be pursued, I think Iraq or Gaza would be the best bets. We know he's been active in Gaza, and there are missions between Iran and Iraq.

'One thing is for certain, payment won't work with Zand – but playing on his ambition and vanity will. The idea of helping him gain further promotion and gongs has a nice ring to it. Penny's idea of working with the US, Israel, and the UK government to create Quds Force successes or rather apparent successes is attractive.

'We know the Israelis defuse and store IEDs and captured munitions, and eventually blow them up. We could arrange with the Israelis for a store on a military base to be blown up. It should be simple to choose a store with reinforced walls so that only the roof is blown off and nobody is hurt. Quds Force claims credit for the attack, the Israelis dispute it, a whistle-blower announces it was an Iranian attack and, yes, Zand gets the credit.

'With a bit of ingenuity, we can devise a series of incidents which are the work of Quds Force and Zand. He gets the credit, and the promotion, and *we* get a mole in the Iranian General Staff who supplies us with Grade One Intel for years.'

'Gene?' asked Tommy.

'I'm not opposed to the idea of recruiting Zand, but it's high risk. We demonstrated how easy it was to create a bank account for Zand, and put money in. What if he feeds us low grade intel for months until he has stashed sufficient cash and then disappears? Even worse, lures us into a trap with multiple casualties and unbelievably bad press?

'I'd feel happier if we outlined the options and passed it upstairs. Haven't we got a meeting with Commander Short on Monday? If we put our heads together, we could assemble the various options and get her reaction.'

It didn't take long to agree Gene's strategy and to start on the options.

Chapter 37

Double agent

Monday 10th April 2023, 1:30 pm

From the evidence assembled, Commander Alice Short was in no doubt; a group within the Islam Revolutionary Guard Corps, the Quds Force, had planned and conducted the bombing of *Monroe Bravo*. The forthcoming meeting with Steel, Preece, Pendleton Price and the US Homeland Security Team would be an opportunity to get a reaction to the proposed action.

Surprisingly, Harry Preece was early for the meeting with Commander Short; he was sitting outside her office.

'Harry, why don't you come through whilst we wait for the others?' she suggested.

Harry didn't reply, but merely stood up and followed Alice through her secretary's office and into hers. She picked up a file from her desk and sat at the large round table that dominated her office, Harry joined her.

'How well do you know Colonel Zand and what's he like as a person?'

'I don't know him … but our paths have crossed several times.'

Harry was silent for a moment whilst he pondered what to say next.

'I'd describe him as smart, ambitious, vain and ruthless. He's not a leader, more a driver, but he gets results, though he doesn't get his hands dirty anymore.'

'Elaborate.'

'I first came across him in Syria during the civil war about ten years ago. I was part of a UN Peace Keeping Team when I first met him. It was a routine meeting designed to "keep channels of communication open". He was a junior military intelligence officer, a Lieutenant within the IRGC, and I was surprised he was present because he was so junior, but he had a certain presence within the Iranian contingent. I remember him being confident, opinionated, verging on arrogant, in front of his more senior officers. A short while later, he came to our attention as a particularly brutal interrogator of both military and civilian personnel.

'Our paths crossed again in Yemen under similar circumstances. He was now a combat officer and had been promoted to captain. There were disturbing stories emerging of summary executions, forcing villagers at gun point to walk through mine fields, and gas attacks. We raised this with the Iranian commander who said the young officer responsible had been redeployed. I remember because he called his colleague a "zealot" – an odd choice of word. Zand was later credited with organising one of the Palestinian uprisings on the West Bank. When the Israelis reacted so firmly, we gather he returned to Iran, and was later made Commander of the Quds Force and promoted to colonel.'

There was a noise in the next office as Steel, Pendleton Price and the Americans arrived for the meeting with Alice. The secretary showed them through, and they took their seats. There was no agenda, and there would be no minutes, but the outcome could be serious. Alice didn't waste any time.

'This morning I attended a COBRA meeting with government ministers, the Commissioner and Head of MI6 regarding the fire on *Monroe Bravo*'.

Alice turned to Gene and explained.

'It's a high level, government, emergency response committee that meets to handle potentially disruptive or significant matters of national, regional or international significance. This morning it was chaired by the Prime Minister.'

'The committee were in no doubt that agents of the Iranian Quds Force, led by Colonel Hussein Zand, planned and executed the bombing. On the basis of the report you submitted on Zand, a decision has been made to recruit him as an informer with immediate effect.

'I'm aware there are several existing lines of enquiry, and these need to be pursued. However, I'm hoping these can be concluded in the near future and this incident wound down.'

Alice looked around the table, her eyes settling on Special Agent Dilks.

'I'd welcome your comments.'

Gene turned to his colleagues around the table, and smiled.

'Commander, before I comment I'd like to make an observation. You've got a great trio here and great teams in the field. It was a pleasure to be part of it. You'll be aware of Washington's reservations about recruiting Zand but we accept that if successful, it could provide valuable intelligence. We'd only urge the closest of surveillance and termination if he tries to play us. We're working on Shirin Mousari – she's already given us some valuable information; the Israelis are delighted. We'll obviously keep you informed.'

Gene paused for a moment before continuing.

'I've been recalled to Washington ... there's been an incident in Kansas City. Pamela will head our team until such time as you decide to scale down the current operation and the team returns to Washington.'

'Tommy?'

'We're systematically investigating every contact and friend of Callum Jeffrey and his wife Nazarene. It looks as though they'll be cleared of any complicity. We believe that Nazarene knew nothing of her husband's intentions and action. It also looks as though her husband's contacts at the Mosques have returned to Iran. I doubt they will be travelling outside the country in the near future.'

'Penny?'

'Nothing that isn't in the report.'

'Harry?'

'An update from Captain Stanford this morning. He's confirmed the military grade explosive in the bomb he retrieved is similar to that used by the Iranian Army. It's not been possible, so far, to link it to a specific source of production. We've been unable to determine how the devices were brought into the country but the Diplomatic Bag was not discounted.'

In the coordination office, afternoon tea and cakes, coffee and doughnuts marked the start of scaling down the wider operation. It would soon be replaced by the long slog of data gathering, analysis, and interpretation. It would no doubt culminate in a report by some official board of enquiry.

As Gene washed down the remains of a doughnut with coffee, be grabbed Harry by the hand.

'Harry, it's been a pleasure. You certainly lived up to Oscar's hype. I reckon if anyone can keep on top of Zand, and get the most out of him, it's you.'

Next, he turned to Tommy.

'You've got a great team here and most of it is because of you. If you are passing through Washington, call in. There's a lot our guys can learn from you.

With a big smile on his face, and with open arms, Gene hugged Penny.

'Penny, I'll never forget your comments on Lord Byron's raven-haired beauty. You'll be pleased to know I've even read the poem. That comment alone helped us crack a case. Jack's a lucky guy.'

Chapter 38

Playing the long game

Monday 10th April 2023, 6:00 pm, Ouds Headquarters, Tehran

Colonel Zand had been stunned by the speed at which the British had uncovered his plan to destroy the *Monroe Bravo* Platform. He'd also been shocked to learn he had been under surveillance, and incriminating evidence had been collected against him. He needed time to think, time to mitigate the fallout from the failed operation, and eliminate dangers. The most immediate danger was posed by his fellow Quds Force Officer. It was the threat of passing on the folder of compromising photos and videos, lists of times and dates. He knew that if he wasn't killed by this officer, one of his relatives would willingly take on the task; he knew he wouldn't be able to survive the affair.

Hussein didn't agonise over his decision. He accepted the proposal from Harry Preece and, well before the eleven o'clock deadline, passed on the names of those who had designed and manufactured the bombs. He assumed they would be eliminated – but better them than him. Hussein was still angry about the fifth bomb. If it had exploded, nothing could have saved the Platform from destruction. He recalled the computer simulation that revealed the devastation the submerged bomb would have caused. The Diving Bell and several Platform legs would have been totally destroyed. The weakened structure would have collapsed into the sea – a massive blow against the West. On reflection, he knew he could always find other bomb designers and makers. Whilst he reluctantly accepted he had lost the last battle, he would win the war. It was time to play the long game.

Hussein was further surprised by the speed at which the British Cultural Attaché made contact, outlined their plans and their demands. Perversely he realised these could be to his advantage. At one level, it was merely a case of carefully revising the proposed dossier, blending fact and fiction, to create a traitor within the Army Central Command. At another, it provided opportunities for self-promotion and to undermine rivals. It was when the Cultural Attaché suggested the current head of Military Intelligence could be targeted as a traitor that Zand actually warmed to the idea. The brigadier general had been his commanding officer when he was in Military Intelligence. It was him who had questioned his interrogation methods and had him transferred to Syria, and almost got him killed. If he played it correctly, there could be a significant reward for the person who identified a traitor. There would also be a vacancy for the head of Military Intelligence, at the rank of Brigadier General, perhaps, and a place within Army Central Command.

However, Zand was no fool. Whilst he knew it would take weeks and months to create a fool-proof dossier, the cultural attaché and Harry Preece would be wanting information from him. They would carefully assess any intel he provided and if they thought he was being less than forthcoming, he would be exposed. They'd simply cut him loose.

He reassured himself that as long as he was regarded as a valuable asset to them, he was safe. Whilst this was happening, he would eliminate close threats and start to amass funds that would allow him to disappear and start a new life elsewhere. When this happened, he would send a clear message to Harry Preece and the British Government. The two men that saved the *Monroe Bravo* Platform would have an unfortunate accident.

Chapter 39

A Good News Day

Tuesday 11th April 2023, 3:00 pm

On return to their *Marine Salvage & Investigation Company* office in Salford, Jack and Sandro faced a one week backlog of correspondence. They'd spent the morning wading through dozens of emails and messages – deleting some but replying to many. In the afternoon, they started on the Calls for Tender file that was waiting for them. The good news was that their main asset, the MV *Stavanger*, was under a lucrative standby contract to TransGlobal Oil. However, they still had to find work for the MV *Sultano*, and look ahead for work when the *Stavanger* contract expired.

Jack reached across the desk for the Calls for Tender file, and remarked:

'I've seen nothing so far that is worth tendering for and in a few minutes we've got to drive to Salford Quays for the interview with the BBC. I now regret being talked into it. We're going to hit all the rush hour traffic on the way back.'

'Oh, come on Jack, it'll be a new experience. Consider it free publicity.'

Jack was about to reply when Lesley rang to transfer a call.

'Jack, it's Walter Brachs, TransGlobal Oil, phoning from Houston, Texas. I'll put him through.'

'Good morning, Mr Brachs. It's a pleasant surprise to hear from you. The phone is on speaker, and Sandro is with me. How can we help?'

'Good afternoon Mr Collier ... Mr Calovarlo,' announced Walter Brachs in a distinct Texan drawl. 'You will be pleased to know that thanks to your efforts, and that of your colleagues, *Monroe Bravo* will resume full production in the near future. Rick Johnson also tells me he's reassured by the presence of your ship, the *Stavanger*.'

'That's good to hear.'

'Gentlemen, the TransGlobal Board have considered reports by Norton Flynn, Rick Johnson, and a statement from Commander Alice Short of the Office for Security and Counter Terrorism, New Scotland Yard, in relation to the explosions and fire on *Monroe Bravo*. It wishes to acknowledge the service you and your company gave to us at a critical time.'

'We were just doing the job we were contracted to do.'

'Let me correct you. Your contract with TransGlobal was not due to start until Wednesday 5th April 2023; you were on station early. What's more, diving to ninety metres in the British North Sea, locating a bomb, and saving the lives of nine of our staff was over and above the terms of any contract.'

Jack and Sandro did not reply.

'The Board has approved a financial reward to Gunnar Larson, to you, and Sandro for your roles in rescuing our divers from the damaged Diving Bell. You will find that TransGlobal Oil is a generous partner.

'It has also asked me, on behalf of TransGlobal Oil, to offer the *Marine Salvage & Investigation Company* a proposal. We would like to extend the current standby contract for the MV *Stavanger* for a further two years. The terms and conditions of the existing contract would remain. It would be merely extended to a three year period. If you accept the offer, and I hope you do, our lawyers could have a revised contract to you in the near future.'

Jack and Sandro were stunned. A reward and a two year

extension, on the same terms and conditions, was better than their wildest dreams! Furthermore, everyone in the industry would be aware of the significance of the offer. Being courted by TransGlobal Oil, one of the largest and most profitable companies in the world, was too good to miss.

'Mr Brachs, I don't know what to say ... that's an unexpected reward and a very generous offer. Could you hold for a few moments whilst Sandro and I chat?'

'Sure ... as long as it is only a few moments.'

Jack cupped his hand over the mouthpiece.

'It's a no-brainer,' said Sandro immediately. 'We thought the one-year contract was good. An extension to three years would be great. It keeps the ship working and represents a massive show of confidence in us. I say yes.'

Jack moved his hand from the phone's mouthpiece.

'Mr Brachs, we'd be delighted to accept the proposal. We'll look forward to receiving the revised contract and will return it promptly.'

'That's excellent. Have a nice day,' said Brachs before putting the phone down.

The phone call left Jack and Sandro with a delicious quandary and a different perspective on the pile of tenders in front of them. What to do with the unexpected windfall, and how they could now be selective when seeking work for the *Sultano*. However, a vastly different scenario was unfolding in Walter Brachs' office.

No sooner had Brachs spoken to Jack and Sandro than Norton T. Flynn was ushered into his office. Brachs gestured for him to sit as he arranged several slim booklets on his desk.

'Norton, the TransGlobal Board has considered your report, one from Rick Johnson, and a statement from Commander Alice Short, OSCT, into the explosions and fire on *Monroe Bravo*. It notes your achievement since the fire, and your effort in returning the Platform to full production.

'You're no doubt aware that the authorities believe you were targeted, and manipulated, by a terrorist group to circumvent the very security procedures you had installed. Your decision to switch off your phone before the attack took place, and being unavailable at a critical time is a direct breach of our operating procedure. It led to a delay in your response and is inexcusable.'

Norton Flynn sat forwards on the edge of his chair, hands on his thighs, looking at the carpet. He knew precisely what was coming.

'The Board has asked for your resignation as Vice President, Scotland. We expect you to vacate the post at the end of the month.'

Well, there it was. At least he could resign, and not be sacked. Except everyone in the industry would know. It was doubtful he'd get an equivalent job anywhere, even if he wanted one. He'd be a pariah, but he could go with some dignity.

'Sir, I have already written my letter of resignation. I'd like to offer it now,' said Norton as he retrieved the envelope and placed it in front of Brachs.

'Thank you,' Brachs said, ignoring the envelope on his desk.

Norton started to get up, believing the meeting was over, but Brachs gestured for him to remain seated.

'The Board would like to invite you apply for the post of Vice President, exploration, South Georgia, to commence one month after you vacate your current post. We believe the incident in Aberdeen, whilst regrettable, does not invalidate your value to the company. I'm sure you will strive to make our venture in South Georgia a success.'

'I'm humbled, sir. I was resigned to leaving TransGlobal Oil and feel I've been given another chance. I'm grateful, but I wasn't aware we had plans for oil or gas exploration in South Georgia. I understood those deposits were unviable.'

'We are not talking about South Georgia USA or even South Georgia, Eastern Europe. We're talking about the British Overseas Territory of South Georgia and Sandwich Islands. It lies 1400 kilometres east of the Falklands Islands, off the tip of southern Argentina. If all goes well, I'd expect you to be transferred to a more, er … comfortable post in the future.'

Chapter 40

A few minutes of fame

Tuesday 11th April 2023, 4:30 pm

Lucy Rottmuller was the consummate professional. She didn't dwell on setbacks, but looked forwards. She knew the fire on *Monroe Bravo* was a big story and she was determined to claim as much of it as she could. There would be time to arrange news items about the dead and injured, and coverage of a future public enquiry. She also heard rumours that terrorist action was being considered. If so, the story would run for a while longer. In the short term, she had the chance to interview the heroes of the hour; it was too good to miss.

With Norton's help, Lucy's PA had been able to contact Jack and Sandro when they'd emerged from decompression, and arranged an interview at the BBC studios in Salford Quays near Manchester. The interview could cement Lucy's position as the lead journalist on this story. A studio slot had been booked, and Lucy was trying to persuade the evening news producers to make space for a short piece with the two divers who had shut down *Monroe Bravo* and saved nine divers from suffocation. She was also researching the backgrounds of both Jack and Sandro.

As Lucy walked into the hospitality suite at the BBC studios, she spotted her PA with the two interviewees. As she got closer, one of the men captured her complete attention. Initially, it was the way the man was standing and how he towered over her PA. He had a certain poise – like a dancer or an athlete. When she got up close, she changed her initial impression: he looked like a male model with slightly long, black curly hair, a tanned complexion, and trendy 'five o'clock shadow'. He was wearing an orange polo shirt that set off his tanned, muscular arms. It had been a long time since Lucy was so enchanted by a man.

She turned on a genuine, million-dollar smile, held out her hand, and introduced herself. Sandro returned the smile and held her hand for a couple of seconds longer than normal as he returned her gaze. Both felt the warm softness of their hands and recognised an instance rapport between them. It was the PA who broke the spell, introduced Jack Collier, and focused the group on the forthcoming interview. Lucy had drafted a series of questions that would be the core of the interview. They'd been drafted to lead the divers into saying Rick Johnson had manipulated them into undertaking the dive, and then the rescue of the stranded divers. Lucy was briefing her two interviewees on how the interview would work when her PA returned.

'We've got three minutes, live, on the six o'clock news, and repeated on other services.'

Jack and Sandro were ushered through make-up, sound checks and interview set-up well before the news started. They were gazing at themselves on the TV monitor. Over three hundred kilometres away, in London, Tommy switched on the six o'clock news and the team gathered around. With a backdrop of *Monroe Bravo* ablaze, the news presenter introduced Lucy Rottmuller for her item. Lucy paused for a split second before announcing:

'Just one week ago a series of explosions tore through the *Monroe Bravo* Oil & Gas Platform. We now understand forty two men and women are reported as dead or missing, while others are receiving treatment in hospital. At the time, we thought millions of cubic metres of gas and millions of barrels of crude oil would pour into the North Sea. We believed the fires were out of control and an environmental disaster was unfolding.

'However, we now know that two visitors to the Platform, Jack Collier and Sandro Calovarlo, owners of the *Marine Salvage &*

Investigation Company, risked their lives to dive to the seabed.'

The camera panned to Jack and Sandro. Penny was suddenly overwhelmed by emotion. There was Jack, there was Sandro. The feeling seemed to rise from the tips of her toes and burst all over her. Tears welled and began to roll down her face; her throat was clamped shut; she was speechless as the presenter continued.

'... shut down both the natural gas and crude oil pipelines within minutes of the explosions. Any oil that escaped in those first few minutes has been recovered or dispersed ... it will not end up in the ocean or on Scottish beaches.

'Not content with saving the Platform, they remained at ninety metres below the North Sea, and towed nine divers from a damaged Diving Bell to the safety of a separate Diving Bell.'

Penny fought to gain control as she stared at the TV screen and listened intently.

'I have with me those two heroes, Jack Collier and Alessandro Calovarlo.'

Addressing Sandro, she asked:

'What were you doing on the *Monroe Bravo* Platform, Mr Calovarlo?'

'Just visiting – we were celebrating our contract with TransGlobal Oil, to provide a standby ship, the *MV Stavanger,* and were invited onto the Platform. I'm afraid we were in the wrong place at the wrong time.'

Sandro looked relaxed. His fluent English, with an obvious Italian accent, merely added to his charm. It was clear to Penny that the interviewer was captivated.

'When did you first realise there was a problem?'

'When an explosion blows you off your feet, and sends you skidding across a steel deck, you realise there's a problem pretty quickly,' replied Sandro with a smile.

Were you hurt?' Lucy asked with genuine concern.

'No, just a bruise on my backside, but Rick Johnson broke a couple of ribs and suffered a nasty gash on his forehead.'

In that moment, Lucy realised she'd never asked Dr Johnson about any injuries. She recalled the blackened plaster on his forehead but had dismissed it … she didn't know why.

'In an earlier interview, Dr Rick Johnson vividly described your journey along walkways and down ladders. He described the intense heat, the burning oil cascading all around you, clothing smouldering and the soles of your boots melting …'

'Yes, we only survived because we were with Rick Johnson and Konrad, the dive supervisor. It was their knowledge of the Platform that guided our route to safety … we just followed them.'

'When did Dr Rick Johnson, the OIM on *Monroe Bravo*, ask you to dive to the seabed and shut down the Platform?'

'He didn't; we volunteered. We could see the crane supporting the Diving Bell was on fire and had failed … the pipes delivering oxygen and helium to the dives were ablaze, and the divers had told us the reserve oxygen tank had been ruptured. They were going to suffocate in a couple of hours if they didn't get gases to breathe, or get out.'

'Have you ever dived to those depths before?'

'Yes … but not often, and not in the North Sea and not without back up. We knew that if we didn't tow them to safety, they'd die.'

Lucy turned to Jack, glanced at her notes, and asked:

'What was it like … towing divers from the stricken Diving Bell to the safety of another Bell?'

'Pretty cold for the divers we were towing, and tiring for us.'

'I understand you had a problem … you were reported as missing … what happened?'

There was no way Jack was going to tell the world what

actually happened. He'd heard that the diver he had saved had made a full physical recovery, but was still undergoing psychiatric assessment.

'The conditions in the North Sea, and at ninety metres on the seabed, are extreme: it's cold, very cold, and dark. We'd stirred up sediment around the Diving Bell and so the visibility was poor. Even with a torch, you couldn't see more than a couple of metres. It was like swimming in a dark, grey void ...'

Jack's description took Sandro back to that desolate, unforgiving place.

'The divers had been inside the Bell for almost two hours, with no fresh gases to breathe and only emergency lighting. When I entered the Bell to explain what we were going to do, I struggled to breathe ... it was hot, humid and fetid. In less than one hour, I think they would all have been dead ... suffocated.

'If you've ever jumped into freezing cold water, you know what it's like ... it takes your breath away. People react differently to the thermal shock. Typically, you try to swim, to move, to warm up. When the last diver left the warmth of the Diving Bell and into freezing water, I had to give him a mouthpiece so he could breathe. I had to attach a safety strap and begin the swim to our Bell.

'In the flurry of arms and legs we became entangled. I lost my torch and somehow we tumbled into the remains of the crane that had fallen off the Platform and missed the Bell by centimetres.'

Jack had everyone's attention in the studio, and those watching.

'The current was strong around the Bell, and pushed us inside the mangled wreckage that had fallen off the Platform. The more we struggled to untangle ourselves, the more sediment we stirred up. As we bounced around inside that steel cage, I broke my strobe light ... we were invisible and the guy I was towing was getting colder by the minute.

'As I tried to pull us out of the wreckage, I saw a light in the distance, and guessed it was either Sandro or Gunnar looking for us. I used a carabiner to tap out an SOS on the steel beam I was holding. Sandro found us, and with Gunnar, we made our way back to the safety of the Bell. By this time, the diver I was towing was hypothermic … he wouldn't have survived much longer in those conditions.'

Lucy could see the Floor Manager giving her cut-throat signals to bring the interview to a close. She turned to the camera, didn't smile, but her expression signalled her reaction to Jack's story.

'Without the bravery of Alessandro Calovarlo and Jack Collier, the death toll on *Monroe Bravo* would be over 50 men and women.'

Glancing off camera, towards Sandro and Jack, she commented:

'You were obviously in the *right* place at the *right* time.'

As the interview drew to an end, there was a ripple of applause in the background.

Postscript

Eddie, the crane driver, was amongst the 42 declared missing, presumed lost, in the explosions and fires on *Monroe Bravo*.

The two men who delivered a crate, destined for the *Monroe Bravo* Platform and believed to contain bombs, were identified and traced. It was later confirmed they were acting upon a request by their Iman. Unfortunately, the Iman returned to Iran on the day of the bombing.

Shirin Mousari, also known as Sonya Aslan and Maria Carla Mendez, is currently assisting US Homeland Security officers with their enquiries.

Shortly after *Monroe Bravo* recommenced operation, Dr Rick Johnson left the Platform for a vacation in Utah. He later joined the Board of TransGlobal Oil as Vice President, Worldwide Production.

Norton T. Flynn took up his post in South Georgia, off the tip of South America. TransGlobal Oil are hopeful that viable crude oil deposits can be located.

Hussein Zand was promoted to Brigadier General, made Head of Military Intelligence, and attached to the Army General Staff.

It was announced that a captain, attached to the Quds Force, his wife and their families were killed during an unexplained explosion at a family reunion. An investigation into their deaths continues.

The accidental deaths of four prominent scientists and engineers was reported by the Iranian News Agency. A structural engineer was shot dead during a burglary in his home. A senior metallurgist was killed in a hit-and-run accident. An Army bomb disposal officer was killed during an explosion at a military base on the outskirts of Tehran and a professor of industrial chemistry died after a fall down a staircase in the university.

The evening after the last BBC interview, Lucy Rottmuller joined Sandro Calovarlo for a meal at the exclusive Twilight Club in Manchester. They had a mutually enjoyable evening … and subsequent morning.

Here's a chance to read the first chapter of the next book in the Jack Collier Series.

ONE WAY TICKET

A Jack Collier novel

Fred Lockwood

Chapter 1

Decoy

At 10 knots, the MV *Sultano* was coasting. The twin Caterpillar diesel engines were barely turning over but could push the ex-Italian Navy Patrol Boat to 28 knots if necessary. The high pressure area over the south-east coast of the UK and Northern France had created perfect sailing weather. Even though it was the early hours of the morning, it was warm, and the sea was calm, with only the movement of the boat creating any breeze. The half-moon gave them just enough light to see the outline of other vessels in their shipping lane.

Ahead of them were the narrows of the Straits of Dover. The *Sultano* was at a point due east of Dover and north-west of Dunkirk where the two land masses of England and France come together. It was time for the final check of positions before synchronisation.

The self-assured young man acting as navigator checked the monitor and noted the position, bearing, and speed of the boat. He walked over to the chart table and added the information to the chart before entering the same information into a bespoke computer programme on his laptop. No one had mentioned his name since the time the gang boarded the *Sultano*; he was simply referred to as "navigateur". The way he moved and acted gave the impression of an experienced sailor – perhaps former French Navy. He had a thin, pale face and a slight build. Dark patches under his eyes suggested he was either very tired or unwell. However, he displayed a quiet confidence in his ability to get the *Sultano,* and other ships, to their destination. The computer programme would then tell him what adjustment to the speed and bearing of the *Sultano*, or a second ship, the MPSV *Røsseren*, was needed to ensure they did so without interference. However, before he connected to the software, he wanted to check the position of the other ships in the vicinity.

He dragged the cursor across the laptop screen to a drop-down menu. A simple 'click', and the position of boats and ships in the vicinity were revealed. He didn't need to check all the AIS codes associated with individual ships – there were dozens of them. These were the codes linked to each ship via the Automatic Identification of Ships system; he was only interested in four codes, four ships.

One of the codes was for their 'companion ship', the MPSV *Røsseren.* It looked as though it was on course but he'd confirm in a few moments. He then searched for the position of the closest French high-speed Patrol Boat, the P692 *Maroni* of the Maritime Gendarmerie. It was smaller than the *Sultano,* at only 80 tonnes, but with a maximum speed of 32 knots it was marginally faster. It was also armed but heading away from them on its patrol pattern between Dover and Calais, and was too far away to pose a threat. The mild weather and calm seas would encourage the small rubber dinghies to attempt the crossing between Calais and Dover. It would keep the *Maroni* and UK Border Force vessels busy.

He then searched for two UK Border Force vessels in the vicinity: the HMC *Vigilant* and the HMC *Valiant*. At over two hundred and fifty tonnes, they were twice the size of the *Sultano* but with a maximum speed of 26 knots they were marginally slower. *Valiant* was some distance away, but *Vigilant* could pose a threat. Two other UK Border Force cutters were in the North Sea, one hundred and one hundred and forty nautical miles away respectively, and a fifth was stationary off the Isle of Wight. It was probably inspecting a ship that was negotiating the Channel and, again, too far away to be a threat. It was looking like the perfect moment. He mimed a hand signal to Franco, the leader of the gang, to indicate he needed to make the phone call.

Franco looked like a caricature of a Mexican bandit. A mop of straight black hair, thick moustache that curved to the sides of his mouth. A swarthy complexion, enhanced by dark stubble and a barrel chest. It was only when he spoke that the image he presented changed. He was softly spoken, polite, articulate, and considerate to the point of being apologetic. However, his language and tone only thinly disguised his ruthless and often violent behaviour. Franco slipped the satellite phone from his jacket pocket and handed it over. The "Navigateur" hit the speed dial button for his counterpart on the MPSV *Røsseren,* and waited. The single phrase, "We're on track and on schedule", told him everything was fine.

'Synchronise watches … after the countdown it will be 04:13 precisely … five, four, three, two, one – now. Commence manoeuvrer at 04:15 precisely, confirm,' he said. The strong French accent confirmed his nationality.

'Confirmed,' was the one-word answer.

The "Navigateur" checked his watch, and when two minutes had passed, he called out his orders.

'Come to bearing 320 degrees, and maintain current speed.'

The *Sultano* veered to starboard and settled on her new course. It was aiming directly towards the small seaside town of Broadstairs on the tip of the east coast of England. The "Navigateur" dragged the cursor across the screen and clicked on the red button marked *Synchronise*. The computer programme would now track the speed, bearing, and position of both the *Sultano*, the *Røsseren,* and the two nearest UK Border Force ships. It would calculate the required speed and bearing of two ships to reach their destinations, thirty minutes ahead of the nearest UK Border Force vessel.

Barely a minute passed before the marine radio burst into life.

'*Sultano, Sultano, Sultano*. This is Dover Straits Traffic Separation. Repeat, this is Dover Straits Traffic Separation. You have made an unexpected change of course and left your shipping lane. Please explain, over.'

Franco merely moved towards the marine radio and turned the volume down. There would be more urgent calls, but he would ignore all of them. All attention now was on HMC *Vigilant*, the UK Border Force Cutter. The "Navigateur" studied the data on the laptop. In strongly accented English, he commented:

'*Vigilant* has changed course, increasing speed to 20 … 24 knots. Interception in forty seven minutes. Maintain bearing, maintain speed.'

Vigilant would be making the same calculations as those on the *Sultano*. They would have discovered that the MV *Sultano* was an ex-Italian Patrol Boat, and capable of 28 knots. However, whilst they were on an intercept course, and would be planning to investigate why the *Sultano* had made an abrupt change of course and left the shipping lane, there could be a simple explanation. By continuing at the leisurely speed of 10 knots, it suggested the boat wasn't making a high-speed dash for the coast. "Maintain bearing, maintain speed" was all the "Navigateur" had said. He was allowing the *Vigilant* to close on them, and would monitor their respective positions. He didn't want to provoke a reaction that would elevate the incident. If helicopters or drones were deployed, it could complicate matters. He let the *Vigilant* close to within thirteen nautical miles before giving his next orders.

'Come to bearing 290 degrees and increase speed to 26 knots.'

The effect was exhilarating – they were flying. The engine sound increased, the *Sultano* swung to port, and the bow lifted out of the water. In the early dawn light, the *Sultano* had burst into life. A bow wave streamed from the deep red hull and contrasted with the brilliant white of the superstructure as they maintained a thirty-minute gap between themselves and UK Border Force. The "Navigateur" checked his laptop again, and spoke to Franco.

'ETA in twenty two minutes. Time to confirm final arrangements,' he said as he hit the speed dial button and spoke to his counterpart.

'ETA twenty two minutes, confirm.'

Almost immediately, there was a one-word reply: "Confirmed." The "Navigateur" gave a slight smile as he handed the satellite phone back to Franco.

Suddenly there was a flurry of activity on the boat. Franco left the bridge to talk to one of his associates on deck, and two others in the engine room. When he returned to the bridge, he used the Public Address system to talk to the passengers. In excellent English, with only the faintest trace of a French accent, he announced:

'My friends, thank you for your patience. We expect to arrive in England in about fifteen minutes. As we approach our destination, I will announce, "Brace, brace, brace" for the first time. Please place your luggage against the steel bulkhead and sit with your back against it. Wherever possible, please link arms. We are expecting the grounding of this boat to be gentle; it is a sandy, gently sloping beach. However, I do not want anyone to fall and be hurt.

'Just as we approach the beach I will call "Brace, brace, brace" again. We will run aground within seconds. Once we come to a standstill, I will ask our young men to roll the cargo nets over the sides so that you may disembark. I suggest you drop your luggage onto the beach and climb down the cargo nets to collect it. I urge you not to jump. It will only be a few metres but we do not want damaged ankles and legs. The cargo nets are wide and we expect everyone to be off the boat and walking towards your new life in ten minutes.'

Franco sounded charming and was behaving like any other businessman. He wanted to keep his customers informed and reassured. Satisfied customers would tell their friends, and lead to more customers.

'Brace, brace, brace,' Franco commanded over the loud speakers to the passengers as the MV *Sultano* entered the approach channel to the Western Marine Terminal at Ramsgate.

The long journey from the small port of Terneuzen in the Netherlands to the south-east coast of England, was coming to an end. The one hundred plus passengers were all obeying Franco's instructions. Most were lining each side of the deck, sitting with their backs to a bulkhead, and facing out to sea. Their single piece of luggage was trapped behind them, and they had linked arms. As they huddled together, some stared into the early morning light, looking for land. Others bowed their heads and tensed as they waited for the impact. Considering they were about to run aground, the noise and vibration from the engine was still frighteningly loud.

A hundred plus passengers was a lot to accommodate on the *Sultano*. In addition to those lining the midship decks, there was a small group on the for'ard open deck and a larger group aft, on the covered diving platform. They clung onto rails, stairwells, pipework, and each other.

As the *Sultano* entered the approach channel to the harbour, the captain cut the engines. In the sudden silence, the bow of the boat sank in the water as the boat bled off its speed. It was now down to the skill of the helmsman and the accuracy of the chart. Were they carrying too much speed? Had the sandbank moved? Just before the harbour entrance, the *Sultano* turned violently to starboard and entered a narrow channel between the beach and a shallow sandbank. The sandbank was on the chart … but sandbanks move, and they couldn't afford to run aground now.

The helmsman was checking the monitor and the read-out from the electronic depth sounder. They had 3.2 metres under the keel and the *Sultano* had a draft of 2.1 metres fully loaded. A hundred passengers and their luggage would add another ten thousand kilos to the weight of the boat, which was now fully loaded, but the draft would still be about 2.1 metres. The helmsman held his breath. Fifty metres along the channel, a hundred metres … any moment now. The read-out on the monitor indicated the channel curved to port and towards the beach. Delicately he held the *Sultano* on her course before flinging her into a violent turn to port. He gave the engines a sudden burst of power.

Franco could see the depth under the keel dropping quickly as the seabed shelved to the beach.

'Brace, brace, brace!' he shouted.

The command was followed by silence when the engines were shut down. The previous noise and vibration stopped for a few seconds as the boat glided towards the beach. There was a dull scraping sound as the boat touched the bottom, then she slowed gently as she ran up on the beach and stopped. The sharp curve of the bow, and the first few metres of the hull, were high and dry. They'd made it to England.

'Cargo nets over the side and disembark!' shouted Franco.

Ten strong young men had been positioned near the bow of the boat, both port and starboard. Franco had made them rehearse the process of lifting the roll of cargo netting and getting it ready to push over the side. It took less than a minute for them to do so and for the first passengers to throw a suitcase onto the beach and clamber after it. Some of the passengers would have the good fortune of stepping onto a sandy beach, but others would end up knee-deep in water.

Franco turned to the captain of the *Sultano*.

'That was an extremely impressive manoeuvre ... well done. We will be leaving you now. As soon as we are away from the town, I will speak to my associates and tell them you did everything I asked. Your friends will not be harmed. The tide is coming in and I'd expect your boat to be re-floated in a couple of hours. Apart from superficial scraping of the hull, I expect there to be no damage.'

Franco, his "Navigateur", and the other gang members made their way along the deck to the stern. They had estimated it would take less than ten minutes for the one hundred plus passengers to disembark and start making their way to the shop-lined road next to the beach. Franco and his friends would be taking a different route. At the stern, their deck hand was waiting beside a heavy rope ladder with broad wooden steps. He had dropped it over the side to the waiting RIB (Rigid Inflatable Boat) below. Whilst the passengers disembarked at the bow, Franco and his gang climbed down the rope ladder and into the RIB. They reversed their route, entered the Western Marine Terminal, and then the marina.

There was a surprising amount of activity this early in the morning as those sailors planning to leave on the high tide began to make ready. Some were walking back to their sailboats after an early morning shower, and the smell of cooking wafted over the still water, lights glowing from port-holes. The RIB continued its steady pace, and tucked in between two sail boats. They systematically unloaded fishing rods, tackle, and backpacks; there was no rush. Just a group of friends returning from a night-time fishing trip. Chatting and laughing, they strolled along the pier, around the marina buildings to the car park. An innocuous looking, white multi-seater van was waiting for them, tailgate open. As the luggage was stowed, coffee and sandwiches were shared. A group of fishmen having breakfast in the car park would attract little attention; the same group of men rushing around certainly would. The sound of sirens in the distance was the cue to finish the coffee and get underway. It was about one hundred and seventy kilometres to Heathrow Airport; less than two hours. By lunch time, they would be in Paris – by which time the *Sultano* would be re-floated. As the driver negotiated the carpark, Franco settled back in his seat and did a mental calculation. One hundred and seven passengers at €10,000 each had just generated over one million Euros. Their role as a decoy was complete. It was now a case of the *Røsseren* delivering the main prize.

FUTURE READING

If you enjoyed *Fire on Monroe Bravo* you will probably enjoy earlier books in the Jack Collier series.

Total Loss (2016) traces the lives of three groups of people before they intersect dramatically when an ageing freighter sinks off the coast of Kenya. A routine marine inspection of the wreck by the fledgling *Marine Salvage & Investigation Company*, established by Jack Collier and Sandro Calovarlo, brings them together.

The Sacranie brothers and sister, who own the vessel and have cargo on board, risk their secret being uncovered. Soloman Mbano, a powerful underworld figure in East Africa, is desperate to salvage valuable merchandise he is transporting and to do so at any cost.

The action above and below water is relentless. *Total Loss* takes you from Liverpool to Dar es Salaam, from Dubai to Delhi, from the depths of the Atlantic to the warm waters of the Indian Ocean.

Two heavy, sealed plastic tubs are salvaged from a light aircraft in a remote part of the Celebes Sea, off the coast of Indonesia. Within hours of informing the authorities, strangers are asking about the whereabouts of the salvors and their boat.

Jack Collier and Sandro Calovarlo, co-owners of the fledgling *Marine Salvage & Investigation Company*, are thrust into a deadly "cat and mouse" game. They face ruthless opponents, both above water and below, who want to retrieve the tubs … at any cost.

Overdue (2017) will take you from the Celebes Sea to the Caribbean, from Jakarta to Salford, and a whole new world in-between.

In *Missing, Presumed Lost* (2018) a sailboat is lost during a sudden, violent storm off the coast of Croatia. On board was a battered briefcase – but where is it? People inextricably linked to the briefcase cannot ignore its disappearance and must recover the contents or destroy them.

Jack Collier and Sandro Calovarlo, co-owners of the *Marine Salvage & Investigation Company*, accept contracts to locate the wreck and then salvage it. They become unwittingly involved in an attempt to recover the briefcase or destroy it.

The stakes are high. Is it Jack, Sandro, or the briefcase that becomes … *Missing, Presumed Lost?*

A modern-day treasure hunt locates the wreck of a freighter, sunk by the Japanese in 1941. The *Unlisted Cargo* on board has special significance for a religious community in Myanmar, a community that previously placed this cargo into the safe keeping of the British over seventy-five years previously. It is also of interest to international art criminals trading in antiquities and, for different reasons, both the Myanmar and British Governments. All are determined to get their hands on it.

In the corridors of power, the possession of the *Unlisted Cargo* becomes a battle of wills with high stakes. Within the criminal group their actions are not personal – it's merely business. Who will be successful in securing the contents of the wreck? Will it be worth the price?

A derelict ship is towed from a South American backwater to be scuttled to create an artificial reef of the coast of a Caribbean Island. This previously neglected part of the island, and a new dive centre, are set to benefit – but at a cost to a local entrepreneur.

The entrepreneur is determined the artificial reef project will fail and has ingenious ways of funding his plans and destroying those of others.

The bizarre death of divers on the newly scuttled ship and a series of unexplained accidents around it cause the wreck and dive centre to be shunned. *The Marine Salvage &Investigation Company*, that stripped out and prepared the ship for sinking, is charged with *Gross Negligence*. The dive centre is also under investigation and both could face financial ruin.

The remains of a ninth-century wreck, which may contain ancient Chinese artefacts, is discovered in shallow water in the Quirimbas Archipelago, Mozambique. A Chinese-led archaeological expedition contracts the *Marine Salvage & Investigation Company* to provide onsite support.

Whilst marine archaeologists excavate the submerged wreck site, corrupt officials and a ruthless coastguard captain collude to steal any Tang Dynasty porcelain and ceramics that have survived. They also eliminate witnesses and anyone who stands in their way. Unknown to all are the political decisions that will dictate the fate of any recovered items.

Accidents and deaths decimate the teams associated with the expedition. Who will survive? What will survive? Who will decide?

Sandro Calovarlo awoke, in a police cell, to the start of his worst nightmare. He is accused of assault and rape. "Overwhelming evidence" is paraded before him but he has no memory of what happened. He doesn't know if he's innocent or guilty.

Then, a proposition by an unknown man: successfully salvage illegal cargo from an ageing freighter on the seabed in the unpredictable North Sea, and the victim will withdraw her complaint. Sandro will not face a trial and will not go to prison.

The Police and Sandro's lawyers search for evidence to confirm or challenge the charges against him whilst the *Marine Salvage & Investigation Company* race to salvage the cargo before the court case commences.

Is Sandro Calovarlo innocent or guilty? Is the *Marine Salvage & Investigation Company* aiding criminals?

Printed in Great Britain
by Amazon